# PRAISE FOR
# MERCÈ RODOREDA

D1648091

"Rodoreda had bedazzled me by the sensuality with which she reveals things within the atmosphere of her novels."
—Gabriel García Márquez

"The humor in the stories, as well as their thrill of realism, comes from a Nabokovian precision of observation and transformation of plain experience into enchanting prose."
—*Los Angeles Times*

"Rodoreda plumbs a sadness that reaches beyond historic circumstances . . . an almost voluptuous vulnerability."
—Natasha Wimmer, *The Nation*

"Uncompromising, terrifying, and often stirringly beautiful Rodoreda's *Death in Spring* shares a brutal moral force with Cormac McCarthy's *Blood Meridian*, but her dense, carefully wrought prose style more readily brings to mind the writing of Toni Morrison."
—*Rain Taxi*

# ALSO BY
# MERCÈ RODOREDA

# THE SELECTED
# STORIES
## OF MERCÈ RODOREDA

Translated from the Catalan by Martha Tennent

OPEN LETTER
LITERARY TRANSLATIONS FROM THE UNIVERSITY OF ROCHESTER

Copyright © by Institut d'Estudis Catalans
Translation copyright © 2011 by Martha Tennent
Stories collected here were originally published in three Catalan volumes:
*Vint-i-dos contes, Semblava de seda i altres contes, La meva Cristina i altres contes*

First edition, 2011
All rights reserved

"Blood," "Threaded Needle," "Summer," "Guinea Fowls," "The Mirror,"
"Happiness," "Afternoon at the Cinema," "Ice Cream," "Carnival," "Engaged,"
"In a Whisper," "Departure," "Friday, June 8," "The Beginning," "Nocturnal,"
"The Red Blouse," "The Fate of Lisa Sperling," "The Bath," "On the Train,"
and "Before I Die" are all taken from *Vint-i-dos contes* (Twenty-two stories).
"Ada Liz," "On a Dark Night," "Night and Fog," "Orléans, Three Kilometers,"
"The Thousand Franc Bill," "Paralysis," and "It Seemed Like Silk" are from
*Semblava de seda i alters contes* (It seemed like silk and other stories). "The
Salamander," "Love," and "White Geranium" are from *La meva Cristina i
alters contes* (*My Christina and Other Stories*).

Library of Congress Cataloging-in-Publication Data:

Rodoreda, Mercè, 1908-1983.
    [Short stories. English. Selections]
    The selected stories of Mercè Rodoreda / Mercè Rodoreda ; translated
from the Catalan by Martha Tennent. − 1st ed.
        p. cm.
    ISBN-13: 978-1-934824-31-3 (pbk. : alk. paper)
    ISBN-10: 1-934824-31-3 (pbk. : alk. paper)
    I. Tennent, Martha. II. Title.

    PC3941.R57A27 2011
    849'.9352−dc22

                                                        2010038976

Translation of this novel was made possible thanks to the support of
the Institut Ramon Llull.

**LLLL** institut
ramon llull
Catalan Language and Culture

Printed on acid-free paper in the United States of America.

Text set in Bodoni, a serif typeface first designed by Giambattista Bodoni
(1740–1813) in 1798.

*Design by N. J. Furl*

Open Letter is the University of Rochester's nonprofit, literary translation press:
Lattimore Hall 411, Box 270082, Rochester, NY 14627

www.openletterbooks.org

# CONTENTS

# THE SELECTED
# STORIES
## OF MERCÈ RODOREDA

# BLOOD

**"See this?" she said to me. "Every year my husband planted** dahlias in this empty basket. With a sharp tool he'd dig a hole in the spongy earth; then I'd hand him the bulbs, one by one, and he'd hold them up, slowly covering them with dirt. At night he used to call to me: 'Come here,' he'd say, wanting me to rest my head on his shoulder. He'd put his arm around me, said he couldn't sleep unless I was right beside him, and even though he'd washed his hands, I could catch that scent of good earth. My husband would say the dahlias were our children. He was like that, you know, full of funny little stories, always wanting to joke around, make me laugh. Every afternoon I'd water the basket of flowers. He'd walk through the garden on his way back from work and notice the earth was damp, but still he'd say, as he gave me a kiss, 'Have you watered the dahlias?' You see, when I was a young thing, I didn't like those flowers. They smelled bad. But now, when I pass a florist or a garden that has dahlias, I always stop to look at them. It's like a huge, strong hand grabs my heart and squeezes it. Makes me dizzy.

"You have to understand that when we got married, my father almost damned me to hell. He didn't want me to marry my husband, who was illegitimate, but I was madly in love and ignored my father's wishes. When he died a year later, I always thought it was because he was old, but as time passed, I realized my disobedience upset him so much, it killed him. Some nights I'd feel like weeping when my husband called, 'Come here.'

3

"We were happy, we loved each other, and we were managing well enough because I was working too, sewing children's clothes, and they thought well of me at work. We put a little bit aside in case we got sick. You look at me and maybe you think she's always been like this. If only you knew how pretty I used to be. When we were courting, my husband would sometimes stare at me for a while, not saying a word; then he'd run his finger over my cheek and whisper 'Beautiful,' like he was embarrassed. I wasn't what you'd call attractive, but I had sweet, shiny eyes, velvety. Forgive me, but I can say this, because it's like I was talking about a daughter who had died. You understand? I think the trouble began because I became a woman when I was really young. But things got worse when I stopped being a woman. Before, I'd only be grumpy a few days a month. When the dark mood came over me, my husband used to laugh and say, 'I know what's going to happen!' And he was always right. Around the time I'm telling you about my husband lost his job. His boss went bankrupt. He stayed at home for several months—was really down even though I told him not to worry, we had enough put aside to carry us through—till a friend started telling him that waiting on tables was good, easy work. So, despite the fact that my husband was much more of an office man, he became a waiter.

"About seven or eight months after my husband started the job, I found out I was anemic from working too hard and not sleeping at night. You see, I used to wait up for my husband when he came home late, and then I'd have trouble falling asleep, because even though he slept pretty well, he'd keep turning, pulling on the sheet. We sold the double bed and bought two single ones. You know what? That started driving us apart. When there was a moon, I'd look over at him from my bed: he seemed so far away. It was like our feelings for each other had died a little, because we couldn't touch. 'Are you asleep?' I'd whisper. If he said 'No,' it calmed me because I heard his voice; and if he was asleep, he didn't answer. You see the kind of things that make

4

people miserable? Little by little, I started to believe he didn't answer because he was pretending to be asleep, and I would cry, all alone, quietly, because my husband worked in a café on the Rambla where women were constantly coming and going. One night I cried. I was thinking about my father who died like he'd been abandoned, all on account of losing me when I fell in love with my husband, and my husband got up, sat on my bed, and asked, 'What's the matter?' But instead of calming down, I burst out sobbing, filled with sadness. My husband lay beside me, put his arm around me, my head against his shoulder like before, and said, 'The day after tomorrow is Sunday, we'll plant dahlias. You go to sleep now. You hear me?' But we couldn't sleep, we were still awake when the sun came up. When he got home from work the next day, he said he had a headache, he felt exhausted, it was my fault. I made him a cup of linden tea, but he didn't want it. Finally he took an aspirin, but he was white as a sheet.

"A few days later, he said to me, 'You remember that girl two doors down?' 'I don't know who you're referring to.' I stared at him as if he'd just said, 'I've fallen in love with her.' I couldn't help it, even though I didn't know what girl he meant or why he was mentioning her. 'The house with the two brothers.' 'Oh, I know who she is. What about her?' 'Well, she works in the café with me; she sits at the cash register.'

"The two boys and the girl lived down the street. They had only been there three years. When they moved in the girl was really young, she looked like a child; in summer she always wore a white dress with a red flower embroidered on the bodice. I don't know why, but after that day I felt like I needed to wait for my husband by the gate. He'd arrive around two, and as soon as I glimpsed his little shadow at the end of the street, I'd run inside. As I waited I sometimes thought about my father: he used to send me to the druggist when I was little, and he'd lean against the railing on the balcony, waiting for me. I hated it. I could hardly walk, because I knew my father's eyes never missed a gesture of mine. That's why, before my husband could see me, I'd run back into the house and slip into bed, or take up my sewing. If he found me sewing, I'd tell him I'd stayed up because it was something urgent. Then one night I saw him walking with the girl; after that they always returned together. There's nothing strange about it, of course, living as we did right beside each other. I didn't think anything of it. My husband wasn't like other men; since the day we married, he'd loved only me. They would stroll along slowly. I never, ever, saw her take his arm. Absolutely not! But then I started to agonize. If I hadn't seen them together, maybe the strange change in me would never have happened. I began to feel like I was a nuisance to my husband; something was different, and without wanting to, I started to distance myself from him. I hardly said a word to him, for fear I'd let slip that I waited for him by the gate. One day I ran into the girl in the bakery. She didn't notice me. I would've liked her to recognize me, greet me, tell me she and my husband were friends. 'Your husband and I work at the same place, and since we take the same route home, we come back together at night.' My old friend Roser, who sometimes helped me sew, used to say, 'The more you do for men, the worse it gets. When you grow old and worn down, they look for a young girl. Best not to be upset.' I felt like telling her, 'My husband's not like other men; that's why I chose him. When we look at each other, we don't see what we are, but what we were.'

"One night my husband stormed in, not like himself at all. 'What will Maria think when she discovers you wait for me every night? One of her brothers sees you from his bedroom window and told me today. He says when you see us, you run inside. Can't you understand my embarrassment?' The following day I went to the bakery at noon to see if I'd run into the girl again. I didn't catch up with her until the third day. She had curly black hair and very dark, moist eyes. When she asked for bread, her teeth looked like rows of pearls. I never waited for him by the street again, but inside with my face glued to the window, the room completely dark. When he opened the gate, I'd jump into bed. I kept thinking while I waited that one night he wouldn't return, and I'd never see him again. Obsessions of mine, I know. Because you see, when a woman stops being a woman, her head fills with obsessions. Sometimes, on my way to deliver some sewing, I'd walk past the café where my husband worked and, if I saw him, I'd wave without stopping. After that, I avoided the café, but it was an effort. I'd ask myself, 'What's happened to us? We're like strangers; he thinks about things that I can't know.' I felt abandoned. But just wait. Without knowing why, I switched from never uttering a word to complaining all the time. One night I cried because I was in such agony. I'm sure he hadn't fallen asleep yet, was just pretending he didn't hear me. I lay there till the sun rose, filled with sadness, no one to console me. I cried a lot in those days, and my eyes hurt when I sewed. I was consumed by a terrible unhappiness. I had grown so thin the doctor told me I needed rest and should leave town that summer. We rented a little house in Premià de Mar. After lunch, I would fix supper, and we'd eat it on the beach. I felt calm, didn't think about the girl. I missed the house, though, and my garden full of jasmine blossoms, the kind that have little stars. My husband missed the house too, but he went to the café every night to play a game of *manille*, and right away made a group of friends.

"One afternoon my husband had gone to the beach a good bit earlier than me, and when I arrived I found him lying near a girl. The girl got up and went in the water. My husband said he didn't know her, and he'd lain beside her just to see the face I'd make. I went swimming before we ate, and when I sat back down on the sand, I realized my knees were no longer young. You see, I used to have white, round knees. While the honeymoon lasted, my husband would kiss them, tell me they seemed like silk. That afternoon, as the sun was setting, I stretched out my legs and saw all the wrinkles around my kneecaps. I realized then, truly realized, that I was no longer young. Before, when I would catch sight of an old man, I saw him as he was, I mean, without ever thinking that he'd been young at one point, as if old folks were just a certain kind of people who were born ugly, wrinkled, toothless, hairless. From another world. At that moment, I missed the blood, the same blood that had made me weep the first time I glimpsed it, believing I was flawed and no one would want to marry me because of the flaw. Every month I used to be grumpy for a few days, but when it was over I was in heaven, like I'd been remade. Whereas, without the blood, I was always the same, which is to say mostly not good. Or neither good nor bad, if you prefer. That's the way I put it to the doctor.

"When I started to feel like my husband didn't love me as much, I started to feel the same way about him, because he couldn't possibly like me the way I was, and everything that happened—not that anything in particular did—was all my fault. Whenever I stopped to think that it was my fault, a sense of tenderness came over me and I wanted to love him like I had twenty years before. The tenderness ended the day I realized my knees were old. Once again, I lay awake all night, stretched out in bed, facing the sky. When a woman feels these things, she wants a hand to hold hers, a voice to whisper, 'I understand.' But how could a woman like me find a voice that spoke the words I needed if I can hardly understand the way I am myself? See what I mean? The last days by the sea . . . life is strange, isn't it? Instead of fretting about the girl on the beach and what my husband had told me with that mischievous little smile of his, I started agonizing over the girl down the street. I thought if there *was* something between my husband and her, it was my fault. Instead of spending my evenings sewing dresses by hand, embroidering leaves and daisies and little animals on children's clothes, I should have dropped it all and gone to meet my husband—like so many women do—the first day I saw them together. I don't mind telling you now that one night I did. Around midnight I combed my hair—mid-afternoon that day I'd washed my hair and curled it—put on a white blouse I hadn't worn for years and a pleated skirt. I headed straight for the Rambla and planted myself on the sidewalk opposite the café. The first thing I caught sight of—partially concealed by people either seated at tables or entering and leaving—was the girl at the cash register. She was so young! Her hair falling across her shoulders, like an angel. I realized then that the moment had passed for me to be doing what I was doing. It was too late. I started to feel that my blouse wasn't properly washed, the skirt too old. I went home.

"I had a dream. I dreamed that my father was coming to the house, followed by a young girl that I thought was me, and my husband was saying, 'Let him come, he's amusing, so fat.' My husband and the girl suddenly disappeared, only my father and me were left. We walked down a stone staircase, till we reached a sandy beach where short, square, wooden stakes had been driven into the ground. A dead fish lay on top of each of them. My father knocked one of the fish off with his hand; it looked dead, but it was breathing. I could hear it. My father said, 'We'll eat them for supper.' Then we started climbing a ladder, like in a circus, straight with bars for steps. I was carrying a bottle of water under each arm and was terrified I'd fall off. My father was in front and kept ordering me, 'Up, up.' Once we reached the top, we had to leap onto a roof. One of the bottles dropped when I jumped, and my heart stood still. 'I've killed someone,' I thought. I guess you can say that my father faded away then, because I found myself in the middle of a village square, at the market. 'I have to buy fruit for my father,' I said as I stood before an apple stand. The saleswoman took a long time to serve me, and I was terribly anxious that I'd be late. I turned around, and my husband was right behind me, laughing like mad. 'You see,' I told him, 'if I have you for a friend, I don't need anything else. But I have to take the fruit to my father. If it wasn't for that, we could go for a stroll.' Then we were walking across a low bridge, and I threw out the wrapping to the apples. The water beneath the bridge was clear as glass, still as sleep. On one side you could see rows of fish of every color imaginable, pale colors. A man said, 'Take a close look, they're all dead. They started dying tonight, one after the other.' Finally I found myself in a hotel-like house where they were having a party, the corridors bustling with people and waiters carrying trays of food. It was so crowded I couldn't take a step. I pushed my way into the dining room where I discovered Roser seated at a table—she's the friend I told you about who worked with me sometimes—and I asked her, 'Have you seen my father?' Just then my husband passed by, quick as lightning. 'No, I haven't seen him, he was tired, I don't know where he's gone.' I heard a loud voice urgently calling out my father's name, repeatedly, and suddenly saw a cripple—a stout man with a cardboard nose—tottering toward me. As he approached, I could see his tiny hands, like a child's, all purple with little swollen fingers. I don't know how, but as I gazed at the hands, I realized the cripple was my father. Somehow I managed to remove the cardboard nose. I held him against me, like a baby. He didn't seem heavy at all as I carried him along the corridors of the hotel. Then I woke up. No one knew how to interpret the dream, but it troubled me terribly.

"The garden looked dreadful when we returned from our holiday. Roser had watered it occasionally, but the sun had scorched the more delicate plants that needed water every day. My husband and I set about redoing the garden, fixing it all up. We had them bring compost, planted dahlias—not the right time to do that, if you ask me—and a couple of weeks later it looked like a garden in some fine house. That year, the last, the dahlias bloomed so large that each flower looked like a child's head. Lots of different colors. Blood red, yellow, white, also rose-colored, with a pink so delicate that each petal was like a silk ribbon. The day the first dahlia bloomed—the bud had been hard as a rock—I learned from the baker that the girl down the street was getting married. By chance I caught a glimpse of the wedding because I happened to be sweeping the sidewalk in front of the house. She was wearing a navy blue suit, white gloves and shoes, and carrying a bouquet of lilies tied with lots of ribbons that dangled down. Don't laugh at me now, but I ran into the garden, singing, filled with joy, running my hand over each dahlia, caressing them like they were my children. I was happy all day, a happiness no words can describe. I couldn't sew, just moved from room to room tidying up. I changed the sheets, put on the silk bedspread, fixed a late snack for when my husband got in, put the embroidered tablecloth on the little table near the window, made some pudding.

"When my husband came in, all the lights in the house were on and I was exhausted. As soon as I saw him, my heart sank. He entered and closed the door with such weariness that I thought he was ill. He headed straight to the bedroom; I followed him like a shadow without saying a word. He took off his jacket, laid it on the bed, walked over to the window, and stood there without moving, like he was made of wood. I didn't dare speak. I picked up his jacket—I remember tiptoeing as if I'd entered a church when the Host of Our Lord was raised—and hung it on the clothes rack behind the door. My husband stood there without moving, facing the garden, his back to me. I went over to him, and before I had time to ask him what was the matter, he turned and hugged me, and you know what? He was weeping. Weeping uncontrollably, like I had during my saddest nights. He didn't say a word, not one. I asked him why he was crying, but he didn't want to tell me. He finally calmed down and said, 'Let's go to sleep.' He was like a little boy, it made me so sad.

"The truth didn't hit me for a long time. When I asked him why he cried that night, he would frown and turn angry. Every now and then during the following days and weeks, I couldn't help but ask him why he cried. It was driving me crazy that he didn't want to tell me. Then I started to want to weep. It was like the world had blackened. We hardly spoke to each other. It was all, 'Yes,' 'No,' 'Yes,' 'No.' Nothing else. I felt like I was drowning.

But then I saw it clear as day: my husband had fallen in love with the girl and was sorry he married me. I was driven to distraction thinking that he started falling in love all that time when I was afraid he would fall in love. 'Are you sad because now you have to come home alone?' I couldn't help but ask. 'Do you want me to come and meet you at work?' He looked like he'd been stung by a wasp. 'All I need now is for you to make me look ridiculous.' Then we started arguing; I told him there was nothing ridiculous about a woman meeting her husband after work, he said there was, I said there wasn't. This went on till morning.

"We didn't speak to each other for two weeks. When we finally did, things had gotten too far out of hand. I looked at my husband and saw him as he was. It made me want to laugh. He was missing three molars and could only chew on one side of his mouth; and when he chewed, he had one sunken cheek, one swollen, distorting his face in a comical way. He ate fast, like an animal, his elbows up in the air, and he walked with a stoop, as if he still had a towel over his arm like in the café. He had a red streak in his eye, and after so many years of being forced to smile at clients, his mouth twisted strangely when he smiled.

"That winter he got sick. Caught a really bad case of the flu that almost turned into pneumonia. That's when he cuddled up to me, all frightened, like a child. Even then I felt a tenderness for him. But the real story began when he got well. He started humiliating me, I mean doing things to humiliate me. I can't explain what kind of things; I'd never finish telling you. You know? Little things, all in bad faith. It was torture.

"The summer ended with a lot of rain. All the dahlias looked at the ground; I had to prop them up with sticks to keep them straight. Little by little, the autumn settled in, the days got shorter, the air cooler. I served my husband as he ate and amused myself by watching him eat with that fury of his. Sometimes I'd have to struggle to keep from laughing. He finally realized, and the following day he came home with a roll of electrical wire. I didn't ask him what he planned to do. He spent the next Sunday installing a switch in the bedroom, 'so I can turn on the light in the garden without having to walk all the way to the front door.' When he finished, he said, 'Try it out. You see? How's that? So, if I'm ever late coming home and you think I'm coming back with some girl, you can turn the light on us, without bothering to go to the door. How's that?' 'Great,' I said.

"When the time came, I pulled up the dahlias, like I did every year, and stored the bulbs on a shelf in the junk room on the rooftop. On October 28—I remember like it was yesterday—he calmly got into bed, turned out the light, and went to sleep. Me too. I don't know how long I'd been asleep when I felt—here, in the middle of my chest—a terrible weight, like a real weight, a kind of oppression, and I started waking up, but it was like I was still asleep and was coming from far away. Then I clearly heard my husband's voice, but as if approaching through the fog, 'Get up, hurry, get up.' I jumped out of bed, and my husband pushed me over to the window. 'Don't you see something?' 'No' 'Nothing at all?' 'Wait a moment.' Then he switched on the light in the garden and I saw . . . first I saw a shadow leaning against the orange tree, and when my eyes grew accustomed to the dark, I saw that it was a girl. 'What is it?' 'A girl. Don't you always think I'm running around with young women? Well, take a look, now I even have them in the garden.' 'It's like a dream,' I said. Then he rapped on the window, and the girl began to move slowly, as if she wasn't of this world, moving toward the gate. If I hadn't heard the sound of the hinges, I'd have thought the whole thing had been a hallucination. My husband held his belly and laughed, you can't imagine how he laughed. The next day he asked me what had happened; I'd started crying out in my sleep that there was a girl in the garden. It made my head spin. "No, I didn't dream it; you'd been planning this little joke for some time, ever since you installed that switch in the bedroom.' When he left for work, I raced out to the garden to see if I could find anything by the orange tree, I don't know what, anything that could be touched, like a feather that a bird had lost. I found nothing. No footprints—the ground was too hard. All day I stormed around like crazy, trying to decide if what I'd seen was real or a dream. The dream I described about my father was different; it was truly a dream, but what happened that night was a joke my husband played, wanting to muddle my brain. When it was dark, I locked the house, barred it, trembling all over with fright. I started rummaging through drawers to conquer my fear, not sure what I was looking for. When I found it, I knew what it was: my father's picture. You see, I'm not one of those women who cover the walls with family photos. It was printed on heavy cardboard, discolored from age and humidity. I took it out of the drawer and knelt down, holding it with both hands like a relic. The lower part of his face was rubbed out, but his eyes were clear, so filled with goodness that mine welled up. I went to the bedroom and placed the photo of my father on the bedside table, propped against a vase. It kept me company. From that day on, I started living with my father. I'd talk to the picture, tell him, 'I'm going shopping, you hear me? Don't worry, I'll be right back.' It seemed like my father looked at me and said, 'Off you go.' My husband and I separated that year. It was hard, because he didn't want to. He said we were too old to do something crazy like that. You have to understand, there was no way round it. As soon as I saw him, an uneasiness rushed through me, and I didn't feel good until he left. He's living with a nephew now, and if we run into each other on the street, we shake hands and he says, 'How are you?' and I respond, 'Fine, and you?'

"Dahlias have never grown in this basket again. Sometimes, when the weeds grow high, I pull them up, and move the earth around so it won't look bad, and if I see dahlias at the florist, a kind of dizziness sweeps over me and I feel like vomiting. Forgive me."

# THREADED NEEDLE

**She sighed deeply, sat down, and picked up her sewing from the**
table. The white satin glistened like sun-pierced water in the light
cast by the floor lamp; a fantastical painter had decorated the
parchment lampshade with pyramids surrounded by a landscape
of sepia palm trees. Gold lettering on the satin selvage indicated
the manufacturer and quality: GERMAIN ET FILS—CARESSANT.

Maria Lluïsa threaded the needle, cut the thread with her
teeth, knotted it, and stuck the threaded needle in her bathrobe,
above her breast. *I wonder what the bride's like?* She never saw the
customers. Mademoiselle Adrienne, the workroom manager, fitted and prepared the clothes; once they had been cut and basted
they were sent to the workers. *I wonder what she's like? Blond?
Brunette?* She only knew the woman's size: forty-eight. *She must
look like a sack of potatoes.*

She laughed and reached up to unfold the nightgown. On
the left was a piece of puckered lace. *It's almost as if they do it
on purpose to waste my time.* She positioned the nightgown on
the mannequin, undid the basting on the puckered section, and
secured it with needles. She worked, lost in thought, her mouth
partially open, the tip of her tongue against her teeth. She was
calculating how long it would take her to sew the lace. Thirty-six
hours, if she was alert. She would tell the shop it was forty-two.
After all, if she was sharp on the job, no reason to do any favors.
Six hours for each garland. She would need to go over the design,

leaf by leaf, flower by flower; then she would cut the tulle and pop it out. It was a delicate job that demanded skill and patience. Forty-two hours at eighteen francs.

She removed the nightgown from the mannequin, put on her thimble, and picked up the needle. She loved her job for many reasons; it allowed her a glimpse of a world of luxury, and because her hands worked mechanically, she could dream. That's why she preferred to work at home and at night. When she arrived from the workroom with a new sewing job, she would undo the package slowly and caress the silks and lace edgings. If a neighbor came up to admire the delicate sewing, she proudly displayed it, as if the fine silks and crêpes were for her. The blues and pinks, the occasional lavender, soothed her tired, unwedded heart.

She sewed quickly. With great confidence she pushed the needle in and jerked the thread out. From time to time she would lift the fabric that slid toward the floor and return it to her lap with a precise gesture. Her light chestnut hair was swept back, revealing a few shiny silver threads. On both sides of her small mouth, two deep wrinkles hardened her congested face.

*Three or four years from now I'll set up business for myself. I'll hang a brass sign on the door: MARIA LLUÏSA, BRIDAL SEAMSTRESS. At the workroom they would be green with envy. Especially Mademoiselle Adrienne.* They had worked together for ten years—and cordially despised each other, both of them living in constant exasperation at not knowing how much money the other had. Sometimes Adrienne came up from the fitting room with a package and hid it under the counter, without a word, like a magpie. When Maria Lluïsa saw her coming back with a package, she would grow pale with irritation, a wave of blood rising to her forehead, spreading slowly, leaving shiny, red blotches on her cheeks and the tip of her nose. *I'll have girls working for me and design the clothes myself. The shop will be in my name and customers will lavish me with presents. Better that than getting married. Cooking for a man, washing his clothes, having to put up with a man day and night, only for him to look at young girls when I'm old.* She smiled and cast a condescending glance at the bridal nightgown.

But before the dream could absorb her . . .

Of course, he would probably die soon enough. She imagined him as he had looked two weeks before, his white hair, his restless, eager eyes and sunken cheeks, shaking with an almost imperceptible tremor beneath his old, stained cassock with the shiny elbows and frayed cuffs. The first day she sat with him at the hospital she heard two nurses whispering: "She's the priest's cousin." She had worn her dark hat with the black bird, its wings spread toward the right. Over the years, one of the bird's eyes had disappeared and dust had settled in the empty eye socket. She didn't dare brush it for fear the feathers would come out. She would have it redone in the spring. *I'll tell them to remove the bird and add a pretty little bunch of flowers.*

She yawned, dug the needle into the sewing, and rubbed her eyes. She had slept badly for seven nights, the nights she had watched over him, half seated, half stretched out in an armchair. When the doctor told her cousin he would have to be admitted to a hospital, he had someone contact her. "I'll deposit a hundred thousand francs in your name; you may need the money if I'm sick for a long time. Operations are expensive, and I'd like you to take care of everything. You know if anything happens to me, everything I have is yours." She had kept the fact that he was sick from the other relatives: What if in the end, in a moment of weakness, he put the old quarrels behind him and decided to leave them something? She alone had watched over him; and she would have spent the night sitting in the armchair by the head of his bed, if the shop hadn't given her the urgent sewing. He would have greeted her like every night, with a feeble, wasted smile. "Thank goodness I have you, Maria Lluïsa." And then, like every night, she would scrutinize his waxen face, marked by vague shadows, life blazing in his eyes.

She removed the thimble, picked up the scissors, and started to cut the extra tulle. She couldn't be distracted now; an irreparable snip of the scissors was easily made. Adrienne went over her work meticulously. Nothing escaped her, not the vaguely crooked seam, not the occasional long stitch. "I don't like these pleats, Maria Lluïsa." She had a stray eye, and to look at the sewing she had to hold the material in front of her nose. It was almost as if the devil had given her some sort of miraculous double vision.

That winter she had gone to work every afternoon so she wouldn't have to light a fire at home. One day she arrived a bit late, and they were talking about her. She stopped on the landing and listened: "When I got there, the priest was sitting in the dining room."

It was the elderly Madame Durand, a tall, pale woman who did the ironing and lived in a perpetual state of irritation. The others were laughing. What were they thinking about her?

They wouldn't be able to say a thing now. When her cousin was released from the hospital, he would live with her. They would hire a maid. He would be an easy patient, a tube to pee in, a saintly man who would spend his days praying, waiting patiently for death.

She finished sewing another flower. This is how she would grown old: bent over her sewing.

"Maria Lluïsa," he used to call to her when they were little, "want to look for frogs with me?"

"When I finish cleaning the chicken coop."

If his parents hadn't made him study to become a priest, he might have married her. But at that time he was the son of the poorest sister and hadn't yet gotten his inheritance from his uncle in Dakar. He was a sickly little boy who always wore a scarf around his neck, fastened with a safety pin.

A sharp thud in the kitchen banished the ghosts. She placed the nightgown on the table and went to see what had happened.

Picarol was sleeping in the corner. The light must have woken him. He got up, stretched his front paws far in front of him, and arched his back.

"Don't be afraid, Picarol."

She examined the kitchen with an anxious eye. Above the stove stood half a dozen white glass jars.

*The tomato must have fermented.*

She found one of the lids lying on the gas burner. She smelled the jar before she replaced the lid. Another liter of canned tomatoes ready to be thrown out. She opened the cupboard and glanced at the provisions with satisfaction. Chocolate, cookies, a tin of coffee, another of tea, five kilos of sugar, a row of ceramic jars filled with duck and chicken covered in animal fat. The marmalades were on the top shelf. And two bottles of rum: two! All that in the middle of the war. *He might want a little glass of rum every day, and rum . . .*

She was filled with sadness as she left the kitchen. Those provisions had cost her a lot of money and maneuvering. A lot of chasing people and doing them favors. She watched over them as if they were a treasure. When her cousin moved in they would share them. At midnight she often drank a cup of hot chocolate, but only on really cold nights, purely out of necessity, to be able to work till dawn. Maybe he liked hot chocolate too.

*╱╱╱*

"Yes?"

Someone had knocked on the door, then pushed it ajar. A head with lively, happy little blue eyes appeared.

"Can I come in?"

Palmira lived in the apartment beneath her. Ever since Maria Lluïsa's cousin had been in the hospital, her neighbor had cooked for her, brought her two hot water bottles every night.

"You mean it's already eleven o'clock? Time goes so fast."

"It flies, it flies! And you work much too hard. Don't move. I'll put them in the bed for you. Better to do it quick, while they're still hot."

Palmira headed to the bedroom. *I should give her a collar; I'll get Simona to sew the edge. She's faster than me.*

"How's your cousin?"

Palmira had come out of the bedroom, rubbing her hands with lotion. She was missing the index finger on her right hand. Folds of skin formed a swirl at the tip of a cluster of useless flesh.

"A bit better. He might be released in a couple of weeks. But he's very weak."

"Poor man! It's one thing if he gets his health back, but I can't see you having another person in the house, someone so sick."

Palmira stood in front of her, admiring the nightgown as Maria Lluïsa continued to sew.

"If only I didn't have to work for a living! I would even enjoy sewing, but . . ." *What a bore. Couldn't she just leave?*

"And all the medication; it must be terribly expensive."

Palmira couldn't take her eyes off the mountain of brilliant snow that she dared not touch. *If I show her the nightgown, she'll stay another hour.*

"Come on, Palmira, off to bed, you have to get up early."

Palmira sighed and headed for the door with a sense of regret. "Good night. Don't be up too late."

⚓

Yes, the medicine was expensive. First the hospital, then the surgeon, now all the medication. What would be left of the hundred thousand francs? The stack of bills would slowly dwindle. "One operation might not be enough. If it isn't, he'll need a second," the physician had said as he looked at her apologetically, wiping his glasses with a splendidly white handkerchief. *What if one operation proved not to be enough, and he decided at the last moment to leave his money to the other relatives? That would really upset things.* Of course she could always . . . Then everything would work out. But how could she do it without anyone realizing? She wouldn't be the first to try it. Or the last. Increase the dose, little by little. He was already so weak; everyone said it was a lost cause. He would probably live only a few months.

Dr. Simon had been her physician for years, a kindly old soul, a bit absentminded, only kept a few of his former patients. He would never even notice. His house calls were more like visits from an elderly, tiresome relative than a doctor. Twenty-five, thirty, thirty-five drops. Two months and it would be over. How could she be sure? When she went to the pharmacy to buy the drops, she would wait until the place was empty. When she had paid and was holding the bottle, her hand on the door about to leave, she would turn around: "Senyor Pons, this medicine isn't dangerous, is it? If I lose count one day, I don't suppose it would matter." Maybe the pharmacist would say: "Oh no, be very careful, only twenty drops." I would have to ask in a very natural tone, with maybe just a touch of uneasiness. "Well, it's best to know." Senyor Pons was very neat. He would scratch his white beard and smile at her above his glasses, lowering his head a bit between the two large glass spheres that stood on the counter, one green, the other a caramel color. A small bottle with a rubber dropper. The glass would be cold, the liquid murky. He wouldn't suffer at all. It would really be for his own good. He would fade away, slowly withering.

She could set herself up right away. An apartment in the center of town, on Cours Clémenceau, for example, near Place Tourny. A parlor with two balconies overlooking the street, half a dozen armchairs upholstered in cream-colored damask, a mirror with a gold frame, a few antique fashion engravings scattered about the walls. She would have the workshop at the back, by the gallery. Nice and sunny. *I'll take Simona with me—she does the best edging— and Rosa, the best embroiderer.* She would take the two girls from

Indochina who worked for hours without opening their mouths, quiet as a pair of cats, only raising their heads to smile. She didn't want Madame Durand; she would find herself a good ironer, that would be easy enough. Adrienne would be dumbstruck when she saw that her best workers had abandoned her, left her high and dry! She would go to Paris every year to look for new designs. She would ride first class, wagon lit, with velvet seats and a shiny ashtray by the window. At the beginning of each season, she would send cards, printed with calligraphic swirls framing her name in English script, to her clients. Perfumed cards. She would keep them in a cushioned box where she had sprinkled drops of perfume . . . If she increased the number of drops too quickly, she could be caught. And he might suffer. Some time ago she had read *The Pink Shadow*, where an attorney poisoned three people over some stolen documents. He laced their coffee with arsenic. She had lent the book to Adrienne; all the girls in the shop had read it. Drops were the surest method. Twenty-five, then thirty. Her hand would shake a bit, and the glass dropper would rattle against the glass. One, two, three, four. Perfect round drops that would become slightly deformed from the weight as they slid from the dropper. When they hit the water they caused a tiny mist. Five, six, seven.

The Cathedral clock struck twelve. She opened wide her round eyes as if she had just woken up. *What was I thinking?*

The needle was out of thread; she would have to start another. She yawned. Suddenly, mid-yawn, she became conscious of what she had been imagining and was terror-stricken. She closed her mouth slowly and rubbed her eyes.

"Oh my God!" She placed the sewing on the table. She was sleepy, her eyes hurt, she should go to bed. She removed her smock, sweater, skirt, wool slip and stood in her undershirt and pink knitted breeches that reached down to her knees. She glanced at the bridal nightgown. *I wonder how it would look on me.* She stood in front of the mirror on the wardrobe and tried it on. She was thin, and the nightgown was much too large for her. She tied it at the waist, held out the skirt with both hands, and spun around.

*If I had married my cousin, I would have made myself a white, white nightgown. Just like this one.*

She felt a knot in her throat, something gripping her neck. Her eyes filled with tears.

"What an idiot you are!"

Slowly she removed the nightgown, folded it carefully, and left it on the chair before switching off the light. She climbed into bed in the dark.

She was still weeping when the sun came up.

# SUMMER

**She stopped in front of a shop window full of umbrellas, and her** friend, who was walking ahead of her, suddenly turned around: "Carme, we'll get separated!" Her name was Carme. He had followed them all the way from Travessera de Gràcia—the street where he had worked for eleven years—to Pàdua.

Now, as he leaned over the railing on the balcony off the gallery, he could still see the sheer, pearl-gray dress with the very pale pink—almost mauve—flowers printed on it. A cool, sweet dress. "Carme, Carme." She stopped at all the shop windows that had pretty things, and her friend had pulled her by the arm, trying to steer her clear of so many temptations. On Pàdua, close to Saragossa, they went inside an ironing shop: WE OFFER TOP-QUALITY PRESSING. The sun shone directly on the shop window, making it impossible for him to see inside. And that was how he lost her: because it was late and a little boy who was playing ball had stopped to look at him with curiosity and distrust. Now he couldn't get her out of his mind. Nor could he forget the dress, the legs, the . . . Her skin was tight, dark, smooth. With each step, the hem of her skirt swayed. With each step. With the slightest movement.

He stood there, hands in his trouser pockets, shirt unbuttoned at the neck, gazing at the darkening sky as it slowly became dotted with stars.

"Why don't you help clear the table instead of playing the gentleman?"

A swallow squawked as it flew in. They had had a nest on the balcony for three years, and every spring they brought a bit more mud.

"My work is never done, but you . . . Did you remember the clothesline broke and the mosquito net on the boy's bed needs to be changed? Of course not. You never think about anything. Why don't we just look at the scenery? Sen-yor is looking at the scenery; don't disturb him. Instead of daydreaming, you should be looking for your son. At this rate, he'll turn into a street urchin."

"He's old enough. He knows the way home."

"We'll see how you feel when he gets hit by a car."

How the devil would a car hit him if there weren't even any carriages on their street? She must have guessed what he was thinking.

"The other day he walked all the way to Wagner by himself, without asking you for permission, as far as I know. If you're not careful, any day now he'll be killed by a truck in Plaça Bonanova."

"Well, we can't tie him up with a rope, can we?" he shouted.

The scent of flowers reached him from the gardens below. He could see them all from the balcony. The palm tree at the Codinas' spread its dusty fans in the thick air. The darkest tree of all was a medlar, old and tall, with a smooth, knotless trunk and leaves so stiff they looked like cardboard. He wiped the sweat from his forehead and neck. A mosquito buzzed furiously around him. What if by magic he suddenly found himself in the woods . . . If he could only spend the night in the woods . . . Life, after all . . . This is the only good thing there is in life. Just this. The night. A girl. Just this. And even then it's so terrible, as if you were suffering or dying. For a girl like that you could do anything. "Carme, Carme." Why does a beautiful girl always have an ugly girlfriend? Her friend was carrying a package. Clothes to be pressed, no doubt. WE OFFER TOP-QUALITY PRESSING. The letters on the sign were black, except the capitals, which were red. Carme. He would utter her name in a low voice until finally, by virtue of repetition, she would belong to him.

"Will you empty the bucket? It's too heavy for me."

"What?"

"Are you asleep? I said, will you empty the bucket into the sink for me; I'm not strong enough to lift it."

"I'm coming."

"What's up with you?"

"I'm hot and sleepy. That's all."

He emptied the bucket. Half the water spilled onto the floor, and a faint smell of bleach filled the kitchen.

"I would've been shocked if you did it right."

He lit a cigarette and returned to the balcony. A moment later, his wife called from the dining room:

"I've had about enough. Do you hear? I'm going to bed. If the boy's not back by ten, please go get him."

"Would you just leave me alone," he said, turning abruptly, his eyes full of anger.

"Go ahead and shout. Maybe the Puig family invited the boy to dinner—that would save us a bit. None of us are overweight."

"Why don't you just go to sleep? You're in a terrible mood."

His wife had never been as pretty as the girl this afternoon. She'd never worn a dress that becoming. Where could she have found the material? For eleven years, he had sold silk and wool, wool and silk, and his fingers had never come across a gray crêpe with pink flowers and vines as perfect as hers. Never had he felt such a precise desire as that night, the desire to seize her and take her away to the woods, woods smelling of pine trees filled with moonlight. Perhaps the years had changed him, but not the way other people changed. Perhaps his youth was now, when he was almost forty. Or perhaps youth lasted longer than they say, true youth, with this taste of fire and earth rising from his heart.

Someone kicked the door violently. He opened it, and his son rushed in, just like the swallow, heading straight for the dining room.

"We caught a cricket!" He was sweaty and red, a strand of hair stuck to his forehead.

"How many times have I told you I don't want you to bang the door like that?"

"Give me a big box. He's going to suffocate in here."

"Time for bed, and make it snappy. Your mother went to sleep a while ago, tired of waiting on you. And wash your face; you look like a gypsy. Your hands too."

The boy obeyed, his eyes gleaming with excitement. When he came back from the kitchen with a clean face, he picked up the matchbox where he was keeping the cricket and took it to his room.

When he and his wife were old, dead even, his son would feel the same thing. When he is married and has children, one summer day, all of a sudden, on his way home from work, he will hunger for a silk skirt over bare legs.

He went out on the balcony once more. Night had fallen. He wiped his forehead and neck. Thirty-eight in the shade. Thirty-eight degrees in the shade. Same as his age. He felt a sting on the back of his hand. The mosquito had bitten him while he was looking at the garden. He realized the carnations were dying of thirst. The basil was yellow; it had always been scrawny. But he didn't feel like watering, or doing anything.

"Son! Come water the carnations."

The boy came out of his bedroom, his shirt hanging out of his pants.

"Did you find me a box for the cricket?"

"No. Tomorrow's another day."

The boy went back to his room. He felt like going after him and slapping him to make him water the carnations. He was sure the boy had heard him. "It doesn't matter." He didn't feel like doing anything either. If it was less hot, he could have gone to the cinema. Gone out. Dropped everything and left.

The boy came back to the dining room and went up to him.

"Good night, Papà."

He knew both of them were thinking about the unwatered carnations. He would go to bed too, and if he couldn't sleep because of the heat, he would go out on the balcony and lie on the floor till morning. He took off his shirt, his trousers, all his clothes, and slipped into bed gently, to avoid waking his wife. Perhaps he would see her again tomorrow. His wife turned over. She was small and weak. She had been very sick three or four years ago and looked the worse for it. She tired easily and coughed all winter. The doctor said it wasn't anything serious. All of a sudden, she sighed. A brief sigh, just enough to show she was alive. He was filled with grief. Yes, a deep grief, without really knowing why.

# GUINEA
# FOWLS

**They had just moved. This was the first night in the new apart-**
ment. Everything was upside down, utter chaos: clothes not hung
in the wardrobes, pans and plates on the dining room floor, lamps
unassembled, bags of coal in the hall beside the sewing machine,
two mirrors parked in a corner facing the wall, some paintings
and a calendar on the table.

Quimet had slept poorly. Through a chink in the poorly ad-
justed shutter, a stream of light, straight as a sword, filtered into
the room as soon as it was day, and with it came all the noise of
the market. He dreamt that an older boy was eating a chocolate
bar and turning black little by little.

His mother washed his face and combed his hair. He had a
stubborn cowlick in the middle of his head that nothing could
tame, a skinned knee, rather dirty nails, a brown freckle on his
forehead, and ears that were somewhat fan-like.

"Go down and play. Just be sure you don't leave the square.
Here's some bread and chocolate. When you've eaten it, come
up and drink your milk. Be a good boy now and don't eat the
chocolate by itself."

Wearing baggy, knee-length trousers, made from an old pair
of his father's, and a white, faded sweater that was a little too
tight, Quimet went out onto the landing.

He bit into the slice of bread; when he finished it, he would
eat the chocolate. It was better by itself: sweet and soft. It stuck to
your teeth and the roof of your mouth. With his tongue he would

gradually loosen it, and it would turn into heavenly syrup. Slowly, he trudged down the stairs, one hand on the banister, moving cautiously, a step at a time.

He went outside and sat down on the doorstep, feeling out of place. The plaça was round, not too large, intersected by four streets. The market stood in the center. It had four tall portals, each one facing a street, draped with large red-and-white-striped canvas curtains.

Quimet glanced around. The sky was cloudy, discolored, an autumn sky free of swallows. The garbage was piled up in front of him, at the edge of the sidewalk. As he munched calmly on the bread, he poked through the pile and discovered a bouquet of wilted flowers, a dark, still fresh carnation, cabbage and lettuce leaves, leak stems, and a few squashed tomatoes full of shiny white seeds. He was tempted to pick up the seeds and put them in the empty matchbox in his pocket; he could plant them in a flowerpot and put it on the balcony. But he was feeling lazy after the sleepless night. His thumb started worming a hole into the chocolate bar.

Women scurried past with their baskets and disappeared into the market, from which a loud din emerged. An old woman with a wart on the tip of her chin marched resolutely by, carrying a shopping basket filled with goods. She almost bumped into him. A rabbit's head was sticking out of one side of the basket. He was spellbound. Those huge ears and the pink, nervous-looking snout, the long whiskers just waiting to be pulled . . .

On the opposite side he saw a man dressed in blue approaching, pushing a wagon filled to the top with poultry cages. Hens and chickens poked their heads through the wooden bars. In the top cage, mixed with the hens, a white Asian goose was stretching its long neck. It had a striking yellow beak and black eyes like pins with glass heads.

If he were mine, Quimet thought, I'd tie a rope around his leg and take him for a walk. I'd call him *Avellaneta*, Little Hazelnut.

He stood up and followed the man with the wagon. When the man reached the entrance to the market, he began to unload the cages.

Quimet planted himself in front of the man and stared intently at him. The man picked up a cage and entered the market; Quimet followed. The boy had the impression that the goose had noticed. Those inexpressive eyes were fixed on him.

The light inside the market was rather gloomy. Huge stacks of vegetables and fruit sat on the shelves and counters. Vendors were talking to shoppers. An explosion of color and life. A large bushel of eggplants was flanked by two small baskets—one holding plump, ripe, red tomatoes, the other thin green beans. A complex scent of flowers and fish wafted from the stalls at the back.

Quimet and the wagon man reached the poultry area. From iron hooks hung dead rabbits, chickens with wings crossed meekly across their backs, dappled partridges, geese partially split open with fatty stomachs, their flesh bloody.

All of a sudden the racket of flapping wings made him raise his head. He was petrified.

Five Guinea fowls were hanging by their necks in a row. The last one was still struggling, flapping its wings, uselessly attempting to fly. Two tall, stout men had stopped to watch.

"They don't kill them like that in my country."

A wasted-looking woman dressed in mourning ran the stall. She was wearing an apron and white oversleeves, her thin lips tightly shut. She was absorbed in her work. Without waiting for the hen to die, she took the whole row off the hooks and threw them in a pile on the counter where another twenty or so lay dead.

She took a piece of string from her apron pocket, went over to the cage that was half filled with hens, and removed one. It immediately began to screech. It was dark gray, its feathers covered with tiny white spots, a touch of white erupting on the tip of each wing.

With considerable difficulty she tied its neck with the string, then pulled with all her strength, and hung it up. The hen seemed startled for a moment, not moving, its small head twisted, eyes protruding. Then it spread its wings, its feet tucked into its stomach, ready for a last, deadly flight.

Quimet watched the scene breathlessly, the entire chocolate bar in his fingers, a half-chewed piece of bread in his mouth.

The woman returned to the cage and pulled out another hen. The creature let loose a terrifying, plaintive coo. The dying hen that had been hung up began to close its eyes and stretch out its legs, string dangling from its neck. The woman tied the leftover string around the neck of the next hen, which she then hung up. The tragedy was repeated. At first the second hen was stunned. Suddenly it spread its wings wide, as if it had been crucified, and started to struggle desperately, till finally, with twitching claws, it grabbed the head of the neighboring hen, which again started to make a racket. The more they struggled, the more the string tightened around them, till the neck feathers were damp on both sides from sweat or blood. A third was hung up to keep them company, then a fourth, then a fifth. The last was gray, but less dark, whitish, with a larger head, but the same elegant neck as the others. This hen's beak remained open for a moment, then it gasped violently, causing its breast feathers to undulate. The beak closed abruptly, then slowly reopened, the thin tongue, pointed like a pistil, throbbing helplessly. This one took longer to die. Every time Quimet thought, "It's over," the hen moved its wings. It spread them slowly, then flapped them furiously, the sudden gust of air making the whole row of hanging hens dance. Finally, without warning, it let out a screech. It was a final cry for help, directed to the fields and blue sky, to the space traversed by birds, filled with light and pollen. Its eyelids rolled back. Behind the motionless curtain the eyes grew glassy.

"How can anyone be so cruel!" mumbled an elderly woman to her wizened, hunchbacked companion as she passed the stand.

They glared indignantly at the vendor, as if she were an executioner. "Hanging those poor creatures!"

The vendor pretended not to hear. When the women left, she addressed the two gentlemen who were still watching:

"They're better like this. All the blood stays inside."

Slowly she began to take down the row of hens, preparing for the next batch.

But an incident occurred. The dead guineas, piled high on the counter, tottered, and many of them fell on the ground. A huge cat with a lustrous coat sauntered by the stall, attentive and cautious. The vendor wasn't pleased at this sight, for she suddenly yelled in alarm:

"Hey, lad, quick. Give me a hand. Help me pick them up!"

As if in a trance, Quimet laid his chocolate and bread on the edge of the counter. Yellow as wax, his eyes round, his legs trembling, he began to collect the warm feathery pillows. They were so soft.

He lifted one at a time, clasped beneath the stomach, and placed them on the counter. He was careful not to touch the tiny heads that waved on the ends of pliant necks. He felt a weight in his chest, as if all the dead birds' suffering was pressing against his lungs, keeping him from breathing. The thought that a lifeless body might suddenly start flapping its wings and hit him in the face sent pearls of sweat dripping down his forehead.

"Thanks, lad. For your help."

The vendor offered him an apple, but he didn't take it. He grabbed the bread and chocolate and ran off. Once outside, he crossed the street, raced up the stairs, and entered the apartment all out of breath. He found his mother in the kitchen and hugged her skirt.

"What's this? You haven't eaten your chocolate?"

Quimet started sobbing uncontrollably. He wept loudly, his mouth open, his eyes all wrinkled from being closed so tight.

"What's the matter? Did someone hit you? What is it?"

He shook his head after each question, but couldn't stop cry-ing. All his grief, all his pent-up pain, came pouring out. When the trauma began to pass, his chest still shaking from the last of his sobs, he announced, as if he had suddenly grown older:

"I'm terribly sad."

# THE
# MIRROR

**The doctor accompanied her to the door and shook her hand.**

"It's up to you now, Madame. I don't think it's anything serious, but bear in mind that, for a diabetic, diet is more important than treatment, or at least *as* important."

Not knowing what to say, she smiled and started down the stairs. Her hands and feet were freezing, her forehead burning.

On the street, the fiery summer light left her in a daze. The girls' sheer dresses, the yellow trams, the polished cars, the green foliage of the trees—everything was ablaze with eager life, but the unrelenting brightness made it all seem unreal. She felt weak. The moving shapes had a touch of excessive color that made her dizzy. "Gluten, Gluten." When uttered in a whisper, the word seemed to fill her mouth with a shapeless, tasteless paste.

She paused in front of the window of a jewelry shop. On the staggered shelves, lined with dark blue velvet, the diamonds rings and brooches emitted icy reflections. In the center stood a gold bird with ruby-encrusted wings and emerald eyes. *When I was coming along,* she thought, *diamonds were the thing. I've strewn all the jewels of my youth across France—the ones my husband gave me. What would he say if he hadn't died? I can't even imagine. The dead are quiet; that's why they frighten us. The things I'll carry with me to the grave! Enough, enough.* She glanced at the jewels one by one, making an effort to forget the unpleasant moment at the doctor's. She had broken into an anxious sweat when her blood pressure was taken. The cold, rubber sleeve around her wan, pale arm, the needle jumping back and forth. She reached up to feel the brooch she was wearing: she wasn't sure she had put it back on when she got dressed. The shop window reflected her hand, a long hand, furrowed with dark veins, the joints of the fingers deformed, a hand that was slow like a sickly animal.

Two girls stopped beside her.

"The ring I like the best is at the back. Do you see it? With the seven diamonds in a row."

"Are you serious?"

Their voices drew her out of her lethargy. French had gradually become familiar, but a few words still escaped her. On some days, it made her furious, and she would tell herself that she was going back to Barcelona, alone, even if she had to walk. *What am I doing, standing here?* she thought. As she was about to cross the street, a gentleman with a straw hat took her arm and escorted her to the opposite sidewalk.

"Thank you. Thank you very much. All these cars, at my age, they're rather frightening."

∗∗∗

Place Gambetta was filled with people, the outdoor cafés overflowing. The air was tepid, though the sun continued to burn hot. She stopped in the center of the square, beneath a magnolia tree. Some ladies were sitting in the shade, knitting or calmly chatting while their children ran around and yelled. Bees swarmed over the open magnolias and an acidic smell reached her. From her bag she removed a handkerchief embroidered with drupelets and carefully wiped her left eye. *This happens to people who have been too happy,* her oculist had told her with a smile many years ago. *One way or the other, tears need to find a way out.* Nothing had ever been able to stop that little bit of involuntary weeping that occasionally dampened her eyes.

She walked slowly along, small and bent. Her dark green

poplin coat, with its threadbare elbows and underarms, looked shiny in the sun. With a slight caress, as if from feverish fingers, the perfume from the magnolias wafted across to her, weakened by the distance.

When she reached *L'abeille d'or* she hesitated, then entered. A dense smell of cream-filled puff pastries made her mouth water. Her cheeks were rosy now. With an unconscious gesture she anxiously opened and closed her hand. Trays stacked with pastries were spread out before her. Some were golden, spongy, light, apt to melt in your mouth; others were heavy, buttery, dripping with liqueur, covered with a caramel topping that shone like glass.

"What would you like, Madame?"

"Half a kilo of cookies."

The shop attendant smiled at her and picked up a paper cone. While the woman filled it, she studied the trays.

"Vanilla as well?"

"Yes, please, and some of those wafers over there. The ones with the little cherries, just two of them. I'll eat them right now."

As she strolled up the shady side of rue Judaïque, her mouth felt all sweet and a tooth began to hurt. In her bag she was carrying two paper cones, one with cookies, the other with candy.

*～*

Her daughter-in-law, Elena, was seated by the garden gate, sewing.

"What did the doctor say?"

"The doctor? What doctor?"

Just beyond, her grandson was digging around a bed of carnations. When he heard his grandmother's voice, he turned around.

"Come here, Grandmother! Watch me plant these sunflowers!"

"I told my son not to buy him that hoe. He'll dig up the whole garden."

Elena raised her head from the sewing.

"Don't worry. I'm keeping an eye on him. Didn't you say you were going to the doctor's?"

"I'll go another day. With this wonderful weather, I preferred to go for a walk. What could the doctor tell me?" She tightened her grip around her bag with an irritated reflex; she could feel the weight of the cookies. "What could he say to me?"

She strolled over to her grandson and stood there for a while, observing him as he dug.

"That's it, keep planting."

She wanted to be alone, to rest. Her room was her world, filled with secrets, with pictures of people that not even her son or daughter-in-law knew. As she entered, the mirror on the wardrobe reflected the mysterious-looking green garden, barely visible behind the slats on the partially lowered blinds, a dream-like landscape.

She closed the door, took off her coat, and sat down in the wicker chair by the window. She struggled to remove her shoes. With an effort she reached her feet, her bony feet, just a bit of flesh covered the edges of the tendons. She left the shoes by the armchair, stretched her legs, and wiggled her toes, all the while thinking about the cookies. *The doctors can go to hell, their diets too.* She began to eat the cookies, slowly, so they would remain in her mouth longer. With her tongue she removed the gooey remains lodged in her teeth. Her stomach began to feel heavy, as if a lump of plaster had slowly set up shop inside. She closed her eyes, then picked up the hand mirror, a wedding present from the witness at her marriage. The frame was embossed silver with laurel leaves intertwined with ribbons. She observed the face of a sixty-year-old woman, slightly congested, the delicate skin wrinkled like an old apple, two pulpy, bluish bags under her eyes. She pulled an eyelid up. The inside was damp flesh, pinkish in the center, a brighter color at the edges, the white globe streaked with red veins. *"Green eyes and black hair. Enough to drive you*

*wild*," a suitor had said to Roger before he met her. *Black hair.*
The mirror reflected white, yellowish, thinning hair pulled back
from her wrinkled forehead. Without letting go of the mirror,
she reached for another cookie with her left hand. *"Why won't
you dance with me?"*

Roger didn't dance that day. He was standing by a window of
the drawing room, talking to an elderly gentleman. He seemed
uneasy as he watched someone she couldn't see. Between the
dancing couples she caught a glimpse of the gardenia he was
wearing in his lapel.

"Why won't you dance with me?"

Jaume Mas, her husband, had entered her life in that manner:
timidly, as she gazed at Roger, remembering that afternoon. She
was filled with the terrible wish to scream. Jaume had entered
her life too late, but it was at the precise moment when she was
losing her bearings. *Are you tired?* She was gazing at her fan, the
mother-of-pearl ribs, the silk tassel. She had had a mauve dress
with a lilac posy at the waist made for her. She had it made with
Roger's words in mind. *We've begun to love each other beneath the
sign of the lilacs.* You could see clumps of lilacs in the park, and
branches of them stood in vases around the room. On that afternoon. *If Roger comes near, he'll see the landscape on my fan, tender
apple green with a peach-colored sky.* But he didn't approach. I don't
think he even saw me, and I wanted to scream.

"You don't want to dance?"

I felt sorry for him, a sudden sadness, as if I had just been
shown a condemned man. Had I chosen him as a victim while I
watched Roger? Scarcely a month had passed. The man in charge
of closing the park had scolded us because he had to wait. The
streetlights were beginning to come on and a slight drizzle had
started. In the sand near the bench where we sat, I had written

"Roger" with the tip of my umbrella, and the drizzle had slowly erased the name.

The waltz was sad. Sad as the light that afternoon when we left the park. She passed me. Agata dancing, her shoulders bare. Agata. Her dress was white as daisies, and she was wearing a ruby necklace, shiny as drops of fresh blood. Lovers. Agata and Roger, lovers. I had only been told a few days before. Long-time lovers. Roger and Agata. Roger. When I scribbled "Roger" in the sand that day. He and I were lovers that afternoon. The first and last afternoon. A few drops of blood on a white sheet. Red as Agata's ruby necklace. I could still hear Roger's voice when, with the last embrace, he asked: "Don't you feel well?" All so far away. The kisses, the blood, the lilac perfume.

I found myself dancing in the center of the drawing room. An expressionless face had drawn near mine, its cheeks too round. It belonged to the man who would become my husband.

<hr>

"Get the watering can, little girl, and help me water the plants."

"The sunflowers, too?"

Her daughter-in-law must have locked the gate and was probably watering the geraniums beneath the dining room window, as she did every afternoon. Then she would water the chrysanthemums that were beginning to grow tall. She sighed and turned the mirror sideways. She had small, pearly ears with pinkish lobes. One was slashed. When she was breastfeeding her son—she had wanted to call him Roger—she would often wear her long emerald and diamond earrings. The child, who was just beginning to walk, used to take hold of her lips with his tiny hand and squeeze them tightly. Sometimes the hand seemed to be grasping air. One day he pulled furiously at one of the earrings. With the earring in his hand, he continued to suck the blood-splattered breast.

White lilacs adorned the altar the day she married, like lilacs

from another world, a world of the dead. She was frightened. She
suddenly wanted to flee.

I was sinking. Sinking into a dark well. Two invisible hands had
grabbed hold of my head and were pulling me down, down,
backwards. "Remember when we first met? I asked you: 'Do you
want to dance with me?'" That memory will haunt me all my
life. When he embraced me, he said: "Say my name, say it." In
my mind I said, "Roger." I didn't say it, only thought it, but my
husband moved aside. I didn't understand what he said. I never
knew what he said. I could sense him getting dressed; then I
heard the outside door closing, his footsteps walking across the
pavement. I wasn't sad, nor did I feel like crying. It was as if I had
turned to stone. I stroked my belly. Roger's son would live, and
I could give him a name. I woke when it was still dark. Someone
beside me was weeping. The smell of night and wind reached
me. He had returned. I felt the suffering, and it calmed me. He
wept with his face close to my back; the smell of wind and night
were in his hair. Against my skin I could feel his burning breath
broken by sobs. Another breathing, within my belly, burned me.
Every drop of blood gathered together to create flesh. I lay very
still, observing the shadows in the corners of the room. Dawn
would devour them. I held a monster within me, a footless, hand-
less monster. I thought my belly moved, that hands were forming
as I watched, determined to emerge. A bitter, sour taste coursed
into my mouth. He wept, and I fell asleep.

Beneath the lilac-filled vases lay purple stars; lots of tiny flowers had fallen. Roger was getting dressed. His initials, R.G., were
embroidered on the left side of his shirt. I too needed to get
dressed, but I lingered, afraid that the most insignificant gesture
would shatter that mirror of sad, fragile happiness. As if my dismay could make the afternoon last for years and years. When we

went down to the street, we stopped beneath a streetlight and shook hands, as if we were simply friends, and said good-bye. Yet coming down the stairs, we had stopped to kiss on each step. When I was alone again, I thought, "We'll never see each other again as we have today." I looked around for something to call my own: the light from the streetlamp, the purple sky, a window with a light. Then I started walking. And later? The dance, Agata, the child, my marriage.

I had only the instinct to say: "Don't shout." He walked up and down the bedroom, occasionally opening a drawer in the dresser, only to slam it shut furiously, with an abrupt, brutal gesture.

"Why did you marry me? Why?"

"Don't shout. Everyone will hear. Don't."

"Your past."

He had said "Your past." We were different then, bookish.

"If at least your past were dead! But it isn't; it's alive. Your past has lived with us, breathing day and night as if it were a real person. Always, always. I've reached the point where to continue living I have to feel that someone needs me."

Ill. I'm old now and ill and my youth . . . "For a diabetic, diet is more important than medicine." Cookies don't make me feel bad, the sun does. I was out in the sun too long. This mirror knows it all. My green eyes and black hair are still there, hidden inside it. The first thing they did was hold the mirror up to his lips. This same mirror. At the beginning it didn't turn misty. "We'll save him, I'm sure." The doctor looked at me, as if to cheer me up, as if it were a tragedy that my husband had wished to hang himself. I too had suffered, but I didn't hang myself. "We'll save him." He was left with a purple spot on his neck, a line that lingered for a long time. I watched over him that night. He had chosen our wedding anniversary, and I couldn't forgive him for surviving.

"I keep seeing you with that mauve dress of yours, and the lilac posy on the day I met you, at the dance. You're looking at me as if I frightened you. How could I frighten you?"

How indeed? Especially now that it's like someone else's story. My son, my husband, Roger. Nothing. No one. I've lived alone. I am alone. Alone with this bundle of dead memories, which could be mine or not. Useless, sordid. Sixty years old, ill, with a son I don't love because he looks like Roger. My jewelry has been sold off, little by little, in order to get by; I was forced to leave my country. Stupid. Bald and stupid. I watched over him all night; in the morning he asked for a glass of water. He could hardly speak. He made a tired gesture with his hand. He took a swallow and wouldn't let go of my hand. He asked me to kiss him. "Out of kindness, even if I frighten you." I went over to him. We were alone, everybody was asleep. I leaned down to kiss him, and when his face was close to mine, I spat on him. I spat and ran out. He seemed to be dead already. When he died, a few years later, I didn't cry. And he was probably the only person who had loved me. Not me, the other woman who lived inside me.

           *

Slowly she raised the mirror, held it by the marble edge of the bedside table. She hesitated a moment. Should I break it? *I'm so much a creature of my own time, my own time.* She lowered her arm slowly and threw the mirror on the bed. She heard steps along the corridor. It was her son. He must have left work early.

"Elena, do you know if Mamà went to the doctor's today?

The doctor, the doctor. That would be the dinner conversation.

She picked up the cookie crumbs that had fallen into her lap, raised the blinds, and threw them into the garden.

# HAPPINESS

**Last night, before she fell asleep, she had realized winter was** almost over. "No more cold," she thought, stretching out between the sheets. As if from a limpid world, the clear sounds of the night reached her, restored to their original purity. The ticking of the clock, almost imperceptible during the day, filled the room with a nervous throb, causing her to imagine a clock in a land of giants. The steps on the pavement sounded like an assassin, or a madman escaped from an asylum, and her heart and pulse beat faster. The sound of a woodworm gnawing was the herald of some imminent danger: perhaps the insistent pounding was a friendly ghost endeavoring to keep her awake and vigilant. With, not fear, but a sense of dread, she moved closer to Jaume and snuggled up to him. She felt protected, her mind free of thought.

The moonlight, blending with the glow of the street lamp, reached the foot of the bed, and every now and then a gust of fresh air, full of night perfume, brushed her face. She savored the caress and compared its freshness to the freshness of other spring breezes. The flowers will come, she thought, and blue days with long, pink sunsets and warm waves of sun and pale dresses. Overcrowded trains will carry people whose eyes will shine with the excitement of the big holidays. All the things that accompany fair weather will appear, to be taken away in the autumn by a strong wind and three heavy rainstorms.

She lay there awake in the middle of the night finding pleasure in the thought of leaving winter behind. She raised her arm and shook her hand: the metal jangle made her smile. She stretched voluptuously. The bracelet shone in the light of the arc lamp and the moon. It had been hers since that afternoon, and she watched it shining against her skin, as if it were part of her. She made it jangle again. She wanted three of them. All the same. Three chains to be worn together.

"Can't you sleep?"

"I will in a moment."

If he could know how much she loved him! For everything. Because he was so good, because he knew how to hold her tenderly as if he were afraid of breaking her, with more love in his heart than in his eyes—and she was one to know if there was love in his eyes. Because he lived only for her, the same way she had lived for her cat when she was little: anxiously. She had suffered because she was afraid her cat suffered. With troubled eyes, she would anxiously look for her mother: "He finished the milk; he's still hungry . . . His neck's caught in the ball of yarn; he's going to choke . . . He's playing with the fringe on the curtain, and when he hears someone he stops and pretends he doesn't notice, but he's so scared his heart's pounding . . ."

She felt like kissing him, not letting him sleep, pestering him until in the end he would want the kisses as much as she did. But the night was high, the air sweet, and the bracelet shiny . . . Little by little she lost consciousness and fell asleep.

But now that it was morning, she was miserable. From the bathroom came the sound of running water. It was pouring into the sink. She recognized the unmistakable clink of his razor being placed on the glass shelf, then the bottle of cologne. Every unambiguous sound conveyed the precision of his actions.

She was uncomfortable lying facedown, elbows propped on the bed, hands pressed against her cheeks. She was counting the

*arrondissements* in a Paris guidebook. One, two, three . . . The
sound of the water distracted her, and she lost count. She could
only find nineteen. Where did she go wrong? She started with
Île Saint-Louis and started around. Four, five, six . . . The tender
colors calmed her anger. The blues, pinks, purples, the splashes
of green from the parks, all of them reminded her of the end
of summer, when every tree turned gold or copper. On other
days, the stream of water from the next room brought a rush of
summer happiness, evoking memories of wide rivers reflecting
low-flying birds, of white coves with seaweed on the sand, but
today the sound filled her with melancholy.

Of course, it was ridiculous to worry about a morning without
kisses, and she deliberately chose the word "worry" to avoid a
harsher one that would give rise to waves and waves of resent-
ment. But she had always loved the first morning kisses . . . They
tasted of sleep, as if discarded sleep returned through his lips
and reached her closed eyes that wanted to sleep again. Those
playful kisses were worth everything. One, two, three, four, five
. . . Île Saint-Louis, Châtelet, Rue Montyon . . . seventeen, eighteen . . .

Now the shower. She could see him under it, as the drizzle
began, his eyes shut, groping for the towel he had left on the rim
of the bathtub. When he found it, he would hold out his arm so
it wouldn't get wet; then he would wait five minutes. Peculiar
habits. Like eating candy while taking a bath: your body soaking,
your mouth full of sweetness.

It's over, she thought. Love is ending. And this is how it ends,
quietly. The more she imagined him calmly under the shower, the
angrier she became. She would leave him. She could see herself
packing her bags. And the details were so real, her imagination
evoked them so vividly, that she could almost feel the folded, soft,
silky clothes in her fingertips, the clothes she regretfully placed
in the suitcase that was now too small for all her things. Oh, yes,
she would leave. She could see herself at the door. She would

leave at daybreak. She would go down the stairs without making any noise, almost on tiptoe.

But he would hear her. He wouldn't have been woken by her light step, but rather by a mysterious feeling of loneliness. In a frenzy he would rush down the stairs after her and take her by the arm as she reached the first floor. The conversation would be brief, the silences more eloquent than the words.

"I'm leaving you," she would say in a low voice.

"What are you saying?" he would ask in amazement.

Could she leave so much tenderness? He would look at her with tremendous sadness: so many words, so many Paris streets, so many days drawing to a close at a time when they were just beginning to dream of their love. She wasn't counting now. She was looking at the map. In front of every important building he had told her: "I love you." He had said "I love you" while crossing the street, seated at an outdoor café, under every tree in the Tuileries. He would write "I love you" on a scrap of paper, roll it up, and secretly slip it in her hand when she least expected it. He would write "I love you" on a little piece of wood that he tore off a matchbox or on the foggy window of a bus. That's how he would say "I love you": joyfully, not expecting anything in return, as if happiness was simply being able to say "I love you." Here, where her eyes now rested, at the tip of Île Saint-Louis—the water and sky so blue, the horizon and the river so tenderly blue—here he had also said "I love you." She could see Place de la Concorde on a rainy evening. Lights were reflected on the glistening pavement, and beneath each lamp was born a river of light. She could see an umbrella approaching, as if she were looking down from a roof. At the end of each rib of the tiny umbrella—between the ribs, too—there stood a drop of water. Paris: roofs, chimneys, ribbons of fog, deep streets, bridges over still water. The bad weather had kept inside all the women who knit in parks near their blond children and had left the lovers outside—together with the roses and tulips in gardens. It had left the two of them under the umbrella with their newly exchanged "I love you"s and their tremendous nostalgia for love.

While still on the landing of the first floor, she would tell him: "If we don't love each other anymore, why do you want me to stay?" She would make a point of using the plural, not because it was true, but so he would see that her decision was irrevocable, and so he would be forced to understand that there was no other solution. On the street she would encounter rain. Not the rain of lovers, but the rain of those made sad by life's repeated bitterness, the rain that brings mud and cold, dirty rain that makes the poor complain because it ruins their clothes and shoes and causes children with wet feet to catch cold on their way to school. She would board the train mechanically. A train with dirty windows, with thousands of drops of water trickling down the side. Then there would be the sound of wheels and the shrill whistle. *The End.*

A new life would begin. She would have to attack it without regret, with great willpower, saying: "Today life begins, behind me there is nothing." How would her sister receive her? And her brother-in-law?

She would find Gogol: fat, ungainly, dirty, his hair white, his lifeless eyes marked with red spots. Her brother-in-law had christened him at the time of his passion for Russian literature, a passion that had moved on to crossword puzzles. He had found the dog crouching on the side of the road like a pile of rubbish. Feeling sorry for him, he put him in his Ford and didn't realize he was blind until after he'd had him at home for a while. Marta had complained. A blind dog: what good was that? But it would have been too sad to throw him out . . . He walked slowly, head down, bumping into furniture. He would lie in the corner or the middle of the room, and if someone approached he would raise his head as if looking at the sky. They kept him, but it was depressing.

"Bon dia, Teresa," her sister would say when she saw her, "always the same, never letting us know you're coming. Pere, it's

Teresa, put down your crossword puzzle and come here." Then the rejoicing would begin. She would feel a terrible loneliness. The house on the outskirts of town would seem sordid to her: the covered entrance had no glass—not that the glass had broken, but rather it had never been put in. The walls were full of drawings Pere had made during his leisure time, abominable, surrealistic drawings that made her dizzy.

"What a surprise, sister-in-law!" Twenty years of bureaucracy hadn't taken the liveliness from his voice, or the freshness of his laughter, but his eyes were sad and greedy. It was the look of someone suffocating, with no voice left to cry for help.

Her eyes welled up. She could no longer see the tender colors on the map.

Not a sound came from the bathroom. He must be putting on his tie; he must be combing his hair. Soon he would be coming out. Quick, quick, she thought. If only the clock could be turned back, back to a previous moment. Back to the little house last year by the sea. The sky, water, palm trees, the fiery red of the sun reflected at sunset on the glass of the balcony. Blooming jasmine gripping the balcony. And the clouds, the waves, the wind that furiously blew the windows closed . . . It was all in her heart.

A burst of tears and sighs shook the bed. She cried in despair, as if a river of tears were forcing itself out through her eyes. The more she tried to restrain herself, the sharper the pain. "What's the matter, Teresa?" He was by her side, surprised and hesitant. Oh, if the crying could only be stopped, controlled. But his voice brought on another flood of tears. He sat on the bed, very close to her, put his arm around her and kissed her hair. He didn't know what to say, nor did he understand. She had him once more. She had him by her side, even with all there was on the map, and more. Much more than could possibly be conveyed: the smell of water was the rain on the umbrella, on the still, frightened river; it was the iridescent drops on the tips of leaves, hidden drops on rose leaves. The roses didn't drink them, those iridescent, secret drops. They guarded them jealously, as she did the kisses.

Could she tell him the truth? Now that she had him beside her, his face full of anguish as he leaned toward her, giving himself fully to her, the drama that had arisen in half an hour melted like snow in fire. "Can't you tell me what's wrong?" He gently brushed the hair away from her wrists and kissed her. She couldn't say a word but felt at peace. He threw the map on the floor and hugged her like a child. He truly loved her, she thought, and would never have been able to think the absurd things she sometimes did. They had come so far together. They were one in the midst of so many people.

And the girl full of anger who wanted to catch the train, who wanted to flee, to slip down the stairs unexpectedly without being seen, began to dissolve. She was carried away like witches by the smoke. She went up an imaginary chimney and was swept away by the wind, was slowly picked apart until nothing was left. What remained, all curled up, was a girl without troubles, without agitation, a girl unaware that she was tyrannically imprisoned within four walls and a ceiling of tenderness.

# AFTERNOON
# AT THE CINEMA

**Sunday, 2 June**

Ramon and I went to the Rialto this afternoon. We had quarreled earlier, and I was almost in tears when he was buying the tickets. It was over something stupid, I know. It started like this. I went to bed last night at one o'clock. I stayed up past twelve because of the electric blue thread I misplaced, and without the thread I couldn't finish the smocking. And Mamà was in a bad mood. "You never pay attention to where you put things, just like your father." Which only made me more nervous. Papà gave her an irritated look from the table, and then he went back to staring into a hand mirror he had propped up against a wine bottle and picking the blackheads from his nose. I finally found the thread and could finish the smocking. But I still had to iron the skirt and blouse. I was exhausted when I got in bed, and I thought about Ramon for a while till I fell asleep. When he rang today after lunch I was already dressed; I even had three roses in my hair. He stormed in like he was crazy and didn't even glance at my skirt and blouse— and all that work to iron them. He went straight to Papà, who was sitting in the rocking chair half asleep, and said, "Figueres says it's better for us not to give our names. Just as I thought: They tricked you." Papà opened one eye, immediately closed it again, and started rocking. But Ramon kept on talking, as if he didn't see he was annoying Papà, saying the refugees should do this or that, and all that time he never even looked at me. Finally he said,

51

"Let's go, Caterina," and he took me by the arm and we left. I said to him, "You always say things to upset him. You're so annoying." But that's nothing. We were half way there and weren't talking and suddenly he let go of my arm. Oh, but I immediately saw what was happening: Roser was coming toward us on our side of the street. He always says he and Roser just fooled around a little. Sure, just fooled around. But he let go of my arm. She walked by all tense, not even looking at us. I said to him, "It looks like she's your fiancée instead of me." (I just noticed I wrote this part without any breaks and the *mestressa* always used to tell me to stop every now and then and start a new paragraph. But since I'm only writing this for me, it doesn't matter.)

Well, I felt like crying while he was buying the tickets, and the bell to start the movie made me even sadder. I felt like crying because I love Ramon and I like it when he has that smell of aftershave the days he goes to the barber to get his hair cut, but I like it even more when his hair is long and he looks like Tarzan from the side. I know I'll get married, because I'm pretty, but I want to marry *him*. Mamà always says he'll end up in Guyana with all that black market stuff. But he won't be doing it forever and he says this way we can get married sooner. Maybe he's right.

We sat down without saying anything; the room smelled like disinfectant. First they showed a news reel: a girl skated, then there were lots of bicycles and then four or five men seated around a table. At that point he started to whistle and stomp his feet like he was crazy. The man in front of us turned around and they argued till it was over. After that there was a movie with puppets I didn't like at all: there were all these talking cows. At intermission we went to the bar and drank a *Pampre d'Or* and he ran into a friend who asked him if he had any Nylons and packs of Camels and he answered he'd have some next week because he was going to Le Havre. I worry a lot when he's away because even if I don't say it I'm always afraid they'll catch him and handcuff him.

On account of the black market we missed the first part and when we were about to sit down everyone complained because the wooden soles on my shoes make a lot of noise even if I walk slowly. The couple in the movie was really in love. I can see we're not in love like that. There was a woman spy and a soldier and at the end they were both shot. Movies are lovely because if the ones in love are miserable then you suffer a bit but you think everything will turn out for the best, but when I'm miserable I never know if things will end well. And if sometimes things end badly, like today, everybody's sad, thinking what a pity. The days I'm really desperate it's worse, because no one knows. And if they knew, they'd laugh. When the saddest part came, he put his arm around my shoulder and then we weren't upset any more. I told him, "Don't go to Le Havre this week," and the lady behind us said, "Shhhh."

Now that I've read what I just wrote, I can see this isn't exactly what I wanted to say. This always happens to me: I explain things that at the time seem important and later I see they aren't at all. For example, all that about the blue thread I couldn't find last night. And then, if anyone were to read this diary they'd say I think Ramon doesn't love me and I do think he loves me even though it seems like he only thinks about buying and selling a lot of junk. But this still isn't exactly what I wanted to say. What I'd like to be able to explain is, even though I'm almost always sad, down deep I'm happy. If anyone reads this, they'll really laugh. I know I'm a bit naïve and Papà always tells me Ramon's a fool, and finally that's what makes me saddest because I think the two of us will be miserable. But, really . . .

# ICE
# CREAM

**"Here you are, which do you want: lemon-yellow or rose-pink?"**

He had bought two ice creams, and he was offering them to her with a sad look on his face. The woman at the cart pocketed the money he had just handed her and was already serving other customers, all the while calling out: "Best ice cream in town."

It was always the same: As the moment of parting approached, it seemed as if a bucket of sadness was being poured over him, and he would hardly utter a word during the time they had left together.

As the long afternoon was just beginning to unfold before them, he had sat beside her in the park, beneath the whispering trees and the splendor of the sun, happy and communicative. The band played the *Lohengrin* prelude, and they listened to it religiously, hand in hand. The ducks and a pair of straight-necked swans floated, as if made of plastic, across the blue-crystal lake. The men, women, and children seemed like walking, smiling figurines that were moved by some delicate mechanism in an artificial landscape made for real men.

As the sun began to set, they sat on a green bench beneath the damp shade of a linden tree, and filled with a mixture of shyness and emotion, he presented the engagement ring to her: a small diamond with a clearly visible imperfection. "Swear to me you'll never take it off." She spread her fingers to look at it, stretched her arm out, and turned her hand from side to side. With secret regret she thought about her hand only a moment before, without a ring, nimble and free. Her eyes welled up.

They left the park and were walking arm in arm, toward the entrance to the metro.

"Here, take the rose."

She took it and felt her legs grow weak. They walked a few steps. "Rose, rose . . ." Suddenly she trembled and a blush swept over her, all the way up to her hairline.

"Oh, the ice cream." She had let it drop on purpose to hide her agitation.

"Want me to buy you another one?"

"No."

Rose, rose . . . please, don't let him notice. *Why are you eating the roses?* And now we'll get married, and I'll have to burn the letters. All of them, even the one from February 15th. If I could only keep it, together with the dried roses. *Are you eating the roses?* I was holding a bouquet, and he was kissing me as we laughed and walked along. He held me by the waist. His hat was tilted to the side and his eyes shone. I was eating a rose leaf. *If you keep eating rose leaves, you'll turn into a rose.* That night I dreamed I was born from an old vine that hugged the wall, and little by little I opened out into petals of blood. He grabbed my arm furiously: *Throw the roses away, throw them away.* I looked at him with half-closed eyes and kept on chewing the rose leaf. My love. When I climbed the stairs I knew where I was, where I was going, and why. An old man opened the door and stepped back to let us inside. No, that dark room with the faded screen and frayed rug gave off no particular smell. It was sordid and sad. *Don't be afraid.* When I opened my eyes I saw his jacket on the back of the chair and his tie on top, green with red stripes. *You don't seem to recall that we have to deliver the violets.* The workshop manager scolded me the following day when I was late. I used a wire to string the purple leaves together. How tight he held me! I got a bruise on my arm and had to wear a blouse with long sleeves. *When I come back we'll get married,* the first letter said. *Do you still eat rose petals?* I'll have to burn them all, as well as the cretonne-lined box. And this ring that hurts my finger. He hasn't written me in two years, two years with no news. Married? Maybe dead. And if he came back, I'd do the same . . . The morning I cried so, the concierge brought the milk up to me: *That's life, and you can thank your lucky stars he didn't leave you a souvenir.* Seventeen letters, seventeen letters I waited for deliriously, sick with so much waiting. *Why are you eating the roses?*

"What are you thinking?"

"Me? Nothing."

# CARNIVAL

**"Taxi! Taxi!"**

A car drove by the girl without stopping. It was one o'clock in the morning, and she was standing on the deserted garden-lined Avinguda del Tibidabo. The only lights still lit shone from the house she had just left. Through the curtains you could see the shadows of people dancing.

"The taxi stand's further down," a young fellow told her as he walked past.

"Where?"

"Right by the tram stop."

The fellow gave the girl a puzzled glance. She was wearing a long, silken cape down to her feet, quite wide but lightweight. She had a shiny star on her forehead. And a mask. The March wind sent ripples through the folds in the cape. Her hair blew to one side.

"And where exactly *is* the tram stop?" she asked, wondering what his disguise was. The white wig was curious, with its tail curling upward at the neck. The socks were white too, the tight trousers red satin. The frock coat was a shade of beige. Some large cardboard scissors hung from his waist.

"Would you like for me to accompany you? I'm heading that way."

"We'll pretend like we're water flowing down the hill," the girl said as she burst out laughing. A fresh, contagious laugh.

They started walking. The boy strolling timidly, not too close

57

to the girl, from time to time glancing at the shadow on the ground caused by the star on the girl's forehead.

"The day after tomorrow I'm leaving for Paris," she suddenly announced. "I'll be there a couple of weeks, then on to Nice."

"Ah."

Not knowing what to say, he gazed straight at her, determined to give his look a surprised, intelligent air, one of admiration.

The girl must have been thinking about something else, because for several minutes she made no attempt to continue the conversation. Her head was slightly canted as she hummed a monotonous little tune of just three notes, always the same. She kept running her hand through her hair. Just when it seemed that she'd forgotten about the boy next to her, she stopped humming and pointed to a little package he was holding carefully in his hand.

"What's that?"

"This? Nothing. Just some pastries for my little brother," he said with a forced smile, a bit embarrassed.

"And that?" In his other hand he held an indistinguishable object.

"It's a mask."

"Why aren't you wearing it?"

The boy hesitated, not knowing what to say, but she insisted; so with a serious air, he put it on.

"I must look silly, no? I wouldn't have chosen a clown's face, but some friends gave it to me and they—"

"Like comical things?"

"Sometimes I think they go too far, but, you see, they—"

"Well, if a mask doesn't make people laugh, maybe it's best to go with your own face."

"You're right. Want a pastry?"

The girl stopped suddenly and with a mischievous twinkle said, "I'm going to get something. Will you wait for me?"

He nodded and the girl took off running, up the avenue. Her cape fell to the ground, but she didn't stop. He picked it up and closed his eyes, fingering the delicate material. Standing there all alone, the girl's cape over his arm, he felt out of place, removed from this world. He looked up at the sky for a long time. The trees were just beginning to bud, the tram tracks gleamed in the moonlight. The rough tips of his fingers against the silk sent a shiver up his spine. He hung the cape over his arm, not daring to touch it. He glanced up, glanced down, then started all over. The sky, the trees . . . Finally he sat down on a stone bench, but the cold immediately shot through his thin sateen trousers, sending another shiver up his spine.

After a long while the girl reappeared, tiny and pale, weightless, her sheer dress fluttering in the wind, like a bird with its wings extended downward.

"They let me have a bottle of champagne, and now the two of us are going to empty it. Do you like champagne?"

He was about to say, "Si, Senyora," but caught himself in time and exclaimed with a blush, "Immensely. Would you like your cape?"

"Not now. Later."

They had reached a tiny triangle of a plaza. A rickety evergreen stood in the center. She turned, facing west, and cried out "Titania!" A feeble echo from the houses on the other side repeated, "Titania!"

"The echo's not too bad here, but further up, by the house where the party is, you can hear the words repeated three times, loudly."

Feeling moved, he dared to exclaim, "So, it is my pleasure to accompany the queen of the fairies?"

"Purely by chance. With the same dress and a string of pearls, I could have been Juliet. Or with a garland of flowers and leaves in my hair, Ophelia," she added flirtatiously. "But with my temperament, I prefer to be, even if for just one night, a powerful character. So, why did you take me for Titania?"

"Because that's what you cried out, and my uncle used to tell me those stories."

"He died?"

"Many years ago."

"Well, now that you know who I am, introduce yourself."

The boy hesitated, but she insisted.

"Say your name, loud."

He swallowed and said in a low voice,

"My name's Pere."

Cheerfully, the girl shouted his name very loudly, and the echo replied, "Pere, Pere!"

"Twice? This echo's a bit crazy. Now that we've introduced ourselves, open the champagne. I might spill it on myself and a fairy's dress has to be immaculate." She handed him the bottle and added, "It seems like we've been friends for a long time."

"For years." *I wonder how much she's drunk tonight?* he thought. But she had walked a straight line the whole time, without any effort.

The cork came out without a pop and no foam.

"It's flat," she exclaimed in disappointment. "But it'll quench our thirst," and she took a long sip straight from the bottle.

"Would you like a pastry?"

They sat down on the edge of the sidewalk and started eating and drinking. He moved the cardboard nose with the mustache to one side, but it bothered him, so he pushed it up onto his forehead.

"The owner of the house," the girl began explaining, "is . . . I guess I should confess—after all, we're friends. He's my lover. He's the one I'm going to Paris with. He has to go on business, so we have an opportunity. His wife was at the dance. She's rarely at home, travels all the time. Since she was there, I decided to leave. The situation was really tense, especially for me of course.

I left without saying good-bye to anyone, and now I'm guessing he's searching for me all through the house and garden. But if he wanted me to stay, why didn't he lock his wife up in the dark room. For one night . . . I don't want to give the impression she's nasty. She's very nice, dresses really well, knows how to be welcoming. I'd say she's *una gran senyora*, a real lady. But I have the feeling that when she climbs in bed, covers her face with cream . . . He doesn't love her any more; he likes me. As we danced he told me, 'You're the most charming girl at the party; you're like a flower.' And a little while later he said, 'I'll love you eternally' or something like that."

The girl gave him a surprised, vexed look and didn't speak for a moment. Finally she said, "Shall we go?"

"Of course."

They left the empty bottle upright in the center of the street and started walking. His lids were heavy, the bones in his legs weak. Further down the street, the girl stopped in front of a gate. He paused beside her. She took his hand and whispered, very low, as if sharing a secret:

"Can you smell the gardenias?"

He couldn't smell anything except the scent of night, of green and trees. Besides, so much familiarity made him feel uneasy. The wind hit them in the face and droned plaintively through the branches.

When the boy didn't respond, she murmured in a gentle voice, her forehead leaning against the iron bars:

"The wind is always sad. When I was little I used to think that I'd like to live in a solitary house pounded by the wind, and every morning I'd take my two greyhounds and go to the forest to see the trees that had fallen during the night. The wind's bringing us the scent of gardenia, isn't it?"

"You should put on your cape," he said, still carrying it in his hand. He shivered just glimpsing her naked arms, but all the enthusiasm over the gardenias was starting to frighten him a bit.

"Would you help me?"

He put the cape around her, thinking, *If I were just a little more daring, I'd kiss her now.*

"I can see them, over there, at the back. Come closer, at the foot of the tall tree. You see it? If I could have just one."

His head was spinning, everything seemed foggy. In the end there was no other solution. *The gate's not that high*, he thought.

"You want me to get you some?"

She turned toward him, her hands together, imploring.

"Would you? That would make me very happy."

He attached the scissors to the strap and jumped effortlessly over the gate. He walked across the grass without making a sound. But then the grass ended and the path began. The sand grated beneath his feet. He didn't hear the wind, only the sand. He tiptoed, but the sand seemed to make more noise. He stepped back onto the grass, wiping the sweat from his forehead. The white flowers lay before him. He picked some, wrapping them in his handkerchief. Slowly he retreated, his heart pounding. The champagne, his pulsing blood, his fear—all of it left him in a daze.

"Did you get it?" she called impatiently from the street.

Suddenly, right by the boy a dog began barking furiously. You could hear the noise of the chain rattling as it grew taut, the dog pulling violently on it.

He threw the handkerchief with the flowers to the other side and climbed quickly over the gate. Just as he was about to jump to the street he was startled by the feeling of the back of his trousers splitting.

"My trousers," he managed to say.

"Did they rip?"

"Pretty badly, I think, but we need to hurry before someone comes out of the house."

He picked up the handkerchief with the flowers and they set off running.

"Let me see your trousers."

There was a huge tear at the back of his left thigh.

"There's quite a hole, but it can be sewed," she said.

"I know, but they're rented."

He said it with a dry tone, making an effort to conceal his sudden irritation. It had only lasted a second.

There were no taxis when they reached the tram stop.

"Not a good night for catching a taxi. Especially up here."

They stood for a while under a streetlight and he could look at her calmly. She was blonde, with very dark skin, well-defined lips—the lower jutted out a bit—her chin gently round with a dimple in the middle. Behind her mask he could see her tiny black eyes gleaming.

"I still haven't looked at the gardenias, or thanked you."

She gently removed a flower from the handkerchief, but as she was about to smell it, she said with a surprise, "What kind of flowers did you pick?"

"The ones by the tree."

"These aren't gardenias. They have no scent at all."

She glanced at the unfamiliar flower with an obvious expression of disappointment.

"Don't give it another thought. If you don't like them, toss them away."

Without realizing, he'd used the familiar "tu." He liked her, standing there absorbed in thought. He would have forgotten about the trousers had it not been for the cold wind that blew through the hole, bothering him.

"Now that I think of it, I'd have been surprised it they were gardenias. What month is it?" she asked in disappointment.

"The beginning of March."

"And gardenias bloom in the summer, for Saint Joan's feast day. It doesn't matter, I'm just sorry about your trousers. I wish I knew the name of these flowers." She again sniffed the flower, making him do the same. "What do they smell like? Doesn't it remind you of something? Such a faint scent, almost nonexistent, but it reminds me vaguely of elderberry flowers. You see? Without giving it a thought I've discovered what they smelled of. What if they were begonias?"

"They're smaller. I mean larger. I mean gardenias are smaller."

"Maybe they're stunted begonias."

"They're probably camellias." Both had started playing the game.

"Camellias? No, I'd recognize a camellia anywhere. These, I can assure you, are mysterious flowers. Flowers that bloom on the night of Carnival."

She wrapped the flowers back in the handkerchief and stood there, pensive. He was glad she hadn't thrown them away, and felt an irresistible desire to kiss her. But he thought, *I'm a man*, and with a protective tone he said, "There are no taxis, which means we can only do one of two things: wait till the sun comes out, if necessary, or walk. I'll accompany you to the end of the world."

They heard a car approaching, coming from Passeig de la Bonanova. When it got closer they could see the inside of it lit up, full of people. It drove right by them. The people were shouting and laughing. The man seated beside the driver, wearing a feather hat, threw them a handful of confetti.

"It's probably better if we don't wait. Let's walk," she said, adding, "but I live a good ways from here."

"How far?"

"Consell de Cent."

"Why don't we walk down Balmes? There's always the chance we'll find a taxi."

*Let's hope we don't find one.* He took her arm happily to help her across the street.

Barcelona lay below them, gleaming with a reddish halo that blazed across the sky, creating a magical arch of light. To the left, the lights on the top of the Putxet gleamed, but the houses sheltered on the side of the mountain had their windows closed. If the wind stopped blowing for an instant, their sole companions were the silence and the night.

They walked for a long while without speaking. She was the first to say something.

"What are you disguised as?"

"A tailor."

"A tailor?" she laughed. "If you hadn't told me . . ."

"Louis XV's Jewish tailor," he stated, sure of himself.

Then he began to explain that he was studying Greek and composed poetry, was writing a book, "Persephone's smile," and he'd spent the afternoon at the Carnival parade and was just returning from a party.

"When I finish my studies, I'll travel. I want to know the world. I'll leave without a penny in my pocket. Maybe I'll get myself hired as a stoker. Poets here all tend to die in bed surrounded by family, and the newspaper prints their dying words, describing the force of their last breath, the whole bit. I want to die alone, with my boots on, face down, an arrow in my back."

Until now she had led the conversation; she began to grow impatient with his outburst of eloquence.

"Ai!" she exclaimed suddenly, her hand on her chest as if her heart wanted to take flight.

"What's the matter?"

She took a moment to respond.

"Nothing, my heart. I was just dizzy all of a sudden."

He looked at her in alarm, not knowing what to say, whether he should hold her, let her go. She sighed deeply and ran her hand across her forehead.

"I'm all right now, it's starting to pass. I have a weak heart. It must be the kind of life I lead."

"What does your family say about it?"

"It doesn't seem to worry them."

"You should lead a healthier life. Fresh air, exercise, get to bed early."

"I know the story: lots of fish and vegetables."

"No," he responded, a bit disconcerted. "That's not what I mean. I mean to love more honestly."

"And die of boredom. No thanks. I decided long ago the kind of life I wanted. I plan only to pick the flowers, as my concierge would put it," she said, lowering her voice and shooting him a quick, amused look.

He was strolling, staring at the ground, distracted, and hadn't noticed she had looked at him. He raised his head with a certain regret, "And make a terrible mistake."

"A mistake? Oh, I don't want to get married, if that's what you're thinking. When I'm fifty and look back on my life, evaluate it, I'm convinced that I'll be pleased with the results. At least I'll have had love, dreams, kind words. I'll have avoided—as we do a puddle on a rainy day—everything that was tedious and vulgar."

"Even so, old age without children—"

"And no grandchildren, no aunts and uncles, nieces and nephews, or any other relatives. The funeral at noon."

"It's useless."

"I should redeem myself?"

A wind blew across their feet, coming from the sea, creating abrupt whirlwinds of dust. It bore thick clouds that traveled quickly across the sky, devouring the stars.

By the time they reached Plaça Molina, the sky was completely overcast and the wind panted ominously at the cross streets and above the rooftops.

"The night's going to end dramatically!"

"I've already told you, I love the wind."

Her cape was blowing horizontally. She took it off and handed it to him.

"Hold it for me."

He took it, stopped, and glanced at the sky.

"Which side of Consell de Cent do you live on?"

"Facing the sea, going down Passeig de Gràcia, on the left. Why?"

"Let's take the shortcut along Via Augusta. They're working on the street, not an easy walk, but it's quicker. I mean because of the weather."

He was neither in a hurry nor concerned about the rain. He simply wanted to stroll down the broad, deserted street. *It'll seem like we're alone in this world.* Midway between Plaça Molina and the train platform at Gràcia was a garden with a very old plane tree right beside a gate, its foliage falling over onto the street. He knew he'd never forget the sound of the wind blowing through the branches of the tree as he walked beside the girl.

Suddenly raindrops began to fall. Scattered drops, round and fat, striking the ground with a dull sound that increased the intensity of the moment.

"Just what we needed." The girl looked from one side to another, searching for shelter.

"If we want to find a doorway, we'll have to run down to the pink house. There are only gardens along this stretch," he said anxiously.

They would have to run like a couple of idiots. Damn rain that was ruining his reverie.

"Put on your cape, it'll keep you from getting quite so wet." He pulled up the ends of it and tied them at the level of her knees. "Will you be able to run?"

"I think so."

Holding hands, they ran down the street, pursued by the rain, driven by the wind that pushed them to one side. From the ground rose a hot, asphyxiating smell of damp dust. The rain slackened for a moment; the cloud that had borne it passed, but a darker one was approaching.

By the time they reached the first portal a real downpour had started. They were too exhausted to speak. Their hearts and pulses raced. She took off the cape and shook the water off her, as a bird might.

She looked at the boy and burst out laughing.

"Poor costume," she exclaimed, glancing down at her pleated skirt, all wet, the hem dirty. "If it were just a bit warmer, I would stand in the rain. When we're out of town in the summer and it rains, I put on my bathing suit and go for a stroll along the beach. It's wonderful."

The wind blew the rain toward the other side of the street. In front of the house where they had taken shelter lay a patch of dry ground, some two meters wide. A streetlight shone on the opposite sidewalk. The girl gazed at it in silence for a long time, wrinkling her forehead. She kept opening and closing her eyes as if she were alone.

"Do what I'm doing and you won't be so sad," she said without turning her head. "Close your eyes a bit and look at the light. You'll be amazed at the colors. You see? Green, red, blue."

He closed his eyes and opened them slowly.

"I don't see any colors."

The girl was engrossed in the game and didn't respond, as if she hadn't heard him. After a while, she exclaimed, slightly annoyed.

"You must not be doing it right. You have to close your eyes, but not all the way. Leave a tiny crack, really small."

The boy tried again, closing his lids, then opening them a little. But the yellowish light was unchanged.

"I don't see a thing."

"That means you'll have a long life," she said with a touch of disdain. "People who see seven colors die the following day. Today I've seen five. Wait, let me try again, see if it changes."

The boy felt depressed, as if having a long life was a true sign of mediocrity. The girl held her breath, still submerged in her experiment.

"No. I can only see five. There was a blue that looked like it was going to turn purple. I was really scared."

The game entertained them for a while before they noticed that the rain had stopped. Above the roofs, a cloud was slowly ripping apart, displaying a band of dark sky with a few stars visible on the edge. But you could still hear water falling all around, the sewers incapable of absorbing it all.

The boy sighed as if a nightmare had lifted.

"I was afraid we'd have rain all night. If you want my opinion, I think we need to hurry."

"Wouldn't you have enjoyed sleeping here in the doorway? I was starting to like the idea."

For some time the boy had begun to feel impatient. His legs were cold, his back soaking wet, and he was unable to control the tremble in his knees.

"It's stopped raining. We need to go."

The girl stretched out her arm, looked up, but didn't move.

"Where's your mask?"

He'd removed the cardboard nose when they started running in the rain and was holding it by the elastic band.

"I'm not coming unless you put it on."

With a condescending air he put on the mustache and nose without uttering a word. She noticed his forehead was full of bumps.

"You must have eaten something that didn't agree with you."

"Who, me? You mean because of my forehead? The doctor says it's because I'm growing so fast." *Why did she have to notice these things?* he thought.

They left the bright area by the doorway and entered a dimly lit neighborhood, walking along a seemingly abandoned street. Two dogs were rummaging through a pile of garbage, attracted by the nauseating stink. At the end of the street they could see the lights of the Diagonal.

They walked side by side, without saying a word. She held up her skirt and walked very slowly, hardly able to see where she stepped. Midway down the street, a shadow appeared and planted itself directly in front of them, demanding a light.

The man was tall and stocky, with a husky voice. A shorter shadow, as if it had just sprung from the earth, stood alongside.

"Sorry, I don't have a light." The boy was about to continue on when a hand as heavy as a hoof struck him across the chest.

"Hey, not so fast. Your money, first."

The boy felt his stomach contracting and his eyes well up. Instinctively he tried to keep his head.

"Look, it may be Carnival time, but it's too late for jokes."

"I wonder what you look like without that disguise of yours. Listen to the little sparrow chirping. Does your mamma bring you worms?"

Suddenly he was blinded by the man's flashlight.

"Send us a note when you get more hair on that face of yours. The little shit thinks I want to play games. Hand it over."

The girl intervened, her voice trembling slightly.

"It's not worth arguing," she said, handing her purse to the large man.

"Well, I'll be damned! Take a look at that star. Did it just pop out on your forehead like the Mother of God?"

As he spoke, the large man handed the purse to his companion.

"Count the money, Gabriel."

The short man opened the purse and took out two bills.

"Twenty-five and twenty-five, fifty," he said without enthusiasm.

"And you, brave little boy, you made up your mind yet?"

The boy was about to explode with anger.

"I'm not giving you anything."

The large man shone the flashlight on him again. Using his index finger and thumb he pulled on the cardboard nose, as far as the elastic allowed, then let go of it.

"That's for starters, and to wind this up—" and the man slapped him so hard he fell on the ground.

"Get up, you shit. Learned a lesson? Gabriel, get the girl's chain and medal. When you make your first communion, your godfather'll buy you another one."

The little man walked behind the girl and tried to unfasten the chain.

"Shine the light over here. The clasp's small, I can't see." The hefty man joined him, pointing the light. "Got it," he said, handing over the chain and medal.

The boy had struggled to stand up. He was covered in mud, his mask bent sideways, his cheek aching.

"Don't you want the star?" the girl asked, making an effort to smile.

The men didn't bother replying.

"Clean out the kid, Gabriel."

The short fellow went over and began going through his pockets. The stocky man laughed, "Don't cut yourself, he has scissors."

"But he's short on dough." From his pocket the man had pulled out a small, old wallet, its edges worn down.

"Two pesetas plus a five-peseta coin, seven pinched pesetas."

The large man looked at the boy curiously and said: "All that hullabaloo for this, you ass?"

He buttoned his jacket, raised the lapels, and spat.

"Down the street."

He turned to face the girl, tipped his hat, and said, "We'll accompany you a while, princess. You'll be safer with us. Want to take your mask off? No? As you like."

They headed down the street, one man on either side of the girl, the boy following behind. He felt like crying. He could feel a lump in his throat, his eyes damp. The girl was talking to the men.

"You could at least have left me a few pesetas, enough to catch a taxi home. You did a great job, a bit over the top, but you can't just leave a girl without a penny."

"Maybe she's right," said the shorter man.

"Gabriel, stop being so romantic. Think about that steak."

They reached the Diagonal.

"This is where we split. If you're looking for better company, feel free to come along. You won't get very far with this little guy."

She waited till they had walked away. The two men disappeared around the corner, their jackets turned up, their caps set firmly on their heads. Then she went over to the boy, who was standing apart, and said, "Some adventure!"

The boy didn't reply; he had a dark look. His outfit was muddy and wet. She didn't dare say anything else. The wind had calmed; the night was gentle and velvety now. They walked slowly between the stunted palm trees along the Diagonal. Passeig de Gràcia was an explosion of light. The plane trees stood motionless, their branches just beginning to bud. The asphalt was stretched taut like skin, shiny with patches of light, and littered with papers and drooping flowers. Colored confetti hung from the trees and balconies, drops of water still falling from them. That was all that remained of the *festa*. Every now and then a car passed, the lights on inside, displaying sleepy, listless men and women in disguise.

"Why are you so worried?"

He couldn't stand the silence any longer and began speaking with a serious voice.

"It's not that I'm worried. It's something much worse. I wanted to make this evening . . . I don't know how to explain . . . a night like this! I wanted a memory, something I could cling to, keep for the future. Because I will never take any trips, or write poetry. And it's not true that I study. I used to, now I work. I have a younger brother and I'm head of the household. So, now you know it all. You also know what a bad impression I've made. I've made a fool of myself."

She was filled with a deep sadness. It was as if a secret reserve of anguish had melted in the bottom of his chest, risen to his throat, and turned yet again into pain. She stopped and looked at him steadily. Perhaps a long, sweet look from her could raise his spirits. Instinctively she took off her mask and laid it on the bench nearby. He was mesmerized. "You look like an angel."

"Don't make fun, a drop of water just fell on my nose."

He gazed at her with a melancholy infatuation that she found disturbing. He seemed to have lost all sense of where they were or the time of day, as if for him the only thing that existed was her shy smile, those eyes of jet, her soft, flaxen hair falling limp on her round shoulders, smelling no doubt of fields in spring-time. *He must think I'll always laugh at him when I remember this night, those men, laughing at him always, till the end of time.*

They didn't realize that they were walking again, or that houses were passing them by, or that trees were trailing behind as more appeared, inevitable as fate.

"Oh, I lost the flowers," she exclaimed, pausing nervously. "Maybe I left them in the doorway when I was playing with the changing colors, or maybe those men . . ." She stopped because to speak of the men was to confront him with that troubling

memory. She bit her lips. She felt bad that she'd lost the flowers. She would have kept one in a book till it was dry as paper,
had lost its perfume—it wasn't even a gardenia—and when she
stumbled across it in the future, it would have always evoked
the color of night, the sound of the wind, her eighteen years, the
years she felt she had lost as soon as she had gained them.

"The flowers? They're not worth it." He waited a moment,
then smiled as he shrugged his shoulders and murmured, "Don't
give it another thought."

The girl looked at him for a moment without speaking. She
leaned her head to the side and gestured as if she were about to
take his arm. Then she changed her mind.

"I don't know why you're upset over such an insignificant incident. It could have happened to anyone. I'm sure my being there
made you feel inhibited; without me you'd have reacted differ-
ently. Now that you've told me things about yourself, I should tell
you something about me."

Her voice was strange, as if it she were straining to speak.

"You know what? It's not true that I have a lover. I've never
loved anyone. All my brother's friends that liked me a little, I
found them . . . I don't know how to explain it. It's difficult to say
the things the way we think them or feel them. I mean, all the
boys who have liked me up till now left me indifferent. It's probably that I don't like young men and older men scare me a bit.
Sometimes I'm convinced that I'm suffering from some strange
illness, because I feel good all alone in my room, with my books,
my thoughts. I know my thoughts aren't particularly lofty; I'm not
trying to sound grand. I don't really know why I ran way from
the party. I went with my brother and his fiancée. I shouldn't
say it, but I don't like that my brother's engaged. We were best
friends. No brother and sister ever got along better. Nor is it true
that I have a heart condition. Sometimes I can feel it beating fast
and it's because . . . I'll never find a substitute for my brother,
someone who can be what my brother was to me."

He felt a sadness rising from deep within him. He'd have given his life to be able to replace her brother.

"When I saw him dancing with her I felt terribly abandoned. I was filled with this furious desire to go home, gather together all the pictures of us when we were little and look at them one by one, to be able to feel myself again in all the places where they were taken. What *is* true is that I'm going to Paris, but it's because my father's French and he's just signed a three-year contract. He's an engineer and will be working on a dam. We'll just be passing through Paris. Then we'll be cooped up in a sleepy old town, and one day I'll marry a man just like my father, who'll come to me, as if he had been born old, with a certain tendency toward obesity . . ." She laughed.

They heard a clock strike three, resounding in the night, slowly, forlornly. The air was crisp, the stars twinkled like diamonds, the trees gave off a tender, freshwater scent. "And I'll have a proper wedding. Or maybe I'll devote myself to perfecting the education of my brother's children when they visit us in summer." She sighed deeply, affected by the insidious magic of the hour and the night. "I won't marry for love or merely to serve my own interest. Or maybe I'll marry for both these reasons. I'll have an orderly house filled with jars and jars of marmalade and summer preserves made for winter and large wardrobes with neatly folded clothes. If I have children, they'll have what I've had: heat in winter and the broad sea in summer. In other words, I'll be a scullery-maid Titania."

She gave a tired smile that turned unexpectedly into a laugh that was young and frank, crystalline.

"When I ran into you tonight, I suddenly wanted to invent another life for myself."

"Me too. I'd been saving my money for three months so I could rent this costume, not even catching the tram, and I live in Gràcia but work on Carrer de la Princesa. When my father was alive we had everything we needed. One day he went to bed feeling very ill and never got up. What little we had disappeared with his illness and the funeral. It was really hard for me. I had to give up everything I enjoyed, all my plans. Everything. We were really alone, and I was the oldest child. I had to make a real show of pretense, so as not to add to my mother's grief. It's kind of ridiculous that I'm explaining all this, complaining. It shows a poor spirit. My life would make a great dime novel. Here I'd been saving for three months, thinking I'd have fun with my friends, but as soon as I saw myself in this costume, I was embarrassed. I did go out with my friends, but they were all with their girlfriends; and after we'd been in the park up on Tibidabo for a while, they disappeared without my realizing. I walked for a long time, I sat for a while on a bench by the funicular . . . but that's not true. It's painful to tell the truth. I went up Tibidabo because a friend of mine works in a restaurant there, and he told me to stop by and see him. He gave me the pastries we ate. I sat on the park bench, thinking how terribly boring life was, and gazed at the night, the lights of the city below me, till I was tired."

"The kind of things that occur on the night of Carnival, no?"

Carnival had ended. The wind and rain had helped it die. *We too have died a bit*, he thought, *or the ghosts we have left along the way*. No one would be able to see them at the top of Avinguda del Tibidabo, with the pastries and champagne, by the gate with the perfume of the false gardenias, at the door where they had sheltered during the rain. It was all far away, indistinct, a bit absurd, as if it had never happened.

"Will you give me your address in France?"

"I don't even know it yet."

She, however, would never again remember that night. The sound of the train taking her away would erase the last vestiges of it. But he . . . he would never find another girl like her, with that smile, that hair. From time to time he would see her blurred outline standing in front of him, her image evoked by a certain perfume, a sigh of leaves, a swarm of ghostly stars at the back of the sky, a silence that suddenly manifests itself.

"You know what I'm going to do one day?" he said, his voice faltering, pronouncing each word distinctly, cautiously, as if walking a tightrope, afraid of falling into the impenetrable void of melancholy.

"No, I don't."

"I'll go to the little square off Avinguda del Tibidabo and I'll shout 'Titania' and listen for the echo. Then I'll cry 'Titania' again and again till I tire. You know, perhaps it's only when you're young that you wish so desperately that *now* would last, that nothing we have would ever end. We wish it even more when what we have *now* seems the best thing possible."

"I think you're right. You see, my parents are pleased that we're leaving, but for me . . . ? It's like having my hand cut off. If my brother were coming with us, I don't know, maybe I'd be excited about moving to a new country, new people, other friends. But my brother is staying, he's getting married before we leave. All these streets that are part of me, this sky, everything that has made me what I am—it'll all be lost. Some of it will vanish within a few days, some a few months from now, till finally after many years—"

They had reached Consell de Cent and crossed Passeig de Gràcia. The asphalt, still shiny from the rain, was beginning to have large dark patches of dry spots. The night would soon end. A faint suggestion of light began to appear on the horizon, at the end of the streets, above the houses, in the direction of the sea. Soon the sky would prevail and the stars would begin to fade one by one.

The girl stopped in front of a luxurious house. Through the large door made of iron and glass you could see the carpeted marble stairs. *That's it, it's all over*, he thought. He would have liked to find himself lying on a beach beside her, listening to the waves.

"I'm home" she exclaimed cheerfully, with that abrupt change from sadness to joy that was so characteristic of her. "I can say it now: when we met those men, I thought I might never come back."

She wasn't sure what to say, how she should say good-bye to the boy who'd been her companion for the last few hours. She was a little sorry she had confided in him. If she had the power of a real fairy, with a wave of her magic wand she would have made him disappear, or maybe turned him into a tree, and she wouldn't have to think any more about it. But he was there by her side, filled with passion. It struck her that she might never rid herself of him. She was filled with a sense of cruelty. *It's not cruel; it's just that I'm sleepy.* A sweet lethargy pervaded her. Her eyelids grew heavy, and she struggled to keep them open. She wanted to be in her own room, take off her clothes, put on fresh pajamas, lie flat in her bed and sleep a dreamless night.

It was as if he'd been bewitched. He couldn't take his eyes off the reflections in the door; he could see the branches of a tree, its newborn leaves swaying in the air, dappling the glass with lights and shadows.

"The time has come for us to separate," he said with a sigh, then added with a voice filled with regret, "but first I'd like to ask you something."

Through the mist of her exhaustion she thought, *If he can just ask quickly* . . . because exhaustion had enveloped her, her eyes, arms, legs, conquering her whole body and spirit. She felt as if she had never slept and her eighteen years of not sleeping demanded to be rectified in one single night.

When she didn't respond, he struggled to find the right words and continued, "I've been thinking about it for a while, but I don't know how to say it. Before I leave, I'd like to—your beautiful hair—"

The words flew from his thoughts, like birds from a branch, and he was left with only a stammer. He didn't know how to ask her if he could touch her hair.

"I think you have some confetti in—"

"Why don't you get it out?"

She smiled at him, as if encouraging him.

The boy reached out his arm, his hand trembling as if it weren't part of his body. He touched her hair, caressing it.

"Shall we say good-bye now?"

"Adéu."

She opened the door, but before disappearing into the shadow of the stairs, she turned her head and said tenderly,

"Adéu."

"Adéu."

But she probably didn't hear him. The door had shut with a dry, metallic clang.

---

The boy stood for a moment before the house, hesitating, suddenly feeling restored to the night, the street, to his most naked reality, as if the sound of the door banging had cut him off from another world. He had nothing left, only that silken touch on his fingertips, perhaps a bit of golden dust, the kind butterflies leave. *I've fallen madly in love*, he thought. Slowly he began walking beneath the trees. A gust of wind stirred the leaves around him. He felt the cold nipping the back of his thigh and instinctively felt for the rip. He started walking faster.

"What will they say when I return the costume?"

A stray dog spotted him from a distance, ran over, and started following him. An alarm clock rang on the opposite side of the street, disconsolate, as if trying to awaken a corpse.

# ENGAGED

**"You haven't said anything for a while—is anything wrong?"**

"What's the matter with me? Nothing, nothing at all."

"You're so worried you didn't remember today's my birthday. I'm not scolding you; it's just that I was so excited to turn eighteen!"

They strolled slowly. He was taller and rested his arm on her shoulder; she held him by the waist. Waves of cool air rippled through the branches of the linden trees along the Rambla as the last rays of sun began to fade, gilding the leaves.

"Let's stop to look at the flowers."

They had to wait for a tram and a post office van to pass before crossing the street. The tram stirred up dust and specks fell from the trees. They stopped in front of a shop window: it was like paradise, carefully guarded behind the glass that reflected their images. Roses, branches of white lilac, purple iris with fleshy petals dappled with yellow, bouquets of sweet peas (purple, blue, pink)—all of them breathing their final hours of quiet, insolent beauty. Behind the flowers, in the semi-darkness of the shop, a dark hand with painted nails moved forward to grasp two lilac branches. Several white petals floated down onto the iris.

"Okay?"

"What do you mean, 'Okay'?"

"I mean, have you looked enough?"

"Me? I'd never tire of looking. See that rose? The one that's swaying because the woman touched it when she picked up the lilac. It's so dark it's almost black. Have you ever seen roses that dark?"

"I don't understand your obsession with flowers. All that . . ." he made a gesture with his head as if shaking off something that suddenly vexed him. "They only last a day. If the florist left them in the window and you stopped by tomorrow at this time, you wouldn't even bother to look at them. Shall we go?"

"Just a moment."

"I'm dying of thirst."

"You know what I'd like?"

"What?"

"For you to buy me some flowers one day, just a small bouquet."

"Don't you know giving flowers is passé?"

They continued their walk. The sky was almost white, practically devoid of color, and the sun shone dimly from behind thin clouds.

They entered a little café that was empty.

"Want to sit outside?"

"No, the tram makes too much noise."

They chose a table in the corner. From where they were seated they could see the shiny electric coffeemaker that hissed as it spewed plumes of thick steam. Sitting in the café they felt a sense of comfort and freedom. It was all so clean and welcoming: the red leather booths along the wall; the bottles arranged in rows on shelves of light, varnished wood; the mirrors with their reflection. Even the view outside—the edges of the trees, the façades, the sky. Everything seemed recently made, unobserved. A different, gentle world.

"You have really small hands, don't you?"

They were folded on top of her red purse that bore the brass letters A.M. Soft nervous hands. He ran his index finger over her pale fingernails, which were an indefinable pinkish-white color.

"Let me see your life line."

He took her left hand and began to study her palm.

"You'll live longer than me. Senyora Ramon Esplà, widow."

"Since we must die, better that we both die on the same day."

Next to hers, his hands were wide and hard, "a man's hands." She was filled with a wild desire to kiss them. At times they reminded her of a bird.

The fat, bald waiter was leaning against a column; he had forgotten about them. He was gazing out at the street, occasionally running a hand over his shiny head.

"Hey! Two beers!"

The man roused and turned around. His eyes were dreamy.

"Right away."

"There's something I wanted to mention, but please don't get angry." She looked into his limpid and penetrating blue eyes. "I'm nervous because exams are almost here and I'm behind. In order to catch up, I need to study full-time for at least two weeks. I mean without seeing each other. You know what the history professor is like. He acts like he's speaking at an academic conference and doesn't realize we're no more than . . ."

"Two beers."

The waiter placed the glasses on the table and glanced tenderly at the couple.

"How much?"

The boy paid. This way, they could leave when they felt like it, without having to clap their hands. The waiter brought the change, picked up the tip, and returned to his place by the column.

"Do you mind if we don't see each other for a couple of weeks?" she asked.

"Why can't we see each other?"

"I've just told you, because we'd spend too much time going out, and exams are almost here."

He looked at her guardedly. She was drinking, her lips puckered around the white foam.

"Why can't we see each other like always? Are you looking for an excuse? If you don't feel like seeing me, just tell me."

"Ramon!" she begged with anxious eyes. She put the beer down on the table and repeated: "Ramon."

Suddenly he picked up her purse.

"Why did you do that?"

"I don't know. I just needed to. May I?"

"Of course."

She watched disconcertedly as he opened it, inspected it, and began to empty it. A wisp of hair fell across his pale, adolescent forehead, and his hands trembled a bit. He placed everything on the table. The lipstick, the green enamel compact with the dragon inlay in the center, the wallet. The address book he had given her the month before. He had been so self-conscious: it was his first present to her.

"Why are you examining everything?"

"Does it bother you?"

His eyes were hard, a look she'd never seen before.

"Not at all, but . . ."

He read the addresses of the people he knew. The English teacher with the telephone number and the dates and hours of classes: Tuesday, Thursday, Saturday from four to five. The addresses of her hairdresser and her two friends, Marta Roca and Elvira Puig.

After he had removed everything, he put it all back inside. He closed the purse, looked at it closely, then gave it back to her.

"Your turn."

He pulled his wallet out of the inside pocket of his jacket and handed it to her.

"Look at everything; I want you to look at it all."

"What's the matter with you?"

She was holding the wallet in her hand, giving it a troubled look.

"Nothing's the matter. Look at everything. All the papers."

She hesitated as she pulled out the bills, the tickets, the letters she had written him the year before, when they were mere friends holidaying in Tossa. A picture of her taken at the beach: it was too dark because a cloud had suddenly appeared just when he snapped. She found a tiny slip of paper in the corner.

"You kept this too?"

"I'll always keep it, I told you so. You see? I remember and you don't."

She unfolded the paper. "Yes, I'll marry you." She had written it because she was speechless when he asked her if she wanted to be his wife.

As she removed the papers from his wallet, she sensed that he was calmer. Then she put everything back in its place and handed it to him with a smile.

"This is what we have to do, always." he said, slipping the wallet into his pocket. "There can't be any secrets between you and me. Ever. We'll be like brother and sister."

They left the café, both feeling a bit strange, out of place. The air was cool, clean, filled with colors.

"And after we've been married for years, what if you fall in love with another woman?"

"Hush."

She squeezed his arm tenderly, but she wanted to weep. Houses, trees, streets—everything seemed false and useless.

# IN A WHISPER

**It was the last day. The very last.**

She was wearing a pale blue dress with a wide-brimmed hat, its black velvet ribbons dangling down to the middle of her back. Most of all I remember the velvet bow and the color of her dress, because that is what I saw last. That blue: a sky blue. Sometimes in summer the sky takes on a blue like her dress, a gray, sun-gorged blue. On scorching summer days, a blue as bitter as gentian.

The blue dress. Her eyes with the tiny pupils that were black like the velvet bow, her mouth—all milk and roses—her hands. All of it, the shape and the color, was a challenge, an insult to my *propriety*. "There are sad loves and happy loves. Ours is sad," she told me one day long ago with a gray, monotonous voice. It hurt so much that I couldn't put it out of my mind. "Why sad?" "Because you're a proper man." We hadn't seen each other for eight days, because I had accompanied my sick wife to a village in the mountains, for her to convalesce. A proper man. This man, who lived for a simple gesture from her. Everything about her, everything that came to me from her filled me with emotion.

I can still see the canvas awning at the café that morning (orange with a fringe that flapped in the wind), the bushes by the sidewalk, the notice on the mirror about the soccer match. I can hear her deep, cold voice. "I'm getting married." She had lowered her head, and the brim of her hat concealed her face. I could see only her lips and her nervously trembling chin. And the toxic blue of her dress.

Everything around me, everything within me felt empty. It was as if I lived in a shadowless, echoless cavern. It was a terrible period of inescapable magic. All the things that might have seemed a signal, might have engendered hope, had suddenly vanished, as if an invisible hand had snatched them away. They had ceased to be.

But at the age of forty, nothing ceases. No. Nothing ends. The child that I wanted was born and will live when I am dead. The last child. A pale child, light as a bouquet of flowers. When Albert went to peek at her, his Latin book under his arm, his mother asked: "Aren't you pleased to have a little sister?" He looked at the baby with curiosity and disdain, knitted his brow, pouted his arched lips, then left without a word, closing the door without a sound. The last child. I had wished for it darkly, from the depths of my loneliness, hoping to alleviate it, as if I might revive the sweetness that had died, preserve it within a being that was marked and still faltering.

We celebrated her first birthday today. She's beginning to walk but needs to grasp onto the furniture, the wall. If she has to take a few steps alone to get from one chair to another, she looks around anxiously and bursts into tears. I requested that a blue dress be made for her. I picked her up for a moment, and she laughed, making little cries of joy like a bird. I have concentrated all my tenderness in this little ball of warm flesh, in these tiny hands and feet. It is a bitter tenderness. When the child looked at me with sudden attention and curiosity, I had to close my eyes. Her shiny, black pupils are surrounded by a sky-blue shadow.

I had an impetuous desire to write to her. "Just to have a glimpse of you. If only to see you pass. If you would wear the blue dress, the dress you wore that last day." I tore the letter into a thousand pieces. I know she asked about me. She would have used that neutral voice of hers: "Ah, so he's had a daughter?" If I could only explain to her . . . "I'm getting married." If I had only been able to say: "I don't want you to." Her words cast me into a void, left me spinning, falling. "Gracious, you're young!" Her youth frightened me so. Since the child was born, my son looks at me as if he were trying to understand me. I sense him smiling harshly.

I haven't been able to sleep all night, and now my head is splitting. I got up to open the window and came back to bed. Slowly the dark room filled with starlight. I felt cold and pulled the duvet over me. The wind brushed the leaves on the lemon tree against the glass. "She's in Algeria," I was told yesterday afternoon. "She left two months ago." All night I imagined the sea and the ship. I couldn't rid myself of the image of the sea, the ship rocking back and forth like the leaves on the lemon tree. When it was almost day, I went to my daughter's room and lifted her frantically. She grumbled but didn't wake. I held her in my arms for a long time. Slowly the daylight returned the shape and color to objects. I clasped that tiny bit of flesh with its beating heart. I must have hurt her, for suddenly she started crying. "What is it?" My wife rushed in anxiously, tying the sash on her dressing gown. "Has she been crying long?" Then she glanced at me: "If you could only see how ill you look! What's wrong?" "Nothing," I said. "Nothing's the matter. Don't look at me like that. I assure you, it's nothing at all. Don't give me that look." Never, not even on the worst day of those eighteen years, had I wished so furiously to die.

# DEPARTURE

**"What's this soup made of?"**

"No way of knowing . . . The cook probably doesn't even know."

The waitress had just finished filling two bowls with a yellowish liquid: small pieces of green leaves were floating in it. They had left the suitcase sitting on the floor, beside the table. A dog went over to it, smelled it calmly, and moved away to the next table, where an old lady wearing a brown hat with a pheasant feather was holding out a fish bone.

"Don't look at me, eat."

He obeyed and put his spoon in the bowl. A moment later he raised his eyes and looked at her for a while.

"What do you plan to do?"

She wiped her lips, hesitated a moment, then answered:

"I don't know."

"I hate for you to leave like this, not knowing what you're going to do."

"Better not to think about it," she said in a very low voice, looking down at the bowl.

"Yes, I do, I hate it."

"Eat."

The restaurant at the train station was full. The waitresses hurried up and down with little notebooks stuck in their apron pockets, pencils hanging by little metal chains from their waists. Theirs had dark hair. She must have been about forty years old,

forty withered years. You could see she was tired and in a bad
mood. She wore a lot of eye makeup.

From time to time he glanced at his watch: still three quarters
of an hour before the train left.

"Say something."

The waitress took the bowls and set the plate down. A warm
china plate. She served them a piece of boiled hake, covered with
mayonnaise, with two or three lettuce leaves.

"Say whatever you like, just say something."

The waitress came back.

"Excuse me, I forgot to serve you the asparagus." She gave
them half a dozen, placing them beside the piece of hake.

"They count them carefully: six for you, six for me. I'm certain
everyone eating dinner counts the asparagus they're served. Six.
The same number of years you and I . . ."

A train whistled. You could hear the sound of hammering on
wheels mixed with the station boys' cries and the noise of the
loud speakers announcing departures.

"Oh, oh! The glass . . ."

It had been knocked over while he was reaching for a slice
of bread from the little basket. Beer spilled over the paper that
served as a tablecloth, spread to the edge of the table, and began
to drip onto the floor.

"Move the suitcase!"

"Fortunately I didn't break the glass."

A tall, thin gentleman entered, wearing a raincoat the color of
*café amb llet*. With a glance he surveyed the entire room, took a
watch out of his vest pocket, checked it against the clock on the
wall, and walked slowly away.

They continued to eat the hake. They ate mechanically: neither of them was hungry.

"When I think about you leaving with no money . . . I'll be
worried about you."

A black cat had just wandered by and the dog let out a few

barks and started to chase it under the tables. A gentleman who was dining alone, a little further away, turned red, protesting with an air of great dignity.

"Better not to think about it. Ah . . . ! That reminds me: I forgot to tell you I left your ironed shirts on the top shelf of the armoire, the socks in the right-hand drawer, where we kept the aspirin and the electric bills . . . Don't you like the mayonnaise?"

"Yes . . ."

"Then why don't you eat it?"

"I mean . . . I don't like it much."

The gentleman in the raincoat entered again, carrying two large suitcases. He crossed the room and sat down at the table where the lady in the hat with the pheasant feather had been earlier.

The waitress took the plates away.

"Grapes for me. And you?"

"Grapes."

"Grapes for both of us."

The waitress went over to the man in the raincoat, set the tray full of plates down on the table, and wrote the order in her notebook. A man and a woman entered. The man had one eye covered with a black cloth and was carrying a guitar. He started to sing with a hoarse, weary voice. From time to time he brushed the strings with his fingertips.

"I thought that was against the law."

"What?"

"That. Begging. Do you want to smoke?"

He handed her a cigarette. He took another and put it between his lips. The cigarette shook. He lit a match and the flame shook also.

"The last two I have. I gave you the whole one. Mine has a little hole."

"Shall we swap?"

"Oh, I'll just cover it with my finger."

The large hand of the clock moved and jumped a minute. The waitress brought the grapes and then served the gentleman in the raincoat a bowl of soup. At the same time she served him the plate of hake, with the lettuce leaves, the asparagus, and the mayonnaise.

"Let's see if he counts them."

They began to eat the grapes one by one, smoking from time to time. All of a sudden they laughed. The gentleman in the raincoat had put on his glasses: first he examined what was in the bowl, then he took his fork and calmly separated the asparagus, moving his lips slightly.

"Are you cold?"

"No . . ."

"You looked like you were shaking."

"Really?"

Through the window you could see the branches of a plane tree shining in the light from a street lamp. The leaves were yellow and shook gently in the early autumn wind.

"The leaves are already yellow. Did you notice?"

"But it's still not a bit cold."

"Perhaps I'd better start getting ready. Why don't you ask for the check?"

She took a tube of lipstick and some powder out of her purse. She painted her lips, spreading the lipstick with her tongue, and powdered her face. In the mirror her eyes were hard, expressionless, still a bit congested. Suddenly she felt an infinite weariness.

The man with the guitar approached them and held out his hand. A dark hand, large, with long fingers. He gave the man a coin.

"Perhaps we shouldn't linger."

She didn't answer him. A hand like his, the man asking for charity, began to tighten around her throat gently, gently.

"Do you want me to walk you to the platform?"

No, she couldn't answer. It was as if she were choking. The

hand was tightening around her throat. It was painful in two or three places.

"Do you know which platform it is? I'm afraid you might get lost . . ."

The gentleman in the raincoat had opened a suitcase and had taken out a bottle of wine. He poured some into the glass and started to drink slowly. He had eaten the asparagus, stems and all.

He called to the waitress.

"I'm sorry, really sorry. I think without me you'll find yourself . . ."

It was starting to pass. The hand wasn't so tight now. She was even able to say:

"I've always liked traveling by train . . . I loved it as a child . . . Did I ever tell you that once . . . ? Oh, there's no point in my telling you now."

The waitress brought them the check. They paid. She picked up the suitcase.

When they were at the door of the restaurant, she told him: "Don't come. It's better. Do you hear me? Don't come."

Tears welled up in her eyes. Again she felt her throat tightening.

He took her by the arm: "Don't you think we could . . . don't you . . ."

He started to kiss her. She turned her face. He felt her whole body stiffen, and he released her arm.

"Good-Bye."

From a distance he saw her hand the ticket to the control officer. "I won't see her again," he thought, "ever again."

"Excuse me."

The man with the guitar wanted to get by. The woman was behind him. She was short and plump, wearing a soiled black dress, very shiny.

He let them through and went out to the street.

# FRIDAY, JUNE 8

**"Hush, little thing, hush."**

She set her dirty old purse on the grass. The metal glaze that covered the clasp had started to flake off, leaving her fingers smelling of nickel. She rubbed them on the edge of her jacket as she unbuttoned her blouse with one hand. Her sagging breasts were pale and lined with dark blue veins. The baby began sucking hungrily, then slowly closed her eyes; when she opened them again, they had a steady, vacant look. A drop of milk trickled from her mouth.

The girl stood motionless, gazing at the river. The wind droned as it whipped through the iron rods of the high bridge, creating ripples on the water, swirling her skirt, playing with the grass. The baby choked, let go of the breast, then searched for it again with an uncertain gesture of her head, like a blind, newborn kitten. Her fists had been clenched the entire time, but they gradually opened, like a flower.

The bridge shook. The shadow of a train sped across the water, letting out a long whistle that blended with the sounds of the bridge and the wind. A cloud of thick smoke slowly began to dissipate beneath the bridge, downstream.

She gave an indifferent glance at the man beside her. She hadn't heard him approach, nor did she know from what direction he came. He stood in the light, and the sun cast a circle of light on his tattered clothes, which were covered in a yellow dust that sifted as he moved. The neck of a bottle protruded from a leather pouch he was carrying and a half-filled sack rested on his back. He had small, blue eyes, and his mustache and beard were very white. The man glanced at the sleeping baby, her head canted, the skin glistening where the milk had trickled.

"Must be hungry."

The girl didn't reply but clutched the baby against her chest, to protect it. The man didn't notice the gesture. With his finger he gently stroked her rosy forehead.

"You don't think she's too delicate to be out in this wind?"

He was confronted by a hard look and heard the woman hold her breath between clenched teeth. He stood there a moment, hesitating.

"None of my business. I can see you're not the talkative kind. Salut." He limped away, up a diagonal path toward a vineyard that hugged the slope like a green sheet spread across the arid land. Without turning her head, she followed him with her eyes. He walked fast. Soon she could see only a dark smudge against the bright horizon.

She placed the sleeping infant on the ground, then picked up a nearby rock. She pulled a dirty rope from her pocket and began to wind it around the rock. Two red, feverish spots shone on her emaciated cheeks. The sun caught blue reflections in her hair and made her bloodless fingernails shimmer as her hands knotted the rope.

She strode back to the child's side and knelt down. Slowly she slipped the rope under her head. The baby whimpered and clenched its fists without waking up.

"Hush, little thing, Go to sleep," she whispered as she picked up the baby.

The girl had to make an effort to stand up. She placed the rock on the baby's stomach and walked to the water's edge. Her feet plunged into the mud. She took a step forward, glanced around with bulging eyes, and threw it as hard as she could.

She heard the sound of water ripping. The body floated a moment, then suddenly disappeared as if someone had jerked it. A flock of birds screeched as it crossed the calm sky. There were many of them, flying in broad rows, carving a black path through the blue.

She faced the wind, walking stiffly—as if with wooden legs—up the same path the old man had taken, following the birds' screeches.

                            *

In the distance you could see four scattered houses. By the road, in a patio beneath an arbor of ivy and roses, stood a few tables with iron chairs. She was seated at the back. The setting sun blazed across the sky, and far away the winding river flowed blood red.

She hadn't walked far. From the bridge to the arbor was a scant half hour, but she had sat on the ground for a long time gazing at the river. She was exhausted, her back and sides ached. The milk from her swollen breasts had dampened her blouse. She was thirsty, and a vein was pulsing on the left side of her neck.

Two men were coming along the road. They stopped, leaned their bicycles against the wall, crossed the patio, and went inside the building.

"I see you got a new customer, *mestressa*," the man said, addressing the woman who ran the café. He was middle-aged and had shiny black eyes, dark cheeks, a dark chin, and what appeared to be rough skin. Drops of sweat covered his forehead, and he brushed them away with his hand. His shirt was stuck to his chest, soaking wet.

"What do you say, Belcacem?"

He elbowed his companion, a small, olive-skinned Arab with a large scar across his cheek. The Arab laughed, his teeth gleaming for an instant.

From behind the counter the old woman, a black scarf around her head, pulled out two glasses.

"She's been here for close to an hour. What are you doing at the quarry with all that blasting?"

The water from the faucet flowed furiously into the zinc basin, splashing the edges with fat, round drops that immediately dribbled down the sides. The woman picked up a bottle of vermouth. The cork squeaked.

"Passing time, *mestressa*, passing time." The man picked up the glass, held it up to the light. "Evening, Violeta."

The servant girl was wiping the tables. She was wearing a short skirt, and when she leaned over you could see the tops of her stockings.

"You gonna say yes to me tonight, Violeta?"

The Arab had finished his vermouth and was standing at the door looking out.

"I won't have anything to do with family men," she replied. Her cheeks were round and innocent. She had one lazy eye.

The man by the counter clucked his tongue, ran a finger under his nose, and called out, "You hear what she said, Belcacem?"

The Arab turned around, "Shut up. Look what the girl's doing out there."

His companion went over to him, and they stared at the girl through the strings of bamboo beads that served as a curtain. She was seated quietly under the arbor with an empty bottle in front of her. It had been filled with *gasosa*, a lemon-lime soda water. Her eyes were closed, and her hand was inside her blouse, touching her breast. The old woman turned on the faucet again. When the girl outside heard the sound of water, she opened her eyes and glanced around with a frightened look.

"She asked for an anise," Violeta said, all excited. "When I asked if she wanted it straight or with water, she gave me a strange look, like she just dropped from the moon. I don't think she's all there."

The old woman came out from behind the counter and looked through the beaded curtain at the girl.

"She must not be from around here," Violeta said. "I asked her again how she wanted her anise and she said, 'Bring me some *gasosa*.' Must've changed her mind. As I was walking away, I turned back, 'cause I thought she said something. But it wasn't to me." She paused, raised her head, and looked at the men. "She was talking to herself." Violeta stopped drying her hands on her apron and started laughing, a squeaky laugh that sounded like a rat.

"I'll get her chattering, *mestressa*, you'll see. Bring us some wine. Come along, Belcacem."

He pulled aside the bamboo beads and walked out, the Arab following him. When they reached the table, the girl skittered like a frightened animal.

"No reason to be scared, princess. He's black, but he's got a good heart."

They sat down at her table. She stared at them. One of her eyes had a burst blood vessel, and her black, oily hair fell across her face. She brushed it aside with a bony hand, her fingers extended as if they were made of stone. A rose petal floated down onto the table. The thick smell of burning oil wafted from the kitchen, blending with the perfume of evening and roses.

Violeta placed three glasses and a bottle of wine on the table. She went back inside, but stopped at the threshold, staring curiously at them, her mouth open, eyes round. She slipped a hand under her skirt and absentmindedly scratched her thigh. The beaded strings of the curtain flapped against each other, making a sound like the clacking of lace bobbins. It kept her from hearing anything outside. She watched the Arab hand the girl a glass, but she shook her head. After the two men had drunk and refilled their glasses, the girl picked up hers and raised it to her lips. It seemed as if she were going to hold it there forever, but finally she downed it in one sip, her eyes shut. Belcacem whispered in her ear. Only the back of the other man was visible. From time to time his shoulders shook as if he were laughing.

The old woman came out of the kitchen and went behind the counter, locked the drawer, and pocketed the key.

"So is that how you help me fix supper, Violeta, you lazy good-for-nothing? Leave the men alone; they're in the mood for playing around."

Reluctantly Violeta walked away and entered the smoke-filled kitchen. She took off the white apron she used for waiting on customers and put on the navy blue one hanging behind the door. She lifted the lid on the frying pan and stirred the potatoes. Some had burned. Through the window the sky was mauve-colored with a band of pink in the distance. The patio was darkening. The old woman switched on the light. The glasses on the sideboard and the aluminum pans hanging on the wall started to glimmer.

Suddenly, outside, they heard cries and the sound of breaking glass.

"You beast!"

Violeta ran out of the kitchen, followed by the old woman, and they stood at the door to the patio. The Arab had both hands around the girl's arm and was twisting it, to make her drop the broken bottle. She was struggling, hitting his face furiously with her free hand. The other man was wrapping his hand in a handkerchief. There was blood on the table and on the ground. "You beast!" Finally the broken bottle dropped. "Leave her alone. Can't you see she's got the devil in her? Leave her alone." The girl let out a scream as she stood there panting, rubbing her hurt arm. Then she slowly walked away. When she reached the road, she took off running. Violeta felt her head spinning, but the old woman gave her a shove, "Come on, clean the table, and make it snappy." When she saw the blood up close, her eyes filmed over and everything whirled about. She could hear a distant voice, "Just what we needed, a beast like her." Then she heard nothing more.

She lay on the ground, facing the river, beneath the iron bridge. Everything was dark: sky and water. Slowly, the damp air spread a thick fog that enveloped the darkest shadows in a milky sea. Her hair was wet, her legs cold. A green light from the bridge wounded the water near her feet. She removed a handkerchief from her pocket, unbuttoned her blouse, and placed it between her breast and the wet blouse. Feeling better, she closed her eyes.

The river made a dull noise, like someone breathing, broken occasionally by a secret splash. Not even the hum of an insect or the screech of a bird could be heard. Far downstream, muffled by the weight of the air, the intermittent echoes of a motor reached her, creating the impression of a pulsing shadow. From the other side of the bridge came the clear whistle of a maneuvering loco-motive and the metallic clank of freight cars hitting each other. The silence had unshackled the sounds and lessened her unease, leaving her with only a slight tension in her stomach and an acid taste behind her parched lips.

She opened her eyes and noticed that at the very back of the sky, beyond the river, a reddish aura had permeated the fog. She felt as if she could again hear the wood crackling in the fire, the smoke choking her. For about a month she had been sleeping alone in a shack on the edge of an unused strip of land near the road to the base. She'd lost her job and her house, and the dishwasher in the restaurant where she had worked had offered her the key. It was a late September evening, foggy like tonight, but a foul-smelling, fluid fog rose from the marches, thick with angry mosquitoes. She didn't hear the two men enter. They must have used a wire to open the door. When she awoke she glimpsed two shadows by her bed. Both of them covered her—first one, then the other. She knew one of them slightly, but she'd never set eyes on the other. Both stank of wine and machine oil. They argued in the dark about who would be first. The door stood open and the wind carried in the fog, conveying the nervous sound of hammering from the base. Then they left. She heard them roaming around outside; they seemed to be laughing. Just as she was about to fall asleep, a gust of smoke made her cough. At first she thought it was the fog. A tentative red glow was coming from the corner where she kept her trunk. By the time she realized that the shack was on fire she could hardly breathe. She had to jump out of the window, unable to salvage anything. The following day at the police station they asked her one question after another. The officer was a young, abrupt man who wanted to know why she was sleeping in the shack, how she had gotten in. She explained about the two men. An inspector accompanied her to the base to see if she could recognize them. She spotted one of the men standing by a crane but didn't say anything. As they walked along, the inspector kept telling himself, "She ain't very attractive now." One morning a month or two later, she vomited for the first time.

Suddenly she realized that the wind had stopped. She heard footsteps and held her breath. When she opened her eyes, she saw a shadow approaching. Her heart pounded. The beat was quick and irregular, like a frightened, trapped animal. The man stopped beside her.

"If you're waiting for the train, you've got a while yet. No express train passes through till the early morning."

He lit a cigarette and held up the match to her face.

"You the girl from this afternoon? If you stay out in this damp, you'll be full of aches and pains."

On the other side of the river the sky had turned dark orange, as if burnished by the air. Higher up, it was a dense black velvet. The motor in the distance was beginning to sound tired.

"Me? It got me in the knee."

In the flickering flame of the match, his eyes looked shiny and pale, his beard and mustache white. His cigarette shook. He removed it from his lips, glanced at it to see if it were lit, and tossed the match away. It circled as it fell, blazing for an instant in the grass. An impenetrable darkness separated them.

"You better be getting home. That baby of yours must be having a screaming fit, what with you here. You think I don't know what you're waiting for?"

The old man took a few steps and disappeared. The moon rose, round, blood red, like a large red-hot metal disk on the point of disappearing, sharply defined, ripe, dead. The frame of the bridge turned blacker as it emerged from the shadows. The river flowed with a russet shimmer.

Her chest hurt; it felt like it would burst. She slipped a hand under her blouse. Her breasts were hard as rock and her handkerchief soaking wet. The wind had cleansed the night, and the moon had scattered phosphorescent pink dust across the sky. A moment before there had been only a great wall of darkness, but now it had grown transparent. Dark shadowy objects materialized, and the insidious sounds of the night became audible. A piercing anguish overcame her, causing her to moan. Her pulse throbbed. The sporadic sound of wings came from a nearby low-lying shrub. The shadows, the glimmering water, the muted sound of animals in the grass, the pink lakes in the sky—everything seemed like incomprehensible signs meant for someone else. Like the cries of the man at the arbor, the taste of the wine, the rose petals that fell onto the table. Like the strange words of the old man. Signs from some other place. She propped an elbow on the ground and leaned forward. A violent shudder ran up her arm, and her eyes bulged. She bit her hand with rage. She heard a splash, sharper than before. There are fish that jump and fish that devour. Where was she now? A tiny shape at the bottom of the river, surrounded by swift, silent shadows that approach, causing a ripple, halt for an instant, then move away. The current must have swept her downstream. But the rock was large. If her breasts didn't hurt so much, she might still be able to rest, lie down, rest. With great difficulty she stood up, panting. She felt as if her legs had turned to soft clay that only hardened little by little. When she reached the edge of the water, a branch scratched her hand. She tore some leaves from the shrub, then frantically closed her palm. It burned, as if she had hurt herself. Her feet sank into the mud, the cold water climbing up her legs, driving them forward, like a slow wind, glacial and thick. A black nightmarish wind. She hesitated a moment. A dreadful terror quickened her breathing, and a muscle tightened around her neck like a rope. She took two more steps. An icy tongue licked her stomach and breasts. Then the water carried her away. For a moment she thrashed about, her mouth and eyes closed. Above her she could feel something closing, forever. Water, cold, shadow. All at once she ceased struggling.

# THE BEGINNING

**He couldn't have told you how he had gotten the ink stain.** As he waited for the tram, he glanced down at his trousers in despair. They were his only reasonably decent ones. There were three spots of blue-black ink on the right knee, two small ones and one the size of a cherry. No, much larger than a cherry. As large as what? An apple, he thought anxiously. The trousers were the color of *café amb llet*, and as the ink dried, the spot turned darker and seemed to spread.

"So, I see you stained your trousers?"

Senyor Comes was an old acquaintance. They rode the tram together in the morning and afternoon.

"You should have put water on it right away. There's nothing that stains quite like ink. I had to have some trousers dyed once. Maybe they weren't as light as the ones you're wearing, but even so, there was no other solution."

He wasn't listening. All he could still see were Senyoreta Freixes's eyes. She was the typist. He had been so irritated when she lost the files, seven files, that he had snapped at her: "Nothing depresses me as much as having to work with imbeciles." She had looked at him in surprise, her eyes welling up. "Oh!" was the only thing she had mustered the courage to stammer.

"Here it comes."

The obese and cordial Senyor Comes had gestured at the tram with his head. It was crowded, and people were huddled on the running board. As always, Senyor Comes was the first on. It was a specialty of his, elbowing his way through, using his belly, his childlike smile. No one protested.

The tram started with a jerk. Houses, windows, balconies drifted past. The Garatge Internacional, the Cooperative, the Tennis Club. Everything passed in the same order as each day, fated, draining. The tram emptied out slightly, and they sat down.

"I've already bought the ticket," Senyor Comes said with a mysterious air, giving his friend a little slap on the thigh.

Once a month, for close to five years, they had bought and shared a lottery ticket. They had never won anything, but every month Senyor Comes would say to him with a smile, "We're getting closer."

When Senyor Comes noticed his friend reaching for his pocket, he stopped him. "Don't bother. We'll work it out at the first of the month. How's the boy doing?"

"The boy? Better, thanks."

When he reached home he headed straight to the dining room. The sun streaming in from the gallery made the furniture look older, the corners more dusty, the curtains grayer. Everything looked aged, had lost its freshness.

He wife moved back and forth to the kitchen. She had just set the table. She had gained weight. He kissed her perfunctorily on the forehead, sat down, and opened the newspaper.

"What did you do to your trousers? What's that!"

"I know . . . Senyor Comes said the only solution was to have them dyed."

"Everything always happens at the same time. Why this month, when we have the boy's medicine and the doctor?"

"How's he doing? Anything new?"

"No. Doctor Martí says tomorrow we can let him get up. But, what is it with you?"

*Here we go. She's realized something's troubling me.* His wife's knack for grasping his moods had seemed like a blessing when they were courting. It had been reassuring to feel himself understood, to know she could read his state of mind, anticipate it, and he could say, "I'm feeling down, though I don't really know why. Maybe I'm just worried about the exams." But more and more that infallible intuition of hers caused him anguish. He felt naked, defenseless. He would have wished to have a bit of a secret life. The thing that most irritated him was that he would begin explaining everything he didn't want to disclose at her slightest allusion. Occasionally he would decide to keep quiet, his silence an act of discipline, but his will always faltered. He was incapable of keeping anything from her.

"Something upset me this morning. That's how I got the ink stains. I got nervous and knocked over the ink pot."

He explained to her about the seven lost files.

"I said every disagreeable thing one can say to a person."

He saw her face light up. Her large eyes, usually expressionless, shone, and her tallowy, rather sunken cheeks turned rosy. His wife had the thin lips of a blunt, worried person.

A drama occurred every time a new typist joined the office. She had never met any of the girls. She always said, "My place is at home. I'm not one of those women who follow their husbands around." But she always managed, subtly, to extract descriptions of the typists from him, and she would agonize as she imagined them.

"Serves her right, losing seven files! All these girls who work with men, it's because they're looking for something. She had it coming. Now she's seen that you're a man of character."

She placed the steaming soup on the table and served it.

"What's her name?"

He raised his head, his mouth full, the spoon motionless in midair.

"Who?"

"The typist."

"Ah, Freixes."

"No, I mean her first name."

"Eulàlia or Elvira. I don't know."

"Is she very young?"

He swallowed the mouthful of soup.

"I think so."

"What do you mean, 'I think so?' It must be obvious that either she's young or she isn't."

"Oh, you know me, I don't pay much attention."

"Is she engaged?"

"I don't know."

She had only joined the office the week before, a little shy but candid. She had sat down in front of the typewriter and waited to be given work. The next day she took one of the drinking glasses, filled it with water, and placed some violets in it. By the third day she was laughing.

While he was drinking his coffee, his wife entered the boy's room and came out immediately.

"He's sleeping like an angel. Better not to disturb him. You'll see him this evening. Come home early, you hear me?"

*What a beast I was. Such a young girl, probably not yet twenty, I shouldn't have said . . . her hair's like silk and when she laughs . . . I shouldn't have said anything.*

He decided to walk back to work; he didn't feel like talking to Senyor Comes.

*It's curious. I've walked along this street for years, yet today it all seems new.* He noticed a shop window with crisp curtains, a budding rosebush by the gate to a house, some blades of fresh grass springing up between two slabs of pavement. Beyond the hedge of boxwood shrubs at the Tennis Club he could hear two girls chattering; they must have been standing right there. He stopped for a moment in front of the Garatge Internacional: "Important things are taking place in Barcelona now, no doubt about it." A wave of youthfulness surged through him.

There was a flower shop near the office. He deliberated for a moment, then with an effort to overcome his embarrassment he strode in with resolve. He bought a bouquet of tiny roses surrounded by green, russet-tipped leaves.

"They look like porcelain," the florist said kindly.

Standing on the stairs to his office, he wrapped the bouquet in a newspaper. When no one was looking, he would throw away the violets, change the water, and place the roses in the vase. Perhaps . . . Perhaps in the afternoon he would say: "Elvira, would you like for the two of us to go out this evening?" He could already imagine the color of the sky, the evening's perfume.

# NOCTURNAL

**A plaintive moan filled the room. It continued for a while before** suddenly dying, as if it had passed through the walls. It sounded like a whimper from a wounded animal that had not yet lost any blood or energy. The dense silence again invaded everything. A moment later a body moved beneath the sheets as if, rather than a moan, the mysterious echo of a moan had awoken him from a deep sleep. The meowing of a cat on the stairs rose in tone and volume, becoming sharp and urgent. Another moan silenced the cat. A shadow jumped out of the bed, followed by an arpeggio of springs. The sound of bare feet on the floor, two or three coughs, a switch being flipped, and the room was flooded with light.

The man who had turned on the light returned to the bed, racked with worry, and asked: "Are you saying it's time?" The tiny kitchen, just three meters away, had permeated the sheets with the smell of boiled vegetables and a sauce of tomato and onion. A tired voice rose from beneath the sheets: "First put some water on to boil, then go knock on the druggist's door and ask if he'll let you phone the doctor." *She looks so pale,* the man thought to himself. He had never seen her so pale, with such sunken eyes. On the stairs the cat resumed, his meows filled with desire. *Order, order, order,* he told himself, in an attempt to stop the trembling in his hands. He wished he could control them. He used half a dozen matches before he could finally light the gas stove. By the time the orange-blue flame ignited, the atmosphere was unbreathable. *I should have turned on the gas after I lit the match, not before.* Using a blue jug he filled a pot with water and placed it on the stove.

"Maybe you should open the window a moment." Another moan followed. He walked over to his wife, took her hands to encourage her. He didn't know what to say. She looked anxiously at him, her face covered with drops of sweat. "Four children." He could feel how tense her hands were. "At our age," she stammered. All of a sudden, he felt the need to move more quickly: open the door, run down the stairs, knock on the druggist's door, pick up the telephone, and implore the doctor to come right away. But he didn't budge. It was almost as if the three children in his life were holding him back. One in Madrid, a member of Franco's Falange party; another a left-wing exile in Mexico; the third—a daughter—in Reggio, seduced by an Italian officer. *My interior contradictions expressed in the flesh,* he often thought. The last child now eighteen and the fourth about to be born. A feeling of anguish, the kind that precedes nausea, ran though his body. He felt grotesque. During the day, the gas flow was gentle, but now, in the heart of night, it streamed out, making a buzzing sound. The straight flames reached up the sides of the pot, wavered, creating blue reflections. The water was beginning to rumble. *Coat, stairs, telephone . . . order, order, order.* "I'm going now. I'll be right back," he said, but before leaving he went over to the table and cleared away his books and papers. *The Terrible Consequences of Truth.* He had been a geography teacher in a lycée in Barcelona before going into exile, where he had begun writing. When he got off work—he was a dish dryer in an exclusive restaurant—he would surround himself with books and submerge himself in his writing. When he resurfaced he felt entranced. The original title of the book was *The Terrible Consequences of the Desire to be Truthful.* But then he had decided on the other. Truth as the dissolution of all human relations. Truth as the negation of all authentic values. Salvation achieved through systematic deception, applied with a radical spirit, could be transformed into truth. Man could become truthful by means of a lie, in a way that was more real than sincerity. These somewhat confusing ideas nevertheless possessed a coherence: "Order, order, order." His rather verbose study had led to another, entitled "Toward Freedom by Means of Dissimulation." I simulate *ergo* I am free. This was the point of departure for his thesis. "Order, order, order." He cleared away his papers and books, put his coat on over his pajamas, walked over to the bed, glanced sadly at his wife, and went out onto the landing.

The stairs gave off a sickening stench of garbage, the sour odor of something rotten. He felt his way down the stairway in the dark. To save electricity the light hadn't been turned on since the war began. The wooden steps were worn and creaked beneath his feet. The silence of night made the creaking resound, much more than during the day, when children and neighbors coming and going filled the stairs with life and a noisy bustle. "This is what France is," a Frenchman had told him once. "Not Paris or the luxury of the few. But unhygienic houses, streams of dirty water in the streets, water closets—a euphemism—under the stairs at the entrances to buildings, for the use of neighbors and passers-by, chamber pots . . . running water a luxury. Voilà."

He breathed laboriously when he reached the last step. Then, just as he was feeling reassured, he stumbled against a soft body. This wasn't the first night that a drunk had slept on the hard floor in the entrance hall; it was a common occurrence in this working-class neighborhood. Making an effort to maintain his balance, he took a huge step across the obstacle, which groaned gently, removed from the world by sleep.

The street was dark. On the other side, seven or eight houses further up, a red light attracted his attention. A stealthy shadow was visible as it crossed beneath the light and disappeared into the doorway. "A German?" For the last few nights, groups of two or three German soldiers had walked down the street, their boots resonating on the pavement, attracted by the light despite the sign on the door that read "Verboten."

At the top of the stairs two cats started a furious fight. They hissed and growled furiously, no doubt all tooth-and-claw and arched backs. Suddenly, one of the cats, mad with fury, its eyes lit, brushed against his legs and crossed the street. It frightened him. He had been mesmerized by the starry night and the moon that cast steely patches on the roofs and houses across the street. All the splendor of the constellations shimmered in the dark sky. It was offensive, just as a well-lit palace at the end of a park might seem to a passing pauper. He couldn't admire it any longer; he had to knock at the door, do something. The druggist was close by. He heard the sound of steps and ducked back inside his building, closing the door slightly for fear that his light-colored pajamas would give him away. For an instant he saw the outline of a coat beneath the red light. Then it disappeared. He thought he heard a scream and returned to reality. He had to move, had to knock. Cautiously he went out, as the cat slipped back inside between his legs, fast as a curse.

"Knock," he said to himself. The wrought iron door shook, though he had only used his palm. No answer. He waited a few minutes and knocked again, harder this time. He was afraid he would wake the neighbors, who would lean out their windows, shouting crude insults at him. How could a foreigner dare to disturb their rest in this way! A husky voice asked from behind the iron door, "Who is it?" "Your neighbor." "Which one?" The question was disconcerting. He chose the simplest answer. "My wife's sick. Could I use your phone?" An angry voice responded, "The phone's been out since morning."

Not sure what to do, he returned to his room. At the foot of the stairs, he again stumbled against the sleeping, panting obstacle. On the second floor, he passed the fuming cat. He heard voices inside and entered. The neighbor across the landing and the lady from downstairs were there. He realized they were waiting impatiently for him. His news ("The phone's out.") was greeted by expressions of disappointment. *She looks so pale, so terribly pale.* The sheet was rising and falling beneath her belly. It was as if he could see it emerging—naked, majestic and victorious—from a body wasted by years and grief, framed by bony, waxen shoulders, angular sides, emaciated arms and thighs. The body that had attracted him years ago. The group of women deliberated in a low voice. The lady from downstairs found a solution, "As far as I know there's only one other telephone in the neighborhood." "Whose?" asked the woman from next door. "The one at Number Fourteen." "Number Fourteen" was the name all the neighbors in the building used for the house with the red light. "Hurry!" "You have to change your clothes." "Only the trousers." A spasm of pain rocked the bed. *She's so pale, so pale.* Almost without realizing, he found himself behind the folding screen, thinking: *Order, order.* An energetic hand passed him the clothes he needed. Once again: stairs, dark, obstacle, splendid night.

He walked up the street. He had never been in a place like that. He was familiar with them, of course, but only indirectly. As a young man, all his friends had confided in him. He was a good listener and that had made him an innocent father confessor to the bolder lads. He had lived a lot through the lives of others. Too much. Sometimes this surrogacy produced in him a certain sadness that was pasty, cosmic, rough-hewn. *No one cares about me. If I have a problem, I'll have to solve it by myself. I'm like an abandoned soul in a wasteland.* Life had passed him by, just beyond his reach. Like a river, he had captured the sounds, the commotion, had recognized the dangers, but he had remained on the shore. When he *had* thrown himself into the stream, inexpert as he was, it was to follow others. Simply a matter of contagion, as if he had caught typhoid fever. The current had dragged him to France, where he had been discarded like a dead branch. He had married young so he could work calmly, feel himself strong through his child, so he wouldn't lose himself completely. Many years ago, a young girl, a student, had led him to the very edge of sin. The sense of vertigo had frightened him. A more experienced girl could have really derailed him, but this one, with all her charm, had only managed to trouble his spirit for a few months and prompt a spate of sleepless nights, a brief interruption of his moral serenity. The experience had left him with a tremendous attraction to crime novels and blue blouses. He had only known one woman intimately, his wife.

A military march could be heard coming from Number Fourteen. He approached it with determination. The glass door was covered by a sheer curtain. To enter he had merely to turn the knob. He took a deep breath and went inside. He would ask the first person he saw if he could use the phone. He found himself in a narrow hall with doors on either side. The military march was coming from the second door on the right. A whiff of perfume distracted him. "Lilac," he thought. Had it not been for the music, the house would have seemed deserted, like a house recently abandoned in a village filled with the threat of an enemy. He continued along the hall till at the end he reached a comfortable sitting room. Over the sofa, in a gilded frame, presided the portrait of a gentleman. Quite Proustian, with a wing collar, gardenia in his buttonhole, romantic mustache. The gentleman was staring pensively at the door. *He must be the founder.* There were no shiny, golden pillows or lace curtains with pink bows, no trace of the diabolical chiaroscuro that he had always imagined. All together it had a rather grave air, a bit like the waiting room of an austere, provincial lung specialist.

Suddenly the waves of music grew louder. They must have opened the door to the room. A woman's shrill laugh erupted from somewhere, making him jump. A maid passed quickly by, carrying an empty tray. "Madame, s'il vous plaît, the telephone." She disappeared through a small door beyond the sofa. He heard footsteps coming from the floor above: they must be dancing. Without thinking he sat down in an armchair, feeling confused.

*Order, order, order.* Someone was walking down the hall toward
him, probably coming from the room with the music. They had
shut the door, and the music—now a languid waltz—was lower. He
stood up. A stout German soldier in shirt sleeves, with gray hair
and a tanned face, stopped in front of him. He was carrying a bottle of cognac under his arm and an empty champagne glass in his
hand. He clicked his heels. He clearly had some difficulty keeping
his balance. For a moment they stood without moving. The soldier
looked at him with gentle eyes. A secret flow of sympathy seemed
to emerge from deep within the soldier's intense gaze, almost like
a balmy breeze. With a resolute gesture, the soldier had him sit
down and filled the glass. He felt that he had never heard such
a fresh sound as the liquid pouring from the upturned bottle. It
spilled. Instinctively he separated his feet, but he couldn't keep
his trousers and shoes from being splashed by the tiny drops.
The soldier handed him the glass and the bottle, sat on floor,
took out his handkerchief, muttered some unintelligible words
of excuse, and began drying the bottom of his trousers; then he
raised his head and began to laugh. A childish, contagious laugh.
*Order, order,* but he couldn't keep himself from laughing as well.
The jerking motion caused by the laughter made the liquid splash
out of the glass. It rained golden drops. The soldier gestured to
him to drink. He drained half the glass with one swallow. The
soldier took the bottle from his hand, uttered a loud "Prosit,"
and poured some cognac down his own throat, straight from the
bottle. He finished what was left in his glass. The sullen maid
crossed the room again, giving the two men a resentful look.
"Madame . . . the telephone," he murmured with a thin, imploring
voice, but the maid had vanished. Another toast paralyzed his
decisiveness. *Prosit.* He was unsure how to respond to the numer-
ous attentions paid to him by the soldier. He realized he had to
make a decision, that it was urgent to find a phone, make the call,
wake up the doctor, beg, intimidate. A gentle warmth had settled
in his cheeks and began spreading insidiously through his body.

It must have slipped into the obscure region of his will, changing some delicate mechanism within him. He felt a slight tingling in his legs and arms, a deep sense of well-being in his heart. With a brisk gesture he emptied another glass. How many years had it been since he had tasted cognac? Six? Seven? At that moment, mysteriously extracted from his spirit, words sprang to his mouth, vestiges of some remote Latin class. *Animi hominum sunt divini,* he whispered with a smile of satisfaction. The soldier opened his round eyes, nodded his head in agreement and refilled the glass. He raised it to his lips, but a violent hiccup stopped him. *Order, ooooorder.* A string of hiccups followed. The soldier sat down on the armrests and began slapping him on the shoulder. After each slap, he showed his appreciation by offering the soldier a melancholy smile. They returned to their drinking with looks of complicity. The soldier asked, "Franzose?" He hesitated before responding, "Barcelona." "Spanier?" "Oui." They burst out laughing at the same time. "Rotspanier?" "Yes." They laughed louder and resumed drinking.

Another soldier entered the room. He was barefoot; they hadn't heard him. The seated soldier cried out, "Spanier," and passed the bottle to the newcomer. The painting showed two gentlemen with gardenias in their buttonholes and wing collars. The frame slowly split in two, but then the figures reassembled, as if brought together by a stubborn desire for unity. The newcomer was short, dark, and quite slender. "Mister, mister . . . the telephone." He stood halfway up, but a curious softness in his knees made him sit down again. The newcomer was distracted, didn't respond, and began to hum a song. The other followed, then two more soldiers joined them. One had his holster looped across an arm, the other a bottle of champagne in each hand. They began singing in unison, solemnly, a vague expression on their faces.

Ich hatt'einen Kameraden,
einen bessern find'st du nit

They opened the bottles of champagne. It foamed over, spilling onto the floor. They passed it from one to another, all of them drinking.

> Eine Kugel kam geflogen
> gilt es mir, oder gilt es dir?

The painting now held three gentlemen, or four. All with gardenias in their buttonholes. Occasionally one was superimposed on the other, perhaps filled with the hurried wish to share confidences, but then they separated in a disorderly fashion, surrounded by gold. At one point it was possible to make out six or seven of them. A whirlwind. The champagne was followed by cognac. At times the singing resumed. Two girls came in, wearing pajamas. The first soldier stood up, filled with rage and tottering, grabbed one girl by the shoulder, the other by the arm and dragged them brutally out of the room, standing for a moment at the door, facing the hall. Every now and then he yelled with a deafening voice, "Raus!" The room became spongy, ethereal, all cottony. The chairs, floor, walls, all of it was clouds and mist. *Order, order, or* . . . He was filled with a sense of optimism and a loud laugh issued from his mouth. He would have embraced the entire world if he could, all the men, all the birds. "All the birds." He climbed onto the chair, concentrated a moment, and began reciting verses he had memorized twenty years before, forgotten, then retrieved in this moment of joy:

> . . . né dolcezza di figlio, né la pietà
> del vecchio padre, né 'l debito amore
> lo qual doveva Penelope far lieta
> vincer poter dentra da me l'ardore
> ch'i'ebbi a diventir de modo esperto
> e de li vizi umani e del valore . . .

Everything spun madly around, rolling down a moss-covered slope, while the gentleman in the frame multiplied, multiplied all by himself, raised to the third, fourth, fifth power. Four gardenias? A bouquet for the pregnant senyora, shut in her room! Carpe diem. The last drop of . . .

They didn't have time to realize. Two gendarmes with brass and steel badges hanging over their chests emerged out of nowhere, in the center of the room, like two towers. "Feldgendarmerie!" A buxom, irritated woman pointed her finger at the sofa and armchair. "Les voilà, maison verboten, ma maison verboten, les salauds." Boots. Four boots: black, opaque, lugubrious. Dozens of gendarmes. "Sakrament!" A bottle flew through the air. *Order, or . . . der.* The gendarme beside him dragged one of the soldiers toward the hall. He ran after the gendarme and grabbed him by the belt. "Cochon! Vous cochon!" "Was?" A heavy blow from the gendarme's fist sent him crashing against the wall. He was alone, helpless, seated on the floor, the whole side of his face in pain. A woman's screams, hurried footsteps on the stairs, the sound of glass breaking beside him. A shadow was leaning over him: "Papieren!" "Merde!" Two hands grabbed him by the lapel of his coat and stood him up. A slap knocked him down . . . How delightful the air on the street. His whole body was aflame. The air must be coming from the clouds, from the stars. He vomited. "Voyons," shouted a woman who looked ruffled, her nose bleeding. "Bande d'acrobates!" He passed the door to his building, without seeing her. At the corner they loaded him onto a truck. With a tremendous din, everything disappeared forever, down the street, enveloped by silence and the night.

# THE RED BLOUSE

**I'll tell you a story about my student days.**

My desk stood by the window that looked out onto the street. My field of vision was limited by the house in front. Its third-floor window was directly opposite mine, and the blinds had been painted green. On the windowsill sat geraniums and a birdcage with a bird that never sang, although it escaped one day. A neighbor had shouted the news from her window to my concierge. One afternoon I saw beds, chairs, tables, a piano being lowered to the street: the people opposite were moving. I was gazing absentmindedly at the furniture swinging in the air at the end of a rope and listening to the movers shouting at the woman driver. I was slowly growing lethargic. The first signs of a precocious spring had appeared, filling me with a lingering melancholy that one encounters at the age of nineteen when a chance event can highlight the ephemeral. At that point in my life, I would have wished to fix each moment of my existence, making it definitive, so that I might continue to exist among objects that were meant to remain there forever. I don't even know what I wanted! Those dusty pieces of furniture, the parcels and trunks being removed, one after the other: all of it would now belong to the past, out of sight, leaving me with a bitter taste of uncertainty.

By the time I realized the apartment was occupied again, the days had grown long and the sun was predicting an implacable summer.

The window must have been closed for many days, because when I noticed a girl opening it wide one afternoon, I was struck by the vivid impression of the inescapable passing of time. I slowly became aware of two curious things: the girl raised the blinds every afternoon at the same time, and a bit later a young man—more or less like me—closed it.

On my birthday I received a parcel from home. My mother had sent me clothes and books, my sister—in a separate box—half a dozen red gladiolas from our garden and six packs of the best cigarettes. I put the flowers in a vase on the desk—half a dozen flaming swords—and, enveloped by smoke, set to work with a warm sense of comfort.

She must have been attracted by the flowers. Perhaps I had placed them there on purpose. When she raised the blinds, she would lean on the ledge and gaze about. She was pretty. Very pretty, decidedly so. The color of summer. One of my favorite words when I think of a girl is *siren*. The next is *nymph*. But my favorite is *siren*, together with all the others associated with it: *ocean, mariner, nostalgia, lichen, island, sail, ship, beach.* She was wearing a low-cut red blouse. At that time it was the color I least liked (influenced, I suppose, by my sister, who hated it). It was a color that exasperated me, whether the entire dress was red or only some accessory, and I classified everyone who wore it as unworthy of my attention. Yet, paradoxically, a red blouse—furiously, insultingly red—would cause me many sleepless nights and many painfully restless days.

Soon I came to live in hope that the girl would appear. I dreamed about her, sweet and remote as a princess. I sketched her in the margins of my books, in notebooks, and I carved her into the top of the desk, using a penknife. None of my drawings resembled her. This irritated me in a sad sort of way and always led me to start over.

They kissed one day with the window wide open. I stood up so I wouldn't see them. Why did they have to kiss like that—

"shamelessly" was the word I used to criticize them—in front of me? They kissed for a long time, as if the world had been created precisely to witness the spectacle of their happiness. I decided to move my desk, but I missed their presence. I was attracted to what, for me, was morbid and unwholesome. I was obsessed by the vision of the two of them embracing. At night in my dark room, I would conjure up the girl, her blouse, the kisses, her dark, moist eyes that shone like water, all the tenderness that I would have wished for me. I wanted to hold the girl in my arms, naked as a flower, her hair fanned out on my pillow. That girl, not another. I would have risked damnation in order to feel that she was mine—if a nineteen-year-old could be damned for the sin of dreaming of a girl and wanting her with a child's desperation.

How long and sad the mornings seemed to me, filled with the bitter taste of restless nights, exhausted from desire! To avoid missing a single gesture or any expression on her face, I decided to close the blinds partially and watch through the cracks. I would look for the slightest contraction of a muscle, trying to make her seem more and more mine.

I was enthralled. One afternoon he unbuttoned her blouse. I left my room and ran furiously down the stairs. I breathed in the air like men coming out of a mine after an accident. The streets led me nowhere. The people were like larvae, vegetating in my world for the sole purpose of spoiling it. None of them knew why they were born or why they would have to die. They strolled about, indifferent, neither discontented nor happy, greeting each other if they were acquainted. I was alone, the only one alive in a desert. I struggled not to turn back, but to continue amongst people and houses and brightness. When I tired, I sat down in a park. The sun fell at an angle, scorching the earth, making the limp flowers thirsty, creating intense, fleeting reflections on the lake where a boat was sailing. I left, irritated by the sense of perfect happiness coming from the trees, the children's screams, the limpid sky, the air filled with life. I walked for hours and ended up, distressed, at a cinema that was showing only current events. I bought a book that I never read and left my dinner untouched at a restaurant.

That night I thought: Tomorrow I will open the window, stand on the desk, and sing, shaking my arms about, so they will exclaim: "He's gone mad!" I'll address them. The mere thought of it gave me pleasure: I would unsettle them with my feigned (feigned?) madness.

The next day I was calmer. I raised the blinds all the way and sat down, placing a cushion on the chair to make myself more visible. "Maybe that will restrain them," I thought with loathing.

The girl seemed surprised when she saw me. The fact that the blinds had been shut for several days must have made them think I was away on holiday. She was wearing the red blouse that made her look so beautiful. I was filled with a profound sadness, more intense than ever, for her and for me. It was an uncontrollable, noxious pity.

But it didn't last long. Soon the man appeared. He didn't see me. They began to quarrel violently, as if they were taking up an argument that had started long ago. They disappeared from sight, but I could still hear the bitter tone of their voices, though I couldn't make out any of the words. An hour or so passed. The girl returned to the window; soon he joined her and seemed affable. They were leaning on the window ledge; when I looked again they were kissing. It was a hazy afternoon, with a storm threatening. The air was still. I pretended to read. From time to time I glanced at the couple kissing, making an effort not to raise my head too high. Suddenly, my eyes met the girl's. Her gaze was fascinating, impossible to ignore. We looked fixedly at each other. Her eyes seemed to be smiling at me in a complicated way, full of refusal and promise. As if her kisses were for me. The girl seemed to be offering herself diabolically to me. Had it not been for the distance, I could have taken her by the arm and she would have followed me. The torture continued for a moment. I was ablaze, as if enveloped by flames. I felt grotesque, sitting high on the cushion, paralyzed before the creature that absorbed me. She was all kisses, but it was easy to forgive her. The air was unbreathable. The girl kept looking at me as, almost literally, I died.

My father fell gravely ill that summer. In September I was scheduled to retake the exams I had failed, but he died before then. It was a sad summer. I loved my father, and his sudden death made me grow up, grow old. I was overcome by a deep melancholy that the years have not been able to expel. That summer marked a turning point in my life. It altered me forever. I returned to my room, to my desk by the window, to the landscape of my student years where I was now a stranger after an absence of only a few months. The weather was gentle, the afternoons pleasant, less blue, the green of the trees more nuanced. All of it gave the impression of becoming more beautiful so that I might sleep better.

The window of my anguish stood before me with the blinds down. The girl with the red blouse seemed to belong to a remote past. All of it was a dream dispelled by the light, disrobing everything that had been made mysterious by the night. How absurd my anxious ravings now seemed to me. I needed to apply myself to my studies. Why all those fine intentions, if the future seemed inaccessible, life difficult, everything useless? But I had to work hard, make my way, beat a path if necessary, do as others did, offer my mother support (my sister too, until she married), and start a family. Then later I would live in my children, die like my father—quickly, one radiant summer—and be mourned by my family.

Despite all my reasoning, despite the mental discipline I attempted to impose, I have to confess that when the accustomed hour approached, I was again obsessed by the window opposite me. The greater the effort to remain indifferent, the more anxious I grew. Everything that had seemed to vanish the night before my arrival returned in all its intensity. But no one opened the window. Nor the following day. Nor any other day. I felt liberated. I would sit at my desk, calmly, without thinking of anything, my spirit at rest. I remembered what I studied and was slowly but surely making progress, following a straight path. I felt solid and began to feel sure of myself. The sense of inferiority at having failed my June exams began to fade. I was exultant.

When the memory had almost vanished, and I no longer looked up from my desk—as if the window opposite now belonged to another world—I realized one day that the blinds were up. I could see into the room that for so long had been like an extension of mine. But the girl wasn't there. Another girl had appeared, with the same young man, but she didn't awake in me any sense of curiosity. Whether they raised or lowered the blinds, kissed in front of me or not, didn't matter.

One day, toward evening, I heard someone climbing the stairs. I could recognize the footsteps of everyone who came to visit me; I needed to hear them only once to know who was coming to see me. But I had never heard that kind of step. "Somebody must have the wrong address," I thought, since I lived on the top floor. But then I immediately told myself: "No, they're coming here, the steps of someone who has never been here before."

They stopped on the landing outside my door. A few seconds passed. The person was hesitating before knocking. Then I heard him going down. I was intrigued. The steps stopped for a long time on the floor beneath mine. Then they started up again, giving the impression of being tired. The strange visitor had decided to come up again. There was a soft knock on the door, as if they didn't wish to be heard. If it hadn't been for the steps, I might not have even realized someone was knocking.

I opened the door. It was the girl with the red blouse. She was paler, almost ashen. She had lost a lot of weight. Without a word she strode across the room directly to the window, as if we had known each other for years, as if I knew that she would come. And why. From my desk she gazed at the window opposite.

She stood there with a sad, eager look. Speechless, motionless. She remained for an instant, as if alone in the world. I felt I should do something, move her away from the window, not let her look. I could feel she was suffering, but I was paralyzed, out of respect, and because I sensed the situation was unreal. What stood before her must have represented a happiness she would never find again.

It was almost dark. I went toward her. I have never again felt such tenderness as on that evening beside the sad girl who did not know to what degree she had taken possession of my heart. Why I decided to approach her, what words I uttered: these things have been erased from my memory. I recall, with terrible precision, only her heartrending sobs. She burst into tears in my arms, which must have seemed impersonal to her, as if she were crying against a wall. She cried with greater pain than I did when my father died. Never again have I heard a person weep like that. I felt I needed to protect her, as if destiny had brought her to me, as if in some way her future belonged to me, and mysteriously she had become my responsibility. Everything I had learned from literature (which at that time was considerable) was evoked. I carried her in my arms, like a child, shaking as she wept uncontrollably, and laid her on the bed, as if she were something that belonged to me, something not seized, but offered, found. I knelt on the floor with my face by hers, her tears dampening my cheek.

Hours and hours passed. She never said a word. The fits of sobbing became less frequent, and she fell asleep, like a flame that slowly fades. I watched over her. It was a chaste night, but I still recall her soft hair, the salty taste of her tears. How can one let the hand of a sleeping body drop! How lips parch when the heart suffers. I felt as if I held a dead bird in my hand. I must have fallen asleep in the early morning. When I awoke it was day, the room full of sun. I never saw her again. Never again have I lived hours of such passion, a night of love so pure.

# THE FATE OF LISA SPERLING

*. . . here come the lovers . . . where are the lovers?*

Madame Létard picked up two saccharin tablets, put one in her cup, and was about to put the other in her subtenant Lisa Sperling's.

"No!"

She stopped the hand with an abrupt gesture.

"Do you still have some sugar?"

"There's a bit left."

"Then I'll take sugar this evening."

She picked up the steaming cup, said good night, and went into her room. Closed the door and slowly turned the key. She set the cup on the little table in front of the window and stood a while, not sure where to start all the work she wanted to do but perhaps wouldn't.

I'll begin with the suitcase. She took it out from under the bed and put it on top. Letters, pictures. It's all mine, but it seems like it already belongs to someone else. She had thin, bitter lips. The corners of her mouth were pale, slightly purple in the center, and her teeth were yellow, with large spaces between them. It looks like the mouth of a corpse, a friend of hers had once said. She picked up the letter from her son and started reading it for the hundredth time. "Dearest Mother, today we leave. Once we're settled in Minsk, you can come. I hope the trains will soon be running properly. I don't want you to have to make such a long journey if it's going to be difficult for you. Trust me." She folded the letter slowly and kissed it. But then the war with Russia had begun, and she had stayed on alone, isolated, in Limoges, where she had settled after fleeing Paris.

She took out three photos. One was her sister: "To my dear Lisa. Souvenir from Anna Sperling. Odessa, 1916." One was her when she was eighteen. She was wearing a gauze dress, white, with a wide velvet belt. The white gauze dress with the red velvet belt. The bow, tied behind her, hung down over her skirt. I was blonder; she was the one who was going to succeed. How far away that girl is now, how very far! She put the two photos together. Anna had died young, TB. She'd left a diary and a collection of verses. She, at least, hasn't suffered so much. The third photo was of her as a bride. So many dreams then. The only thing I've got left is my son's love. My husband, no, not him. If only the kisses he offered other women had been given to me. She put the photos back in the suitcase and shut it.

She stood in the middle of the room. Now, what do I do? Ah, yes, the books. On the table lay half a dozen. She picked them up one by one, looked at the spines, slowly running her hand across the covers. Where did I put the paper and string? She found them in the drawer of the little table and began packing.

From the next room she could hear the sound of plates. Madame Létard was washing the dishes. A cat was meowing.

On a piece of paper she wrote: Monsieur Jean Schuster, 148, Avenue Carnot, Limoges.

This past winter I thought that . . . He was so attentive to me. He's alone too. It was just friendship. I'm getting old. She put her hands on her cheeks; the skin was loose, full of pores, earth-colored. Skin that has lived.

Clothes. She opened the wardrobe wide and began to remove piles of clothes. She selected them and put them on the chairs. The nightgowns for Maria: she needs them. These blouses for . . . and the dresses? She took out a fox fur and looked at it for a while. The coat I wore how many years ago? Fifteen? A hundred? What was that coat made of? Even if they killed me, I couldn't say. If you could go back in time, I'd choose that moment . . . *I forgot the jewelry, Lisa* . . . My father was so strong! *I'll go get it* . . . I did the eighty kilometers by sled, with the soldiers. I found the jewelry where my father told me. I've never forgotten our house, though I never saw it again. You could hear the canons as I was leaving the village. The last train. I left on the last train, full of poor people with packages and baskets. And the cold. *Are you cold?* We shared his food. He was tall, young like me, handsome in his officer's uniform. All night he stayed beside me: he took off my shoes and warmed my feet with his hands. He put his fur-lined coat around me. He was the age my son is now . . . *Where are the lovers?* my husband used to say to me every day when he came home. My son and I were the *lovers*. We were always, always together. I made him what he is today, if he's still alive. I helped him with his lessons when he was little. He never went to a concert without me. *Here come the lovers.* And now, there's nothing.

She picked up her purse and sat down in front of the table. Opened it and emptied it out. Her identity card. She read out her name: Lisa. She'd had the picture taken in Rouen, before the war, when she was in charge of a dressmaker's workroom. She left two days before the occupation. She couldn't find her son in Paris; without letting her know, he'd gone in search of her and then it was too late to leave Rouen. *Come on, Lisa. We have a place for you in the car. Don't stay, it's dangerous.* Maybe I should have stayed in Paris and not listened to them. She opened her identity card: Israeli. It's been a week now. When will it be someone else's turn? Every month some are taken away. From her purse full of papers, a franc fell out. She picked up the coin and looked at it. A brief, ironic smile crossed her lips. One franc. I've never been this rich. I need absolutely nothing, nothing, nothing. Madame Gendron can keep her rich refugee's diamonds. With her diamonds, she stood politely over everyone's poverty. I don't need anything. Don't want to struggle anymore.

The cup had stopped steaming; the coffee was no doubt cold. Madame Létard must have been in bed; there was no sound from her bedroom next door. The cat was curled up asleep beneath the stove. Only silence seemed to exist.

Lisa, Lisa, Lisa. She pronounced her name slowly, as if she were saying the name of a dead person. She looked at the wide bed with the lace bedspread and the ledge above the fireplace with the clock in the middle, stopped forever, and the sea snails on both sides. She was hot: the air in the room was unbreathable. She walked over to the window and opened it wide, being careful not to make any noise. A violent perfume from the lilacs entered the room. Close to the window, the air was gently swaying the flowery feathers. Behind the lilacs, further away, stood the river. The water flowed silently, dark, reflecting the streetlights from the bridge. The sky was a brazier of stars all ablaze.

She looked for a long time, without moving. *Where are the lovers?* The war had passed through Minsk some months before. Where could my son be? The war, snow, canons. When I got off the train with the jewelry, he took my hand. He laughed. *Are you cold?* They must have killed him. My father said: *Thank you, Lisa. It's all we have left. I would never have returned alive from this trip.* He was crying. I had never seen him cry before.

She put her hands around her neck. A rush of anguish rose from her heart. She clenched her teeth; she didn't want to cry. How cruel. What a cruel moment of loneliness. Surrounded by this poisonous peace saturated with loneliness . . . Like an open door.

She removed her wedding ring and left it in the center of the table, the franc on the ledge by the clock. Took a sheet of paper and tore it into four pieces. For Maria. For Madame Létard. For Monica Werner. For Rosa Ramírez. She placed a slip of paper on each pile of clothes. Burn the pictures and the letters. This last paper she left on top of the suitcase. From a corner of the wardrobe she removed two tubes of Veronal. She took one and emptied it in her cup. Had to shake the tube to empty out the last pills. Stirred the cup with the spoon. It was going to be hard to dissolve all the little white disks. She removed the top from the other bottle and emptied it into her cup. I don't want to ever wake up.

It took a long time to dissolve the pills. She broke them in two with the tip of the spoon, but was afraid of making too much noise. Started cracking them with her teeth. The cup was too small. Took a bowl and poured everything into it. Added water. Half dissolved, half still whole, she drank it down. Horrible, horrible. Less horrible than— . . . She became frightened, very frightened. Afraid of what, now? Afraid of what?

# THE
# BATH

**She was wearing a muslin dress, in carmine, with a white insert.**
The broad pleat on the bodice had a bouquet of forget-me-nots.
She was wearing white socks, black patent-leather shoes, and a
bow in her hair that was the same color as her dress, tied like a
butterfly. Her mouth and nose were swollen, and she spoke with
difficulty. The day before she had fallen from her grandfather's
bed—it was a meter high. She was doing somersaults and had split
her upper lip. It had bled profusely.

Her parents and grandfather were closing doors and windows:
the gate by the kitchen, the balcony off the dining room, the
double doors on the roof terrace. Her mother had brought in the
clothes from the line, still damp. That was the prudent thing to
do. In this quiet, isolated area of Sant Gervasi, leaving a house
closed for too long gave a sense that a surprise was in the air.

They ran into silly little Felipet on the street, his nose full of
snot, his glance sad.

"You're leaving now?"

What would he do the whole afternoon without Mercè? He
felt a little intimidated—this was a different Mercè, a flaming-red
Mercè who was going to participate in a comedy. In the last act
she was pulled, half smothered, from a strongbox. "Your arms
and legs, limp, you hear? You've got to pretend you're dead," the
director told her at every rehearsal, because without realizing,
her whole body would stiffen when the man picked her up.

Felipet watched them walking away, up Carrer de Paris. Mercè, her parents and grandfather growing tiny against the backdrop of Tibidabo.

The house was closed, deserted, its well-tended garden with jasmine, camellias, and gardenias, the old olive tree they used on sunny winter days for a pirate ship, or a lighthouse to guide lost ships—all of it, house and garden, seemed alien to him, as if he had never been inside.

    *∗∗∗∗∗*

They were going to "La Flora," in the Guinardó area. They would pass by Josepets, where the trams were parked, and then by the open land that the neighborhood children used for a soccer field. They would see the square with the palm trees, the gardens along Travessera de Dalt, the flower boxes filled with yellow and pink tulips, lifeless rosebushes, the lilac and syringa by the window grills. The gardens where the wind sometimes carried the deep sound of rustling leaves and the fresh scent of honey, as if a swarm of bees was blending together thousands of scattered perfumes. As a young girl Mercè's mother had danced at "La Flora." Here she wore a long dress for the first time, her hair swept high on her head. Here she met her first suitor, had her first engagement. On Sundays, "La Flora" vibrated with polkas and mazurkas, waltzes and the Lancers Quadrille. Declarations of love, complicated intrigues between mothers of soon-to-be-married daughters created a dull, depressing music beneath the outburst of the cornet and the rather viscous violins and double bass. They danced on a red rug that crackled with nutshells. At the entrance a blind woman, short and obese, sold peanuts and bouquets of cardboard pansies in the shape of a heart. You had to walk up a steep slope to get there.

"What's the surprise going to be, grandfather?"

They were inseparable. Not once had he ever reprimanded this rather unattractive, frail little girl who was as unruly as the

March wind. She combed his hair every evening. Before going to bed, she would sit on the dining room table with a comb and some ribbons. If he was busy doing something, she would call to him, "Grandfather, come here so I can comb you." He would sit in a chair and lower his head. He had long, thin white hair. She parted it with the comb and made little braids that she tied together with a bow. Early the next morning her grandfather would go out to sweep the sidewalk with his hair like that and complain to all the passing neighbors, "The things my grand-daughter does!"

"Will there really be a surprise?"

"A big one."

She was so excited about the surprise that halfway through one of the acts, she exited the scene through the wings. Then she didn't remember she had to close her eyes when the man removed her from the strongbox and carried her in his arms. When they called to her, "Ketty, Ketty," she didn't respond, didn't remember that was her name in the comedy. The curtain fell. When the audience applauded and the curtain went up again, her fat, jovial grandfather appeared on stage wearing his black tailcoat and striped trousers, that still smelled of mothballs, and placed a large doll in her arms.

It came up to her waist. It could move its hands, elbows, knees. It opened and shut its eyes. At first she didn't like it at all. But since everyone kept saying how beautiful it was, and Felipet was almost speechless when he saw it, soon she grew quite proud of it.

She would call her Ketty. All the neighbors participated in the christening. Some old curtains and a few scraps of material were used to make the robes for the priest and altar boys. The garden was full of flowers, happiness, and the haze of a summer after-noon. Her grandfather struggled to fit everyone into the frame of his camera. Mercè was the mother. She wasn't wearing the scarlet dress, but a white one with a large satin bow at the waist. Everybody was dressed up. In a corner of the garden, sitting on the green-colored iron table surrounded by chairs, were two trays overflowing with pastries, permeating everything with the smell of cream, sponge cake, chocolate, and vanilla.

"Quiet, everyone. Quiet!"

Click.

Over the next few days the doll acquired a certain prestige. They talked of her at the table. Friends stopped by to see her. They strolled with her in the Turó Park where all the children turned to stare in amazement. Felipet was thrilled, but he would have wished to play with the doll all by himself. The blue eyes that closed, the soft squeaking of her joints awoke in him a secret tenderness.

"Can I take her home with me?"

"No."

She straightened the doll's dress, fixed her hair, dried her hands, pulled up her socks so they wouldn't be wrinkled. But when she was alone with the doll, she didn't even look at her. The doll was too tall and that caused her anguish. Like a young mother who suddenly finds a ten-year-old daughter sitting on her lap. Little by little she forgot about her.

It was much more exciting to play cops and robbers, hide under the Chinese tomato bush, climb the pomegranate tree with its thin, thorny branches. The trees were in the garden behind the house. The garden in front was elegant: carpeted with sand from the sea, full of shells and pebbles that were white as pine nuts, pink as coral. Every year the family would order a meter of sand to be delivered. They would bring it in the morning, still damp, and the smell of the sea would pervade the entire garden.

Who would remember the doll, if you discovered a whole case of *gasosa*? Felipet and Mercè found it beneath the hydrangea that stood in the shadiest corner of the garden, hidden by a cluster of leaves. They didn't know how to open the bottles. They were scared of being caught, and your teeth had to be really strong if you wanted to hear the loud "pop" when the mist and little bubbles rushed up. They spent long hours, hesitating, beneath the hydrangea. They were always reluctant to leave and returned as soon as possible, anxious to take a peek.

Finally one afternoon Mercè managed to open one of the bottles. They each took a swallow, then closed it again. When they left, their hearts were beating, and when they returned the next day, their hearts were pounding . Every afternoon they opened a bottle, but they took only one swallow. One hot day, her grandfather wanted a cool drink and went to look for a *gasosa*. He found them all open, all flat. "This granddaughter of mine!"

The doll was completely forgotten. Mercè played at Senyora Borràs's house: she would polish the faucets and helped dry the dishes. She would visit Senyora Domingueta, a tall thin widow with tiny, sunken eyes. She was rather dismal looking in her black silk dress, and she spoke slowly, in a low voice, her eyes never moving. Mercè painted the pigeon coop for her. Felipet held the bucket of dark blue paint while the pigeons cooed on the rail and the swallows that nested in the gallery flew back and forth, warbling uneasily. One day she stole a chrysanthemum from Senyora Borràs's garden. It was egg-yolk yellow, large and ruffled like a complicated piece of gold jewelry. She spent an entire morning walking up and down by the clump of flowers, stealing a look at it from the corner of her eye. She snatched it at noon, placed it on her chest, under her apron, and raced into the house panting, her face waxen, the flower crumpled, ugly, dulled.

One gray day when they didn't know what to play, they decided to bathe the doll. At the end of the vegetable garden, leaning against the trunk of a mandarin orange tree, stood a zinc tub, old and dented, with some rainwater in the bottom. A few dry, decayed leaves were floating in it.

"First, we'll put her in the water to soften her," said Mercè.

They undressed her. Her slip was pinned to her back with two tiny nails. Felipet went to the kitchen to look for a knife to pry them out.

They placed her in the tub in all her rosy nakedness, the water up to her neck, her innocent blue eyes half closed beneath the long eyelashes.

"Hands and feet are always the dirtiest. Especially children's, and dolls are children's children," Mercè said when Felipet told her with a frown that dolls shouldn't be bathed.

"What are you doing?" shouted Mercè's mother from the kitchen. It made them jump.

"We're playing!" Mercè called loudly.

"We're playing," echoed Felipet.

"You're awfully quiet. Are you sure you're not up to something?"

All you could see were eyes that day. Both children had their hair cut in bobs, their bangs framing their faces like horseshoes.

"Come inside, it's time for your snack."

They didn't remember the doll until the following day.

There had been a torrential downpour during the night. The rain coursed through the gully nearby, leaving the two gardens filled with golden leaves. The pointed, shiny Chinese tomatoes—

dull red, in clusters of seven—were swaying in the wind, filling the air with a sickly, sour smell. The leaves on the pomegranate tree were bright yellow, the sky limpid.

They found the doll soaked with water. They were distressed to see her delicate pink skin was chipped. The dark gray cardboard oozed out like a purulent sore. Only the porcelain face remained intact, indifferent, lips parted with a smile, cheeks rosy.

When Mercè picked up the doll, her wig fell off.

"Bald."

"Like a melon," Felipet said in dismay, yet unable to keep from smiling.

That was the only thing they said about the tragedy.

Toward the end of the afternoon, while Mercè's mother was shopping, the two children brought the doll inside, feeling as if they were going to a funeral.

"Let's hide her under the bed."

"Maybe we should keep the head and throw the rest away." Felipet said. As soon as he had spoken, his eyes filled with tears.

When Mercè got into bed at night, she would start thinking about the doll. She had cared very little about her before, but now she couldn't live without her. She waited until the house was silent and everyone asleep. Then she would turn on the light and curl up by the edge of the bed. "She's dead," she would murmur as she stroked her cheek, a sad expression on her face.

"What are you doing with the light on for so long?" her mother called to her one night from her room next door.

"Pee pee."

She jumped into bed and turned off the light, trembling.

During the day, Felipet visited the doll. Mercè would take him to see her. In the midst of some lively game, or while reading a story, the memory of the doll would rush feverishly over her, and she would hurry to look at her, pulling her by the arm or leg, gazing silently at the distorted cardboard shape.

Till the day the doll was discovered and the elders created a row.

# ON THE TRAIN

**. . . no, no, just like I was telling you, I ain't never been able** to sleep on the train, I get kinda drowsy, but I always hear the creaking of wheels and wood and besides, with all this wobbling and jerking, I'm afraid to go to the toilet and it frightens me that the train might send me spinning against the wall and me struck dumb and if nobody has a need for hours, even if I holler nobody's gonna hear me and at my age they'd find me dead and I don't want to die without the taking of Our Lord. All of us could be struck by accident, but it'd be mighty sad to die doomed and me, I don't like fire, and the one in hell, judging by what they say, must be one of the fiercest.

They thirsty? Poor creatures, sure they're thirsty. With these half-open beaks, their crests all sad—but I can't help 'em any. The day after tomorrow they'll be dead and roasted 'cause it's Santa Maria and at my gentleman's house they gonna have them a big party 'cause, besides being the Senyora's Saint's Day, the oldest daughter, she looks like a Virgin on one of them religious cards, well she's gonna make her debut. You gonna remember to let me know when we get to Barcelona? I can't read, not one letter, my son now he knew how to read like he was a gentleman's son, but he died from the chest and he wasn't even twenty years old. My husband, he told me: "Don't cry, now he don't have to be a soldier." 'cause we used to live right in Barcelona, I don't remember the name of the street now, but it was near the Estació de França. My husband was a baker and they liked him, and working with

138

flour ain't something disgusting. I used to always tell him—Virgin
Mary, and now it has to rain and these poor little creatures must
be dying of thirst, with this sultry weather, look at them nice
and fat, that's how I raise 'em, no lice, *co-coc, co-coc,* poor little
things, if I could only collect a bit of water for 'em. You see, they
used to run free all day. And I always try to keep their feet all
dry and . . .

I think it was the year they burned the convents, no? I hope
the good Lord don't remember them, and in the village there
was a storm that destroyed all the crops and left us poor as Job's
turkey and my husband said to me: "Let's go to Barcelona, that
way the boy'll learn more than if we stay here, a farmer's always a
farmer, but a gentleman is always a gentleman." And my brother,
who had money 'cause he was the oldest and got everything, he
had it good, good since the day he was born, well he bought the
house and the fields so as to raise the value of his property, 'cause
he could and we couldn't, and when we got to Barcelona we had
a little money, but bit by bit we lost it all, 'cause my husband
couldn't find work straight off and the boy was already sickly,
and doctor here doctor there till good-bye to the money my
brother gave us for the house and the land. And all on account of
the water, 'cause without that spell of bad weather, what must of
been punishment for burning Barcelona, and the good always pay
for the sinners and we had to pay 'cause the land was by the river
and on a slope and the water carried everything away.

Help yourself, if you'd fancy some, it's bad to feel weak and
you know it's the stomach that carries us along. I remember how
we all went hungry . . . Take a peek, a little omelet, ah eggs, the
eggs are fresh this week. When I lived in Barcelona every Sunday
we went to Tibidabo and we took lunch with us, but I was always
afraid of the eggs in Barcelona on account of they was eggs that
was kept. Want a little bit of ham? Just a little slice? Don't say
no, you don't know what you'd be missing. It's nourishing but
it don't make you feel stuffed. I used to go and wash clothes for

some senyors who had four women servants and a man just to
open the door, his name was Julio, and the gentleman he was tall
and thin and he wore glasses of gold, and Carmeta, that was the
housemaid, she told me he was head of a political party and every
once in a while he had to escape to France and no time to pack
his bags, on account of Catalans being so persecuted. Sometimes,
when he saw me passing by with a basket of laundry, he'd say
"Ah, Ramona, on your way to do the clothes, are you? Want a
peach? They're all sugar and honey. They'll cure your thirst." Still
raining. Virgin Mary, and like a simpleton I left my umbrella and
I get all flustered when I get to Barcelona, 'cause since I don't
know how to read I get all agitated when I got to catch the tram
and I always have to ask what name's on the side. Want another
one? Make you healthy, eat up. Well, you got to realize they said
Mass right there in the house, and I still don't know why they
didn't kill 'em all when the revolution came, and the priest, who
was a friend of the family and helped the Senyora's mother to
die good, he was saved too. I never saw his face, I only seen him
twice when he was crossing the hall and he was hurrying like a
rat, but he was small. Where are we? Ah! Cerdanyola. Fancy that.
Talking and laughing away we already got to Cerdanyola.

Not long before, my husband went on strike and I asked my
Senyora, she was tall and slim too like her husband and was
always wearing silk and she spoke in a low voice, all calm like,
and I'd get sleepy just listening to her, well I asked her if she
knew about more houses where I could go and clean 'cause we
was having us a bad stretch and everything was getting more
costly, and she asked me did I want to take charge of the cleaning
of the China room. Everything was from China and embroidered
in fine gold that don't turn black, with these creatures that looked
out at me when I dusted 'em, 'cause Carmeta was kinda careless
and she was always knocking off the mother-of-pearl, cleaning
so hard, you know, slap-bang. I told her I'd clean real slow and
we reached an agreement. Well, when my husband was striking,

Carmeta found herself a man, but she was real proper like, and the day she found out he was married she said enough, but he would hang around the house and spy on her when she went to buy the milk, since she was the housemaid they only made her buy the milk in the afternoons, and there he was following her on her day off when she went out and she not even giving him a look and he was going mad. And one day he wanted to see the Senyora and he told her straight, yes, it was true he was married, but it wasn't his fault, and he was mighty powerful in love with Carmeta, and if she didn't want to speak to him no more, he was sorry but he was gonna do something crazy on account of he was losing his head over her and the Senyora gave him good advice and told him not to think about Carmeta, 'cause she was a good girl and owing to him she was suffering sorely and losing weight. He promised her he wasn't gonna do nothing foolish and to tell Carmeta to talk to him every now and then, even if only once a week, but Carmeta was right when she said he should of told her straight off he was married and she didn't want to speak to him again, not even to say "Bona tarda." And one afternoon she went to fetch the milk and didn't come back 'cause he killed her with a revolver and left her stretched out in the middle of the street and Julio and I went down and covered her with a sheet. Yes, that's how it is, here today, gone tomorrow . . .

The doctor as soon as he entered he looked at me and said: "Your husband has caught it." But I never believed it. He looked like he'd got the evil touch. First he turned yellow and for two days he was unconscious and passing worms, and the doctor said it was the epidemic, but an epidemic without poison, and he'd get well 'cause he was strong as an ox, and the next day I threw away all the medicine 'cause it made him sick at the stomach and he turned all green. The third day he spoke and told me to make him a poultice with white onions for his stomach, by the third one his stomach was real chafed and you could see his skin all raw, and he couldn't stop groaning, and he never stopped groaning till he died, with a heat that burned up everything. When he died it was already the Republic, and he couldn't never be boss, and he would of liked it, 'cause the revolution was on the way and the fellow that took care of the kneading trough when the revolution came he said to me, "Now your husband could of rested, 'cause the workers are the bosses and the bosses are the ones that got to slave away"—excuse me, you're not a member of the Falange Party, are you? Ah, I thought so . . .

I sold the furniture to the wife of a fellow that took part in the revolution and I went to the village alone. My nephew, who loves me like a mother and used to play with Miquel when he was little—Miquel, that was my boy, may he rest in peace—he says to me, "Don't you worry, the land is for them that work it and now it's all mine and you'll always have a place at my table." And he took me in, but that ended soon, 'cause when the fellows with the berets came, he had to go to France and ended up in the camp in Vernet and he had to sell his watch, and he still hasn't got paid, 'cause a Negro—what we call a *negritu*—who was a soldier and guarded the camp tricked him good. But just you wait, my nephew is a bad-tempered sort and you'll see what he done. He told me himself when he got back two years later, all disgusted 'cause speaking French was just too much for him and they moved them up and down and made them pick beets. Ah, thank goodness the sun's come out, the sun is half a life. It bothers you? Sometimes a migraine comes from the stomach . . . you see, the *negritu* would walk up and down the camp and my nephew calls out to him and asks him does he want to buy a watch, it's a good make, chock-full of wheels inside, and he says yes, it's a deal, and my nephew gives him the watch and the *negritu* walks away all happy-like not giving him a cent, and here they made an agreement. The next day, my nephew sees the *negritu* passing by, it seems he was expecting him to pass; he calls out and says: another watch, but this one is even better, it goes tic-tock, tic-tock, and the *negritu* laughs and runs away, and about that time, the Negro is in pieces 'cause my nephew told me the clock that went tic-tock was a time bomb.

Just like I was telling you, my nephew took me in, but when he had to go to France, that same night my brother comes to find me, the one that bought the house from us when the flood left us penniless and he says to me, "Ramona, come with me. I'm not moving, no matter what, the boy did something crazy, but I got the lands, and they're rightly mine, and I didn't fight in the revolution, but if they come looking for explanations you can always tell them what I say is true, for the field and the house I paid you what they was worth, and I'm counting on you to tell if need be, 'cause they burned down the town hall and I don't know if my property is in order, and the deeds I was keeping, when the revolutionaries came they took them and I ain't never seen them again."

Ah, gracious me, here we are; time just flew by. Well what I wanted to tell you is the world's like a play, but the trouble is nobody knows how it ends, 'cause we all die before, and those that's left just plug along as if nothing happened. Sometimes I get cranky, and I'm not one that ought to complain. I always been healthy, I'm not delicate-like. My stomach's all swollen now, like I was pregnant, but I think it's only holding water and it don't bother me. When I think about all them that ain't been so lucky like me, Mother of God, and all the tragedies they have, it'll make you shudder. Well, I got to catch the tram to Bonanova, my Senyora lives on Avinguda de Craywinckel. Thank you, thank you, I'll find it. All roads lead to Rome. Nice to meet you and Bona tarda.

# BEFORE
# I DIE

**Before I die I want to write an account of the last two years of** my life to explain—explain to myself—everything I've been forced to renounce. One afternoon toward the end of winter, I was so cold that I went into a café and ordered a grog. The café was called "Els Ocells," the birds. I sat down at a table by the window. People were hunched over as they hurried past. I was nervous. I'd had an argument with the instructor in my art course; he said my colors were too muted and I didn't agree. I thought he was old fashioned and had terrible judgment. I found it utterly absurd that he didn't want to understand me and realize that the way I painted was the way *I* had to paint. Besides, I was in a bad mood because I should have received a check from my uncle a couple of weeks before, and as I was leaving the pension in the morning, the proprietor asked me when I was going to pay my bill. To top it off, I had dropped my fountain pen on the floor and the tip had broken. I asked the boy in the café for pen and ink; I wanted to write my uncle at once. As I was taking paper and envelopes from my satchel, a man sat down beside me. There was nothing extraordinary about him. I would never have noticed him had he not sat beside me. Such audacity! I considered it offensive, especially as there were so many empty tables.

Among my classmates I was known to be rather wild and unsociable, a person "easily irritable, with unexpected, violent reactions." The man sat there beside me without moving, his briefcase on the table casting a shadow on me. It was a good-quality briefcase, but worn, made of brown leather, with spots on it, a metal lock. He had provoked me, and without giving it a thought, I spilled my drink on him.

"Don't worry."

His voice made me even more indignant. A cold, dark voice, accompanied by an indifferent glance. He pulled out a handkerchief and calmly dried his trousers.

"I did it on purpose."

"I don't believe I have disturbed you."

"Why did you sit at my table?"

"Forgive me, it is you who are sitting at *my* table."

I looked at him in surprise.

"Tables in a café don't have owners; they're for the first person who arrives."

"I am a creature of habit; I come to this café every day at the same hour, and invariably I sit at this table, summer and winter."

The following day I returned to the café. He entered and headed straight to *his* table. I was sitting opposite. We looked at each other and laughed. The previous night, before falling asleep, I had thought about the incident with the drink and felt bad.

As I left the café I noticed he was following me. When I reached the door to the pension he addressed me:

"I would like to ask you something, something that is important to me: Please come to the café every day, if you can. I won't address you, if you don't wish me to. Your presence does me good. I entreat you."

I began going to the café every day. We each sat at our own table, but we would leave together, and he would accompany me part of the way. One day he asked me, "Have you ever thought of getting married?" "No." He said nothing more that day, but on the following he posed the same question, and I had one of my reactions. "I'm not going to respond. Come take a look at my room." It was the perfect day to prove my point: everything was in disarray, a dreadful disorder. "You see? Do you believe a girl like me can consider getting married? And I smoke. I smoke like a madman who's a mad smoker. Look at this." I opened the wardrobe. None of my clothes were folded, everything was all jumbled up, towels mixed in with stockings, face creams, books with bars of soap, tubes of paint. "In a marriage, everything is order and harmony and I—"

"Have you ever been in love?"

"Never."

"Don't you love anything?"

"No."

"Flowers?"

"No."

"Music?"

"No."

"Art!"

"No."

"Animals?"

"No."

"But, doves you do."

"Roasted."

He laughed and left. I accompanied him down the stairs.

The following day at three o'clock a boy arrived at the pension with two white doves in a cage. "For Senyoreta Marta Coll from Senyor Màrius Roig." The following day I invited him to dinner: hors d'oeuvres, roasted dove, fruit and cheese for dessert.

"I thought as much."

"What?"

"That they would be good."

More than spilling the drink on his trousers, I regretted my crime. We went out for a stroll. As we walked I confessed that I had made the cook at the pension kill the doves. "I'm sure you thought I wouldn't be capable of doing it."

I didn't go to the café the following day. I was filled with a strange sense of remorse. I couldn't sleep that night. I kept thinking that he must have waited for me all afternoon. In the morning, I found a letter beside my *café amb llet*. "Please forgive my absence yesterday afternoon. It was impossible for me to come. You cannot imagine how I agonized."

We met that day and were happy to see each other. We had a pleasant time, but I had a terrible dream that night. I was traveling, and everywhere I went—on trains, in hotels, in every country I visited—I encountered two white doves, the feathers on their necks soaked in blood. The afternoon that neither of us had gone to the café changed us. We were different. Closer. As if the day we hadn't met had brought us together.

"Would you mind marrying a miserable man?"

"Why do you ask such strange questions?"

"Would you answer my question?"

"I can only give you one answer: I don't know. I've never given it a thought. I suppose the only thing I'd ask of a man was that he love me."

"I love you."

From my diary:

*I felt suffused by an infinite emptiness on the afternoon I didn't go to the café. Terrible. I've learned something about myself. I don't believe in anything. But I think the least one can ask of intelligent people is that they know how to be happy, how to live, how to accept. When we*

147

*separated, he said, "Thank you." "Thank you for what?" I asked. "For the trust you have shown me since we met." He kissed my hand. As he walked away I stood in the center of the sidewalk, looking at him. I followed his shadow, the shadow of the briefcase attached to his body.*

I moved. I rented a room with a little kitchen in a hotel. Occasionally he would stay for dinner, and then we would go to the cinema. Three months passed.

One day he asked, "Would you like to come to my house?"

"Why?"

"Have you ever realized that when I ask you a question, instead of answering you always say, 'Why?' I need you to come. Would you like to come to my house?"

We took a cab. He held my hand the whole time. The house was in the center of town, but in a quiet area. It had a tiny garden in front with two acacia trees and looked quite bourgeois: two stories, with small, silver-colored iron balconies.

"You'll find it rather disorderly."

We laughed.

We laughed because we both remembered his first visit to my room in the pension. On the door was a metal plaque: MÀRIUS ROIG, ATTORNEY. An elderly woman came to greet us, and he introduced her: "My family. This is Elvira, and she has been in the house for twenty years." He introduced me as "My fiancée."

On the floor in the foyer lay a heap of cement and sand. They must have gotten scattered, because the floor made a scratchy noise as we walked through he house.

"I have asked you to come because I want your opinion. As you can see I am renovating the house and I would like for you to . . ."

"Why did you introduce me as your fiancée?"

"Because that is what you are."

"Since when?"

"Since the day you spilled the drink on me. Ah, do you like the bathroom? Do you want it with a door to the bedroom and a door to the hall, or only to the hall?"

"Two doors."

A wave of happiness flashed across his eyes, so powerful that it frightened me.

"That is the first time you have dispensed with the 'Why?'"

"I haven't dispensed with it. Why do you want my opinion?"

"Can't you guess?"

"Yes, but I find that you do everything without thinking of me."

"Quite the contrary. I do everything with you in mind. Is it not obvious?"

<hr />

From my diary:

> It was starting to grow dark by the time we left, and he walked me along unfamiliar streets. Suddenly we found ourselves in front of the café. I thought to myself, ah, it's close to the house. I remembered the winter, that cold afternoon when I was in such a bad mood. It all seemed so far away, a bit sad compared to now. I'm starting to like flowers.
>
> He took me to a concert. It was my first time in a concert hall. The program had Chopin, Ravel, and Mozart. When they played the last violin sonata by Mozart, I almost jumped out of my seat. He took me by the arm and gently pulled me back down. "I love you." That was the first time he used the familiar form of the pronoun with me.
>
> The world he's offered me is limpid, and I feel good in it.

"What is it you wish to tell me?"
"Don't laugh."
"I promise I won't laugh."
"I'd like to have two doves."
And we burst out laughing.

The dressmaker came to fit my wedding dress today. I had to stand for two hours. I was close to fainting when she finally said, "We're through now. Are you very tired?" I was terribly pale, and I felt as if the dressmaker was still sticking me with her pins. I observed myself in the mirror, surrounded by tulle and silk lace, and thought, "A white ghost is looking at me."

My uncle wrote me an exceptionally long letter. In a very formal style, he gave me permission to marry.

We were married at the end of summer. It was raining. The leached gray clouds, the tired light made my dress and orange blossoms seem whiter and the plants on either side of the church door greener. I remember the sound of the rain on the umbrellas, the red one as I entered the hotel, the black one as I entered the church. I didn't want to take the dress off, ever. I felt like a different person in it, as if I were dead or some very old person traveling about after a long absence. We had dinner at home, alone, in the house that still smelled of damp cement and sand and paint. White roses had been arranged in the dining room, red roses in the bedroom. They gave off a caramel scent that annoyed me. He left me alone, and I opened the window and placed the flowers outside. I sat down in an armchair to rest for a moment and fell asleep. When I awoke he was sitting in front of me, gazing at me. I had an irrepressible desire to go out, stroll about, walk with him along the streets in my white dress. It was a dark night. The clock struck one as we left the house, not a soul on the streets. From time to time a gust of wind blew raindrops off the trees and with them the scent of earth and wet grass.

"Are they acacia trees?"

We stopped, and he embraced me.

"Content?"

"Happy."

We must have been a good fifteen minutes from the house when it started to rain. The drops weren't large, but they fell so heavily that they started to seep through my silk dress, leaving my back icy cold.

We were soaked head to toe by the time we reached the house. As soon as we entered, it began to rain harder. No words can describe how I loved that rain; the dull sound of it made me feel truly at home.

When dawn was breaking, he said, "Call me 'Amor meu,' my love."

"Why?"

"Will you say it?"

"Amor meu."

We spent our honeymoon in Venice and returned in the middle of winter.

The house was large. I ruled over the top floor, Elvira the ground floor: the two rooms overlooking the street—my husband's office and the waiting room—the dining room, the kitchen, and a large parlor with a grand piano. Upstairs were the bedrooms, ours and the guest room; the bath; and a large, well furnished library with two balconies facing west. This is where I spent my time.

Mârius fell ill that winter. Influenza complicated by bronchopneumonia. That was when I met Roger, Mârius's doctor, a friendly, optimistic fellow. Mârius considered him his best friend, his only friend really. One day when Mârius was convalescing, I went to the library to look for a book. When I couldn't find it, I remembered that he had been reading it, and I thought he might have it in the briefcase he always kept by his side. I returned to our bedroom; he was seated facing the balcony, seemingly asleep. The briefcase was in the corner. I opened it and caught sight of a packet of letters between some of the files. A packet of mauve-colored envelopes, thirty perhaps. I'm not sure. I only know, I only recall that Mârius stood up quickly, came to me, and took the briefcase from my hands.

"What are you looking for?"

"The book you were reading, that you asked me for and I couldn't find it in the library."

"Why would you look for it here?"

That night I began to think about the letters and Mârius's reaction. Whose were they? His? Had they been entrusted to him by a client? I sketched an entire novel around the letters. I was still awake when the sun rose. From the moment I met Mârius— since that day at the café—my memory of him had always been associated with the briefcase in his hand. Especially my visual memory.

Everything changed. Those letters . . . he had taken the

briefcase from my hand so abruptly. The letters represented something. What?

It was my birthday, and Roger was coming to dinner. I had been alone all afternoon. I had spent the time getting ready for the evening. I was going to wear what I had bought in Venice, the black crêpe dress and the open-toe shoes, their heels encrusted with green stones. I had pinned up my hair, had carefully made up my face and painted my fingernails. Just as I was about to put the dress on, Mârius came in. He had entered so quietly that he frightened me.

"Today's your birthday, no?"

"Yes sir."

"How many years?"

"Many."

"Splendid."

Splendid. He handed me a little box. I immediately thought: a piece of jewelry. I untied the gold ribbon and removed the tissue paper. Inside the velvet-lined box lay a diamond dove with its wings extended.

"I remember how you longed for a pair of doves; perhaps you will have the second one next year."

I hugged him tightly, very tightly. The room was saturated by shadows and a gray, fleeting light. "Amor meu," I whispered. I felt him bristle. I had the impression he considered those two words sacred, reserved only for the dark hours of the night. I was filled with anguish.

⁂

I forgot about the letters for a few days, but another incident made me wish to see them. I needed to discover who they were from and what they said. I knew practically nothing about Mârius's life. I had never dared to ask him about his past, partly from discretion, partly because I was afraid of being disillusioned. I wondered why he had never spontaneously confided in me. Two weeks after my birthday, Mârius was called to the phone while we were having lunch. His briefcase was standing in the corner. I stood up without giving it a thought. Had I been told that lightning would strike me if I approached the briefcase, I would have done the same. It was locked. When I turned around, Elvira was standing by the table, looking at me. I was vexed and hated her. Suddenly I felt alone in a foreign house. Everything seemed strange and hostile. The walls, the furniture, those two people who could draw near without a sound, startle me, frighten me.

My desire to possess the letters was so intense that I was willing to risk everything.

From my diary:

> *I did something I should never have done. Something that did no one any good, but has hurt me tremendously. I took three letters from the packet. Just as I had resolved, I took the first and last letters, and one from the middle. The last was dated six months before I met Mârius. It tells of an affair that had ended. It is a letter of farewell. I have burned all three of them.*

It isn't true, I didn't burn them. I had taken them while Mârius was in the bathroom undressing. The briefcase lay at the foot of the bed, locked as before. But I had anticipated that and calculated I could squeeze my hand under the flap and pull them out. My heart was pounding furiously at the thought of seizing them, my pulse too. I tiptoed barefoot to the briefcase, ready to act. I knew where they were and slipped my hand in. I pulled out the first letter in the packet, but there wasn't much room beneath the flap and the enveloped got crumpled, making a noise. I held my breath. I reached in again and pulled out the letter at the end of the packet. Then I removed one from the middle. When I was ready to stand up, I couldn't; my legs had no strength. I couldn't think clearly. I could only feel the three letters in my hand; everything whirled around me. I hid them under the rug and, with a huge effort, returned to bed. A moment later Mârius opened the bathroom door and the light fanned out to the foot of the bed.

Mârius had been asleep for a while. He had turned on his side facing me, and I could hear him breathing rhythmically. I was suddenly full of regret. I struggled to compose myself, but I couldn't hold back the tears. I wept silently, the tears gushing out. From time to time I felt one dropping on the pillow. "What's the matter?" How I wished I could simply have disappeared. Mârius pulled me toward him and held me. "It's only nerves, only nerves." He ran his hand through my hair and kissed me on the forehead. I was on the point of confessing what I'd done, telling him how distressed I was, asking him for the love of God to tear up the letters, throw away the briefcase that disturbed my rest. The mere sight of it upset me. He went back to sleep, but I lay awake all night. I finally dozed off in the morning. Mârius had already left when Elvira brought my breakfast. I couldn't eat a thing. My mouth had a bitter taste, my tongue felt thick. I took one sip of coffee and got dressed. Why couldn't I read the letters at home? I don't know. Once I was dressed, I collected them, placed them at the bottom of my purse, and left the house.

Few people were on the street, but I felt like they were all observing me, could see the three stolen letters at the bottom of my purse. Somehow I found myself at a metro station; I don't remember how I arrived there, but it seemed like a good place to read the letters. Who would take note of me seated on a bench with the hustle and bustle of trains and people? Then I caught sight of Roger approaching. I don't know what expression of panic my face must have reflected; all I know is that his was filled with anxiety.

"Are you ill?"

"No, but I've been terribly nervous for some time now and I can't sleep."

He smiled benevolently.

"I can see that I need to pay you a visit."

"Any time you wish."

His presence calmed me, and I was sorry for him to leave.

"You're not getting on the train?"

"No. I'm waiting for a friend."

He waved to me through the window, and I continued sitting on the bench, not daring to open my purse.

When I emerged from the metro, I had the impression of arriving in a big city for the first time. The houses, the light, the sky, nothing was familiar. I felt the way a convalescent must feel after a long illness. I strolled about like an automaton. Instinctively I entered a café, as I had done in my student days. I sat down, removed the letters from my purse, and began reading them, as if the contents were completely irrelevant to me. The first read:

*Dearest,*

*I can still imagine you at the station, I can hear your voice. You should not have come. I am obsessed by our parting, and a terrible sadness consumes me because we will never again live as we have during this time. Such brief happiness. Write to me, above all, write to me. If I had to be punished, the greatest punishment would be never to receive any news of you. Write to me in care of Eliana Porta, at her address. She is completely trustworthy. (Her address followed). I will never forget the months we have lived together. Remember this always: "I will never forget." Elisa.*

The second letter was longer and sadder.

*Amor meu: life is so painful that I do not know when I will ever again find a moment of joy. I have given a lot of thought to what you propose, but it is not possible. I cannot ruin the life of a man who has*

*placed all his trust in me. I cannot. Even yesterday, after a terrible
night, I got up, determined to explain the situation. I couldn't. Perhaps
because I am weak, amor meu. It is too complicated to explain why we
will be spending time in X. Nothing could hurt me as much. Eliana
is coming with us. Write to me under her name as soon as you can.
An occasional letter from you will comfort me in a way that no one,
perhaps not even you, can imagine.*

*I realize the risk involved, but if you could come . . . Just once.
Do you recall the Hotel de Llevant, where we first loved each other,
where we met? "Are you staying at the hotel?" "No, I live in a house
on Avinguda de les Acàcies. I am meeting a friend, a woman who is
staying here, in room number 10." "Be careful not to speak poorly of
me to your friend; I am in number 12." Do you remember room 10, the
balcony over the garden with the climbing jasmine, the sea?*

I didn't finish reading it. I wanted to see the other one, from
the end of the packet, which I assumed would provide the most
information, the most insight into that morsel of life from which
I was barred. It was last letter of the story.

*Amor meu, now we will not even have the consolation of writing to
each other. Eliana is going away with her family for a while, but she
is uncertain for how long. We will be left without even the comfort
of seeing the familiar handwriting, only a shared past, fragmentary
memories, a few sweet hours that slowly fade. You are free. If you
despair, think of me, of my sacrifice, and remember that I suffer as
much as you. Above all, remember that you have been, and will be,
my only love. Elisa.*

It was lunchtime and people had stopped work; the café had
gradually filled by the time I left. It was late when I arrived
home, and Màrius was waiting for me. He was concerned, had not
wanted to eat without me. When he caught sight of me, he asked
if I was ill. Could he have realized the three letters were missing?

I could not be sure, and if he had realized, he dissimulated so well that he will never know how grateful I was. Yes, I was ill. Roger came that evening.

"I ran into your wife this morning and told her I would stop by to pay a visit."

He prescribed a tranquilizer and recommended complete rest. I remained at home for a week, moving between my bed and the library. Before he left each day, Mârius would come to ask me how I was feeling. Sometimes he brought me flowers and magazines; his attentiveness was touching. As soon as I heard the front door close, I would remove the letters from my purse. Why had I not sought a different hiding place? I read and reread them. I knew them by heart. I am convinced that the days of "complete rest" were terrible for me. I tortured myself thinking about the woman that Mârius had loved. That he continued to love. That he loved. If he didn't, why would he keep the letters, never letting them out of his sight? I was ravaged by an unbearable sense of inferiority. I felt as insignificant as a speck of dust. Why had he married me? Out of spite? Why was he lonely? What was I doing there, weary and heavyhearted? What was it that bound me to the four walls that surrounded me? Soon I began to live with a single obsession: meeting that woman, knowing what color her hair was, her eyes. What if it wasn't over? And if there were more letters? When Elvira entered the room, she seemed like a jailer, and I was sure that from deep within her small, steely eyes she could see my truth and was glad.

The first day I left the house, I felt strong and young. Oh, yes. I would win. But it was essential that I meet her in order to know what weapon to choose. Strolling through the crowds, surrounded by noise, the brightness of the radiant day, I realized that I loved my husband deeply. I hailed a taxi and gave Eliana's address. During the days I was shut in the house I had planned what I would do. Surely Eliana had not disappeared for good. The letter said she "was going away with her family for a while, but she is uncertain for how long." As I crossed the threshold of the building, my hands were as icy as the day I read the letters in the café, when I was overwhelmed by a sense of absence, of not being the one in control and making the decisions, feeling that I was someone else obeying orders given by myself. I walked up the stairs to the second floor. My icy hands began to sweat. I rang the bell. A large woman opened the door with a smile. "Senyoreta Eliana?" "Sorry, try ringing the apartment next door, maybe the neighbors who moved in when she left can help you." If the kindhearted woman, full of consideration, had not stood in the door, waiting for me to ring, I would have rushed down the stairs breathlessly. But I rang. A girl, about eleven, opened the door. She had plaid ribbons around her braids and a vivacious face filled with curiosity. "Senyoreta Eliana?" She didn't seem to understand. "I mean, the senyoreta who used to live in this apartment. Would you happen to know where she is now? Did she leave her address?" The girl ran inside, calling, "Mamà, Mamà." A moment passed. The neighbor was still standing at her door. Soon I heard voices from the back of the apartment and steps approaching. A youngish woman appeared, in a bathrobe, a jar of face cream in her hand. As she talked, she continued to plunge two fingers in the cream, spreading it on her face with circular movements. "Looking for Eliana? Yes, she left us her address in case there was a message; you see, the concierge didn't much care for her. But she moved such a long time ago that I'm afraid I've lost it. You know how it is with children. In any event, check with the concierge; maybe she'll be nice to you. I'm sure she has it." She closed the door with a "Come along, girl." The two women and the girl disappeared as if they had been sucked inside.

The concierge had gone out for a moment, so I waited. She arrived, weighted down by packages and a basket full of vegetables. "How can I help you?" she asked as she placed the packages on a table, without even a glance at me. When she had finished, she looked me straight in the face. "What is it?" "By any chance would you have Senyoreta Eliana's address?" "Ah, Eliana. Yet again! I thought the fuss was finally over." "If I'm inconveniencing you . . ." "No, not you. Since she moved, not a month goes by without someone asking for her or bringing her letters." "Letters?" I asked, my heart pounding. "Ah yes, the letters, the mystery surrounding them . . ." "So you have her address?" "Hers? I can give you her friend's address if you wish. She used to stop by here quite often. Always in a hurry, never even a '*Bon dia.*' Who do these ladies think they are? I too can go around with my head high." Still grumbling, she went inside and came back out with a slip of paper in her hand. "Here, you see? Elisa R., Carrer Tenerife 26." My head began to spin, and I had to lean against the wall. Realizing I felt ill, the concierge had me sit down and brought me a cordial. I remember a bouquet of artificial roses in the center of the table, the sideboard lined with blue glasses. Through an open door at the end of the hall I could see a patio and hear pigeons cooing.

From my diary:

*A garden. A cool, shady garden. A garden with no flowers. Wisteria climbing the trellis by the front door, the occasional rustling of leaves. A Japanese room. A screen showing pink ibis, their wings extended, surrounded by yellow chrysanthemums. A small black lacquered table with mother of pearl inlay. Almond branches. A magnificent tiger skin lying on the champagne-colored rug. Rare luxury, a bit overpowering. A woman much older than me. White skin. Very white. Black, rather small eyes and smooth, arched eyebrows. Tall and thin. A voice . . . Yes, above all the voice. Just hearing it would make you fall in love with her. As I faced her, I was forced to view myself: a disorderly, brusque, temperamental girl. A failure. How can one possibly acquire her degree of poise and elegance? Somehow I managed to stammer, "I hope you will forgive me. I announced that Màrius Roig had sent me; that's not the case, nor is he ill. I have come because I wanted to. I am his wife." At the very least I expected a word, a change of expression, a bit of curiosity. She gazed at me, unperturbed. Had I said nothing more, I am sure the visit would have ended here. "I've come because I wanted to meet you. It was such an overwhelming desire that I couldn't control it." "What is it that you wish to know?" "Nothing." "What do you want?" "Nothing." "Only to meet me?" "Only that." "Has he spoken to you of me?" I didn't reply. "Is it because you feel that I stand between you and him?" "No." The question had been so humiliating that I'd been forced to lie. "So?" "If I ask you something directly, will you respond?" "What is it?" "Do you love him?" It was as if the ibis on the screen had moved. It took her a while to reply. I could see her searching for something that would sound good, diplomatic. "Some things never die." I wanted to applaud. Even though I saw that she had chosen her reply as one might choose the smallest needle amongst many, still, she had hurt me. She had said it to hurt me and had succeeded. She spoke the words so calmly, with such control, such a penetrating voice. She hurt me, but I knew it was true. I felt as if suddenly I had been pinned to the wall and left there.*

◆◆◆◆

I was consumed by the desire to die. Not to kill myself, simply to die. To kill yourself you must have the will, the energy. To die, you need nothing. Suddenly I found support in Elvira, and here I had always believed her an enemy.

"I remember the day this Senyora Elisa first visited the house, enveloped in fur and perfume. I think she came about an inheritance. She completely transformed Senyor, like turning a sock inside out. How he changed! He was so cheerful, always in a good mood, but after that hardly a '*Bon dia*' to me. Everything went smoothly while her husband was in the sanatorium. Visits, phone calls, urgent letters. Oh yes, she came to the house. She'd march right in as if she owned it, giving orders like she was the *mestressa*. She showed up and wrecked Mârius's life, poor Senyor.

Her goal was to make him fall in love with her. She needed a man, forgive me for being so frank, but lots of women are like that. Did they take a trip together? Many. You have to remember that the affair lasted five years. Straight away I saw how selfish she was. And all during this time, she'd visit her husband. She'd go to the sanatorium, sometimes stay a week. I could tell just by looking at Senyor's face. When she was away, he wouldn't set foot out of the house, all sad and dull, looking like a sick animal. But the husband regained his health, and she began to withdraw. With plenty of fancy excuses, she abandoned Senyor like an old shoe. But you shouldn't be thinking about these things. Can't you see how much he loves you? As soon as I laid eyes on you, I thought to myself 'He'll be happy with this girl.' You can tell right away you're a fine person. But it's not good to be sad, believe me, it's not good."

That is how I learned what it is to have *"seny,"* good sense.

I went out this afternoon with Elvira. We visited her niece Maria, who is married and has an eleven-month-old baby. The sun was scorching, not a bit of air. We crossed a patio at the back of which was a printing press. Through the open window you could see an office and hear the sound of a linotype. To the right of the patio was a glass door, a window with red geraniums on either side of it. We went straight into the dining room. The table was covered with a blue-and-white checkered oilcloth. Maria was sewing. A cradle covered by a bride's veil stood in the corner, and a sewing machine beneath the window. We had a bite to eat. Maria had fixed sandwiches and prepared fresh peaches and pears doused in sweet wine and sugar. The baby woke up. His skin was like milk, his eyes like stars. He was whimpering. He must have been hot and in a bad mood. Maria breastfed him. Her husband came in at six. He works at the printing office. He went off to wash and change. When he returned to the dining room, he was naked from the waist up, wearing blue trousers. Maria handed the boy to Elvira and served her husband some fruit salad. As she did so, he put his arm around her and pulled her forcefully toward him. "Keep still," she exclaimed, but she didn't move away. He ran his hand through her hair, tangling it. Then she sat down. But her eyes were fixed on her husband's chest, staring at his dark, glossy skin, fascinated.

Sometimes, when I am alone, or when I am bathing, or when Mârius falls asleep before me I think: *my husband.* And when he sleeps, I place my hand on his side and feel his rhythmic breathing against my palm and think: *my husband.*

My first reaction was rather vulgar: I wanted him to find me attractive. I had never been concerned about appearance, but now I needed a weapon. Clothes. I would turn myself into an object of admiration. In three months I succeeded in becoming different. I devoted all my time to me: my hands, his eyes, my body. Roger fell in love with me. The only thing I accomplished was something I didn't wish. I was in love with my husband, and I wanted him to love me deeply. Roger's devotion to me led me to realize that I represented very little to Mârius. I had entered his life in a natural, easy way, like the sun that rises every morning. He had me so close by that he didn't notice me.

I would have liked to leave the house and him. Had I never known Mârius, I could have. Where could I go? Back to my silly art classes? To my uncle's house, which I had left because we didn't get along? From time to time a secret hope came over me. What if everything were dead? What if the Senyora, the ibis, the romantic trips were all dead and buried? But if everything were dead, he wouldn't keep the letters. They were his treasure, his obsession. The briefcase, the letters inside. Briefcase and letters always close by, the key in his pocket. Had he realized that three were missing? Why had he allowed his past to become my present? Why had he allowed my love to . . . ?

I was with Roger on one occasion and asked, "Mârius took a trip to Italy, didn't he?"

"What do you mean?"

"Nothing."

Some days I was filled with lethargy. To get out of bed and dress was torture. Why had I allowed a ghost to separate us? To keep from thinking about her and the letters, I became determined to love him desperately. As if each night of love making were the last. The more my passion was excited, the more depressed I became thinking about that woman. His loyalty to her memory stood between us, breathing gently and, no doubt, panting.

One day I couldn't bear it any longer, and I brought up the subject. It was a gentle spring afternoon, like those I used to enjoy with him.

"I've never demanded anything of you. May I ask you something?"

"What?" he said, glancing at me in alarm, as if he guessed what I meant.

"The letters."

"What letters?"

"Your letters, the ones you always carry in your briefcase."

"I don't know what you are referring to."

I immediately understood, yet still I insisted.

"I realize that I should make an effort to ignore them. I wish I could. It's impossible. They exist, and they cause me pain. Tear them up. I beg of you, tear them up."

He reached into his jacket pocket: "Here, we are going to the theater this evening with Roger. You need a distraction. I think you will enjoy it." And he walked away. When he reached the door, he turned, "Never speak of this again. I would appreciate it."

Mârius always kissed me on the forehead when he left. Not that day.

Roger, dearest Roger. Until now I have tried to be objective in everything I have written. But I can no longer. I began writing this account for me, but in the end, it is for you. Because you have loved me. Because I have hurt you and you don't deserve it. Because I need a friend; I need to feel that I am not alone. I remember you with affection and that memory helps me now. But I have never loved you. Despite the hatred I now feel for Mârius, I have loved only him. He has been the center of my life.

Do you recall the performance of *Ondina*? When the years have passed, if you should think of me, remember me as I was that night. I made you believe things that did not exist. Forgive me. I dressed for you, I smiled for you. Please forgive me. For the first time that night I thought seriously of killing myself. They say that a suicide's last wish always comes true. I thought of killing myself as an act of vengeance against Mârius, to ruin his life, so that he would love me more than . . .

Do you remember the dress? Blue. You said, "Waves." And I wanted to die. I sat between you: Mârius on my right, you on my left. I was wearing the diamond dove that Mârius had given me in my hair. Men looked at me. You commented on it. Mârius seemed absent. "He's thinking about the letters. Thinking about her. When I am dead he will never think of her again." You gave me a prescription for gardenal tablets. I wanted two tubes of them. A few days after you prescribed the first, I told you I had lost the prescription. I thought one might not be enough. I wanted to be sure. I wanted to die. I thought of Odette, who was taking a course in ethics at the Sorbonne. She didn't die. I didn't want anyone to be affected—as I had been when I visited Odette—by a person who slowly returns from death, her face all green, in a large hospital room filled with rows of beds.

Do you remember the summer in Pyla? It was my last effort to live. The smell of pine trees, the dark dunes, the lichen the sea spewed out every night. The couple we talked about. Lovers. What mysterious secret had they discovered? The soul or the flesh?

I know that I am inexperienced, that I should have accepted what was handed to me, not looked beyond, not tried to speculate. Perhaps happiness consists in the capacity for resignation. But I want more. I would have wished for the letters to have ceased to exist. Her as well. For a few days I succeeded in forgetting. Only pine trees, sea, sun, silence. My husband sleeping beside me. "If I commit suicide, he will never again sleep like this."

You said, "Acute neurasthenia. Your nervous system is such that even a change in light can unbalance it." Do you understand now, Roger, what was making me ill? We came back in September, and I went to *our* café. I wanted to relive that first day right down to the smallest detail, poisoning myself even more. I returned to her house, to catch a glimpse of her from the street, to torment myself. The trees were just beginning to turn golden. I returned to the pension where I had lived for three months, truly lived, without anguish, without suspicions, sure of everything. Of him and of myself.

From my diary:

*At times I am almost delirious with the desire to find someone who will love me deeply. But this someone could only be Màrius during the period that we were happy.*

I told Elvira, "I'll be home late this evening, and as soon as I come in, I want you to tell Mârius that he has a phone call." I had already taken my little suitcase to the station with the black crêpe dress and the shoes I had bought in Venice.

When Mârius entered the room, Elvira followed him and announced:

"You are wanted on the phone."

"I'm coming."

I would have wished to gaze at him longer, but I had only a quick glimpse of his shoulders as he walked out of the dining room. Without hesitating I picked up the briefcase and fled. Nothing that I left behind exists, not my house, not my husband. Absolutely nothing.

I am at the Hotel de Llevant, in room number 12. I arrived at midnight. The room was occupied. I couldn't have it until noon today. This allowed me time to stroll about and write. It's almost like a short holiday. I have seen the boulevard with the wisteria and the house. I recognized it because the name is printed in gold lettering on the column to the right of the gate. Before I die, lying on the bed, I endeavor to hear the voices of the man and woman who had loved each other in this room with its art nouveau decor. I know her voice. His is more familiar to me than any other. She called him "Amor meu." He would make me whisper it to him in the dark, so he could imagine that I was her. At the head of the bed are two intertwined lilies. Two large lilies. They also adorn the top of the wardrobe with the mirror and the back of the chairs. Fortunately, there is a wing chair covered in velvet, a faded garnet color, its armrests worn smooth. I sit down in it and close my eyes. I have all the letters on my lap. All of them. The

first three as well. I laughed when I left the house, the briefcase
in my hand. I feel like laughing now too, a clear, healthy laugh.
Everything makes me laugh: the two of them and me and my
regrettable suicide, all of it so passé. The mere fact that someone
makes us suffer should send us straight to our deaths. I am alone,
the letters on my lap, surrounded by wooden lilies and an almost
real hatred. I will die wearing my black crêpe dress and the shoes
I adore with the heels encrusted with green stones.

I stand to look at myself in the mirror, filling it with darkness. Slowly, very slowly, my bridal gown floats past, empty, like
a spindled cloud, followed by a bouquet of fresh roses. But then
it is me in the mirror again, the veritable ghost that I am, and the
ghost is thinking, "It's a shame this girl will die."

I read the letters, one by one, in order, conscientiously. All of
them ridiculous, like love itself. One speaks of Italy, of Florence,
of exceptional days in Pisa, and in Venice. How I laughed. With
the laugh I used to have when I would suddenly realize in the
middle of a lesson that my professor was wearing a dirty tie or
looked hungry. My wedding trip was like a pilgrimage to the Holy
Land. Milan, Lake Como, Pisa, Florence . . . Oh, I forgot Venice.
Ladies and gentlemen, the water, though full of history, is not
transparent. No, it is rather like an opal, disfiguring the faces that
it mirrors. I am not indulging in literature. Senyors, all of you
should travel to Italy, with a woman friend, with your wife. There
will be a mirror for every face. The water flows for everyone.

When you receive this manuscript and packet of letters, Roger,
I will be dead. Return the letters to Mârius. They are all there.
Tell him that he has the contempt of a twenty-year-old girl. No,
don't tell him. It will be abundantly clear to him. I know these
letters will scald his hands. That is all I wish.

# ADA
# LIZ

**Ada Liz slowly counted the money she had left. A measly sum.**
Too little to cover her frustrated yearnings for solitude and
silence. She would have to return to the world from which she
occasionally isolated herself and await the ships bearing officers
and sailors. The former, however, rarely trod the streets where
Ada Liz's steps resounded. The narrow, airless alleys with their
wretched houses frightened them.

Ada Liz strolls barefoot around the room. She's left her purse
on the narrow bed, which is hardly wide enough for one person.
The window stands open, overlooking a square that is lashed by
the first streams of daylight. The glass balconies on the houses
across the way were filled with moon the night before, and a star
had fallen onto the top of the roof of the second house. The first
stands at the corner of Carrer Nelson. For the last eight days Ada
Liz had opened the window at dusk and leaned on the ledge,
not thinking of her youth, which had disappeared in the mists
of time. To recapture that period in her life, she has painted her
lips in a youthful way.

For a few moments the prevailing sound in the tiny room is the jet of water coming from the sink. A face with furiously closed eyes, arms moving under the water, then black hair being shaken, splattering the wall with drops.

What dreams will you dream, Ada Liz?

Her body feels sluggish. No man has held her tightly against his chest today; none could tell her she has bewitching eyes. She is the one who wanders about the port with her strange nostalgia for unfamiliar seas. A warship was docked near the sea-green rocks. The wind has unfurled the flag at the bow and stirred the water, drawing the lights down to the depths.

When Ada Liz walks back to her hotel room, all the cafés are closed and night is fading into rain.

Again, Ada Liz mentally counted the money she had left. With tips and all, she could only live on her own for five more days. Feeling that freedom was escaping her, she stretched out her arms to the night and let the raindrops shatter against her open palms. She imagined a ship being born from each drop. As they set sail, she christened them, even naming one after herself: *Veloce, Ardent, Ignotum, Ada Liz*. The minuscule ships sailed beneath all the skies of the world, across all the seas. Solitary islands awaited them with women like Ada Liz who daydreamed and stored up kisses for the returning mariners.

But Ada Liz—who no longer strolls barefoot around the room, but stands expectant by the window, watching her sea-less vessels suspended in air—saves her money in order to sleep alone, even when maneuvering warships are docked by the rocks at the old port.

So as not to soil the sheets, she dries her feet on the little faded rug. The nights are sultry, and she lies down without covering herself, remembering that a consul, bound for even warmer lands, had once fallen in love with her. Was it Dakar? He was tall and dusky, a strong man of forty. His teeth were white, and he had wanted her three nights in a row. Who knows how long he might have wanted her if she'd agreed to accompany him?

She would have had a house with lovely shutters to keep out the sun and a black servant and a phonograph with lots of music for those hours when the heart desires it.

"No," she had said. The shutters would be real, not a dream, but what would I do with a servant?

"You'd have love," he had exclaimed, still intoxicated by the brilliant, wild eyes that three nights in a row had riveted him, driving him mad.

"I don't want it."

"What then *do* you want?"

"Seamen."

She had lied. Not that she wasn't fond of Edgar and Raul and Esteve and Jim, who sang sad airs accompanied by the accordion, and Maria Clara, with the little monkey on her shoulder that Ada Liz despised. More than anything, she loved the sea that bound her to the earth. She hadn't dared ask if Dakar was on the sea, but she felt certain it wasn't, and inland she'd miss the walks by the still water. More than the port itself.

⁂

Before falling asleep, Ada Liz gazed at the map hanging in front of the bed: it showed her country. Sometimes, with her index finger, she would wistfully trace the black lines of the rivers. When Jim gave it to her, he had explained the meaning of the words "latitude" and "equator." He had told her—purely by chance, because he was going there—that Dakar was on the sea.

⁂

Ada Liz can't sleep and, like other nights, without summoning them, her thoughts lead her to the memory of a man she had truly loved. Suddenly she takes pity on herself. It had happened some years before, when she hadn't yet travelled all alone across the sea, nor slept in any country other than her own, or heard the unfamiliar sound of water lapping against battered rocks. And now that same man controls the destiny of her country. In the obscurity of time, her name wasn't Ada Liz, nor had she learned to undress in front of men. She had entrusted her life to the heart of one who called her "beloved" and placed her destiny in his hands.

Ada Liz is remembering the past. She recreates dawns, candid nights, hours with strange fevers in which the murmur of the wind in the branches could make your heart stand still and sharpen your senses.

She's thinking that she loves, reveres, adores. That young girl, faraway, who had placed her life in the palm of one hand. The girl with the passionate soul, her eyes weary from seeing herself so intently in the lost eyes of another.

"What are you looking at, Ada Liz?"

"Your eyes, sailorman."

In vain she had sought the eyes that had been wrenched from her.

"It disturbs me when you look at me like that, Ada Liz. I want to sleep without feeling the weight of your gaze."

"Are you afraid I'll discover your secrets?"

"That you'll stay here, like the sea . . ."

Lying on the bed, Edgar places his hand on his tanned chest and presses the fingertips, leaving round, white marks on his skin.

"Don't be afraid, sailor, your eyes aren't the ones I want, nor are your teeth made to desire me."

Later, as he dresses, Edgar announces: "I'm getting married, Ada Liz. My fiancée is on the other side of the sea. The night was planted in your hair, the sun in hers. Many men have kissed your breasts; hers are like rosebuds waiting to bloom."

Ada Liz is troubled by his explanation. She feels slighted, the blood flowing through her heart stops. With her tiny hands she takes Edgar's arms and holds him tightly, gazing at him with limpid eyes, as if she wished to captivate him.

"You'll remember Ada Liz, sailorman, and I'll remember everything I couldn't find in you. What does it matter if many men have known me, if you have me now? What's your beloved's name?"

"Her name's not important."

"I don't care if you won't tell me. I don't want to know."

"It's Maria Teresa, and she's humble where you're proud."

"Maria Teresa? She can never be Ada Liz. One day you'll find yourself all alone on the open sea, and the wind will bear my name, the storm my perfumed hair, the calm my caresses, the caresses I gave you knowing you would never be mine. Do you understand? As the years pass, more and more you'll want what you never knew, what you always desired but never had: the air, the white brilliance of the stars, the sea your ship leaves behind. You'll have a house and children. Maria Teresa will open the door wide when she hears your song of return, but one day, on the high sea, like a smarting wound, the memory of me will pierce you, and at that moment you would surrender all the souls you possess in order to spend one night with me. I am everything that one can breathe, sailorman."

Ada Liz, bright and pure, wishes she could remind him of the past. Edgar has written that Maria Teresa had a child and, after suckling him, her breasts withered.

The sailors are all marrying.

So what?

Every day new ships arrive from the other side of the earth. Many are old and storm-battered when they dock. But time passes, and Ada Liz lives only with the obsession of a few memories. Why should she feel lonely now that she's grown accustomed to it, why frightened by the years that have taken away everything?

She'll save her money, not simply so she can spend a few days alone. She'll return to her country. She'll again place her destiny in the hands of the man who loved her. She'll describe her life to him. Can she, if she doesn't really know what has happened?

"I've seen the hours fade away," she'll say. And the days and years, but I could never find your eyes. Never. There came a day when I refused to go to Dakar, because I believed it lay inland, and I was afraid the color of your eyes would be beyond my reach. Later, a sailor friend told me it had a port and ships and seamen. Where were we coming from the day we met? From what light, from what shadows? I who had only lived a few springs, with feelings not yet discovered, hopes that never materialized. Driven by an affection I've never again felt, I'm returning to you because I love you still. Many men have known me. They recognize the color of my skin. My life is such. But I will abandon it in the pause of one breath if you don't care for it."

She'll go to him, her soul stripped bare. What can Ada Liz do with her freedom if she's invested every idle moment in her memories?

She rises. Her eyes have been open all night, fixed on thoughts of things that do not exist. She strides over to the window, closes it, and draws the blinds, leaving day outside, on the square, already noisy with footsteps and voices. Inside her room night persists, the moment when women are most beautiful. She starts to look at herself in the mirror, but for some inexplicable reason she's embarrassed and foregoes the inspection. She has the words with which to enamor and a past as sweet as the present. She strolls about the room, her hands on her head. "I'll turn my voice into wind for your soul and the dark shadow of my hair into green shade for your heart. With a rose in my hand I'll kiss your lips, and in my black eyes you'll find blue paths that will be your gaze in mine. Whatever beauty you find in me will be a reflection of your hands caressing me, and everything you desire will be my desire."

Ada Liz begins to fold her clothes. She tears up passionate letters from an officer who at every moment called her "divine," then a postcard from another man she doesn't remember. In the suitcase pocket she discovers a book of poems she hasn't read for years.

She is resolute: she is leaving. Her only regret is not knowing where she'll be when evening falls on the lateen-rigged ships.

Ada Liz stretched out her hand to catch a bit of waveless sea, but the ship's bow was too high. She stared at the horizon and trembled. The captain passed her, admired the flower she was holding, and invited her to his cabin for a drink. She declined with a smile: the tar-fouled atmosphere made her queasy. She needed air and solitude.

The ship sailed along solitary channels, leaving white foam that slowly dissipated behind it on either side. A cloud scurried across the horizon as Ada Liz's eyes grew dreamy. The captain said a storm was brewing.

Ada Liz sat down on a coil of ropes, lit a cigarette, and was sorry not to glimpse the nascent stars that the clouds would mask. The wind played against her lips and the ship's siren pounded the air mournfully. Ada Liz was thinking of roses, and in her mind she recreated the shadow of every vessel that had plowed majestically through the sea.

How dark the clouds have grown! When the wind rises up furiously, a storm is about to break.

"Ada Liz, off the deck!"

The helmsman knits his brow and stares in front of him. Ada Liz is adamant in her refusal. The captain returns to her side.

"I had you one night," he says, as his lips draw close to Ada's thick, shiny hair. "Your streets were silent, and now I am lost in your silence and in this uncontrollable desire for your hands. I must have you again."

"For that to happen, you'd need to strip me of my dreams," she responds with a vacant heart.

"I'll kiss your naked shoulders and calm my heart that beats for you."

She smiled sadly, and her teeth flashed in the lightning. "Hold your heart in check if you're seeking love. Keep it far from me."

"I want you still. I'll remain quiet as you surrender your dreams to me, till we reach the purest point of nakedness. Don't you know that I parted with my dreams one evening beneath the Southern Cross?"

Here the waves began to rear up. One of the bolder ones crashed against the ship, leaving drops of water on Ada Liz's forehead and closed eyes. She tossed away her cigarette, turned around, and stared straight at the captain:

"If I were a flower, you could pluck me. But, Captain, I am not. Your ship is taking me back to the eyes in which I first discovered life. That's why you'll never know me. Save your vessel from the storm, make it brave for the wintery fogs."

The violent wind thrashed and the ship suddenly pitched, a cloud of foam licking the deck. The captain shouted his orders, his voice hammering the night, ruling it. Ada Liz put aside her listlessness and eagerly breathed in the danger. The waves punished her as she gripped the rail tightly, her hands growing tired, the open sea intent on plunging into her body.

That night was long. The exhausted stokers toiled in the engine room below. The sea continued to batter the deck, sweeping one sailor away. The helmsman's hands were bloody.

⁓

When Ada awoke, she let out a cry. She was sleeping, naked, in the place where she had refused to go. Her wet clothes were piled on a chair beside the bunk. The ship rocked gently, the sea was calm, the maritime routes reopened.

Ada Liz didn't remember where she was headed or why she was there. Perhaps her dreams had carried her out to sea. She heard someone walking on the deck above the cabin, then the sound of footsteps coming down the stairs and along the corridor. She sat up, swung her feet onto the floor, and chastely covered her trembling breasts with the sheet.

The steps paused outside the door, and her heart began to pound. Had they really stopped? A voice she would never have thought so familiar asked:

"Are you asleep, Ada Liz?"

Should she reply?

"The sun is high, and we're lost. I'm sorry for you, Ada Liz, not for me."

Taking her silence for an answer, he entered. He was naked from the waist up, his hair falling across his weary forehead. Their eyes suddenly met, frightened.

"What is it about your eyes, Ada Liz? The storm's turned them green and blue, shifting like aquamarine. Close them!" he shouted wildly.

She refused to obey, and with eyes strangely open, her voice devoid of intonation or nostalgia, she reprimanded him:

"You've stripped me of my dreams, Captain."

He grew pale, and a shudder ran the length of his body as the memory of a certain night rushed over him.

At a loss for words, Ada Liz again envisioned the tiny vessels that grew from raindrops one day and bore the names she had chosen: *Veloce, Ardent, Ignotum.* Without thinking, she added another: *The Southern Cross.*

The captain kissed Ada Liz's knees as her dreams faded, and with gentle fingers he moved the covers aside without touching her.

"If I've stripped you of your dreams, may I fill you with memories? Rest now, Ada Liz, your eyes are frank. May I kiss your knees. You weep?"

Translucent tears shone in Ada Liz's eyes. Had she had been capable of thinking, perhaps she would have discovered that she wept for the bottomless waters, or for the human hearts lost on the high sea. Even these words couldn't help her understand why her eyes were damp. Then, at the point where the clouds die and the horizon begins, the captain asked:

"Dreamy Ada Liz, where were you going if not to me? Who could you yearn for, other than for me, even if I had left you with no memories of me? On every horizon, my heart has found you, and in finding you anew, I will never lose you now. Where were you going, siren, but to the sea? To me."

"I was going—"

"To me!"

"No. I was going . . . Tell me where I was going. Tell me why I climbed aboard this vessel, why yesterday—"

"Today! Look at the sea. Here your memories begin. This morning I held you against my heart. That is why the flower you were holding has been shorn of its petals, and now I lose myself in you. I beg you, set me free."

Ada Liz doesn't understand; he rests his lips on her forehead.

"I hunger for you, Ada Liz. I have no words to offer, only tenderness, and the passion to awaken your heart that now sleeps still as a lake. My arms are made for your body, my lips for your mouth. All my desires lie in you. Will I find no caress from you, Ada Liz? None, Ada Liz?"

Her hands reach toward his head. She brushes away his hair, but it tumbles back down. Silently, her hands move down his neck, pause over his veins, rest briefly on his shoulder. Then a hand grips his furiously beating heart.

The sea washes the body of a dead mariner onto a deserted beach. His eyes are open. From time to time the waves lap across the anchor tattooed on his chest.

# ON A
# DARK NIGHT

**"Why am I in this room?"** I asked myself suddenly, but my
thoughts refused to respond. Along with everything else, they
too were lost.

"You see?" Loki exclaimed as she sat on my lap. "The windows
of my house are for decoration. Neither light nor wind enters
them." Then she added, as if it were the most natural thing, "Did
you know that I was born to live only at night?"

At night I reached this house that has but one room. I don't know
how I arrived, without taking a step I daresay. You'll spot a . . .
but what advantage would there be for me to tell which path to
take? Unless you know how to find it, it will always be the path
that is the easiest to miss. No dream could ever conjure up this
girl; she is like none other. Who could imagine her, much less
find her, in this unfamiliar place, where not even the rumbling
canons keep us from loving each other? I explained to Loki what
war was; she didn't understand. It's better that way: she would
suffer needlessly.

You must think me mad. I had seen many of my fellow soldiers fall. Others lay injured, groaning as they lost blood. One
had empty eyes. Evening was falling when the battle ended. For
three days we never stopped burying men! When the first star
appeared, the clamor of fighting had ceased. Clouds slowly covered the sad, wan sky, engulfing the star. I don't know how or

why I began walking. "Where are you going?" asked the companion we all have but don't want because we wish to be alone with our tedium. For two days and two nights we had fought side by side in the trenches. As he charged, he screamed the words *patria, ideal, freedom.* Hearing him inspired me with courage, although at times I wanted to kill him so I wouldn't hear his voice. "Where are you going?" I didn't reply. We had spent the night nailed to the same spot, all the men, elbow to elbow, eyes that couldn't see from straining to look. Not a drop of alcohol to boost our strength, only nerves and memories. Not even memories now. Complete exhaustion. A sense of animality. All my desires converged: I wanted sleep. But my memories are stubborn. They arrive and take possession of my thoughts, filling them with shadows. Sometimes a man feels an infinite, almost delirious thirst for love, and he embarks upon the quest with the confidence that what he seeks exists. Then he feels cheated. All of us have experienced this. In my case, it was especially baneful. The more passionate we are, the worse off we are. Look at it this way: they say I'm a brave man. That is false. Disappointments make us strong. If courage stems from contempt for life and death, it lacks merit. When my dreams were thwarted, I became what I am. We stumble through life more or less mechanically. You know you have a soul or that you are filled with a passion that dares not manifest itself because . . . I'm drifting away from what I wanted to say. Dark night crept in, and I pushed forward, on and on, driven mad by all those days of gunfire and deafening explosions. Not an inch of land had been seized.

I left the war behind.

I paused to listen to the river that was barring my way. I couldn't see the water, but I caught its freshness. I breathed in its scent until I felt myself drenched. The monotonous murmur calmed my sick nerves. The darkness grew more and more intense. The sound of leaves rustling in the gentle wind blended with that of the river. I leaned against a tree. Not even a scrap of tobacco to roll a cigarette! The sky must have observed the clouds scurrying past, not I. "In order for someone to live, someone must die," I found myself thinking. I lived thanks to the stupidity of that discovery. A series of absurd ideas surfaced: I could change the course of the river, rearrange the mountains. Suddenly one thought stood out: What river is this? Why is it here in this barren, desolate land? From where could this tree have sprung—and all the trees I sensed from the wind in the branches—if I have walked kilometers without encountering a single blade of grass? I assure you it was no mirage: I could feel the cool water against my face and chest. I was soaked.

I continued down the path, following the river, attempting to convince myself that it was real. No matter which way I turned, it never left my side. My feet stumbled on the dense undergrowth that blocked my way until finally I reached the high wall of her house, although I did not know then that it was hers. The wall was made of logs, as were the other three, the first ones with two windows each, the last with a tiny door.

I walked around the outside of the house. The windows had no shutters or blinds, and the light streaming from them drew my gaze inside, to the figure of a smiling girl. She was seated. My eyes paused on her hands, but I could not make out what she was holding. Allow me to speak of the girl. What will I gain? If I tell you that she was quite pretty, you may believe me, though perhaps you will think it a lie. Who can say? In truth, she was beautiful, but beauty is not everything in a girl. Now that I have held her in my arms, heard her sighing with love against my chest, now that I have grown drunk from the perfume of her hair, I can tell you that the shape of the eyes or the perfection of lips are not the only thing one should love.

Perhaps a certain way of speaking, looking, smiling drives us wild, but it is best to put aside what is difficult to explain, or take it up another day when we don't know what to say.

The girl rose, moved toward the door, out of sight, then came outside to breathe the night which was suddenly filled with her presence.

My desire led me to her. She gazed at me without the slightest fear, and her voice reached me, as sweet as the bitterness of those who have suffered greatly.

"Come."

Together we entered the room that I have often recalled. There was a faint light, a soft atmosphere.

"Sit down," she said pointing to a low seat. "And now I would like . . ." she continued, sitting on my lap as a child might, "I would like for the light to be extinguished, leaving only the glow of night." She gently placed her arms around my neck, resting her lips there as she spoke.

"It's as if I have always waited for you, from a moment beyond time, before I ever began to wait."

I thought of distant loves of mine; they no longer seemed to be real love. I considered how my hate had vanished and my anxieties quieted. I would have wished to know why she was there, who her parents were, what sky had seen her come into being, what country had seen her as a child. Yet at the same time, I was afraid I might shatter what didn't seem to exist, despite the fact that I held the girl so tightly against me that my heart could feel hers. She had always waited for me; I had always desired her. A girl like her, filled with tenderness, bringing peace to my spirit, penetrating it before making me hers in the flesh.

A calendar with the days marked with a cross hung on the wall in front of where we were sitting. She noticed my gaze and explained:

"I was counting the days. Every night I counted them. I didn't know which path would lead you to me. I would have wished it to be through the stars."

"I've followed the road of desire and will return by the road of memories."

"What are memories?" The question seemed to frighten her, so I didn't reply. Her lips searched mine. Nothing in this world can equal the sweetness of her kisses.

When I left her, only my body departed. My thoughts—no will was involved—could not accompany me because they were the prisoners of her soul.

There was a truce that day. An inventory of the spoils. We needed to fortify recently conquered positions. Enemy aviation appeared at dusk. I thought of Loki as I lay on the ground. Why that name and not another, since I was certain that she hadn't mentioned it? I realized that she was becoming my obsession: I lived *in* her, *for* her, *with* her. She had penetrated my soul, taken possession of my spirit, as no other woman ever had. But was she real?

The sky was covered with clouds, as it had been on the previous day. The evening was impregnated with an overpowering sadness. Loki . . . How could such an absurd name charm me to this degree? I realized how deeply I loved her. It was true love, its intensity perhaps possible only because we were immersed in the awareness of death.

"Loki," I said, holding her clumsily. I had found her in her house with the tiny windows. "Listen to me. Do you understand what death is? I'm here because I'm fighting a war." I spoke to her as I would a child. "I have to defend my country. My country's desire for freedom." I used my companion's ideas, communicating them with the same faith he professed, although my skepticism had mocked them. I had gone to war out of a desire for adventure, the need to see new lands, fleeing from the person I despised—myself—leaping into whatever awaited me as long as it allowed me to feel that some good was derived from my uselessness. I was surprised by Loki's sincerity and by the words I whispered close to her face. I saw in her eyes the reflection of the war. "War is hard, it is cruel. How fortunate to hold you in my arms, hear your voice!" In a strange surge of desperation, I screamed, "War destroys everything, everything!" Then I continued with great tenderness, "I might die one of these days. So what? You'll always be mine, no matter what happens. I could take on the entire world and not be frightened because . . . *he* doesn't know how much I love you."

I have no idea how long I spoke. I was intoxicated by the words that her eyes absorbed. The young girl of the previous day became a woman. Her incorporeal beauty became human and all my senses desired her. Her eyes were fastened on mine, incapable of closing. "I may not return tomorrow." Did she understand me? "You are the only good I've encountered in life. You hold in your tiny hand all my past, all my future." Then my hand, without my wishing it, was filled with desire and ran slowly up her waist, until it found the breast my lips longed for.

We gave ourselves to each other. Close to her mouth, I drank in a word as old as the earth. *Life.* She infused it with emotion and meaning. *Life.*

I uttered her name, as she breathed against my chest, and the day dawned.

"Loki."

*Despite strong enemy resistance, we have occupied new positions.*

The soldiers advance, their uniforms blending with the earth, their bayonets gleaming in the sun. They enter the remains of a village. A dead horse blocks the way, obliging them to separate. The soldiers are from far away; they have left their homes behind. They've come from all walks in life, but to come this far they have had to cross rivers and march along broad roads. They arrive with their youth, which only now begins to acquire a past. If they are alive when this has ended, they will have become men. The ruined roads are flooded with soldiers. A site must be chosen to set up headquarters. Curtains of fire billowed from the village yesterday. Today silent ruins stand in the sun. The day is bright, the sky a diaphanous blue. Most of the enemy prisoners have died of gangrene.

I feel a raging pain in my back, as if knives were probing an open wound. The nurse who cares for me is middle-aged. Her face is flushed. She has whitish-blonde hair, a wisp of which pokes out from beneath her dingy white cap. She is clearly skilled and explains that she is always assigned to the hospitals closest to the front. She takes my pulse, places her hard, rough hand on my forehead with a masculine gesture of someone who never hesitates. Can a person retain such energy and strength of mind amidst such . . . ? I don't finish the question. The pain in my back causes me to desist. I grit my teeth and think of Loki. I wonder how long it's been since I was able to think of her. I'll escape tonight and search for her. I'm filled with an irrepressible desire to weep, because . . . Suddenly I remember that I wanted to go yesterday. I escaped from my bed and jumped out the window. The night was clear, and I could plainly see where I stepped. One kiss from the person I loved would have sufficed. Not a sweet kiss, but passionate, interminable, like those of the last night. In this dreary room I conjure up her presence and speak to her. *I was wounded and fell. I couldn't find your house with the windows for decoration. I know you are without equal and that, like the land where I was born, for me there is no other. You are better than all the women I will never meet. It is impossible to compare you to those I have known. I long to be alone with you, hear your voice when my breath touches yours. I'll whisper your name, close to your lips that I dare not touch. I'll speak to you of all the things you cannot comprehend, and your eyes will be agape with understanding. You will mark the days on the calendar with a cross, not for what must come about, but for what must depart. I yearn for your always lively presence, long for the nights that were worth more than all the nights of my life. They have brought me to you. I glimpse your house, the windows, the silence, your footsteps, your eyes in which dreams are born. I want you.* I thought these things, and you were mine.

I died at dawn. Wanting to be with Loki, I had ripped off my bandages, and the wound had immediately spread, deepened. I would never have imagined that my body could hold so much blood. The pain in my back lessened. Slowly the light grew dim, the colors paler. I watched as the bullet holes in the wall in front of me—the hospital where I lie had been the town hall, the scene of terrible fighting—began to fade. "Everything flees," I thought to myself. Soon I will be out of here. If that's the case, I can go wherever I want. The land is free of obstacles. Not like here, where the legs on the bed keep me from reaching the window, or if it is closed, I run the danger of smashing my head against the walls. Then something strange happens: I lose my feet, then my hands. I hear a drip. Blood sputtering, escaping the prison of my veins. I'm overcome by sleep, a deeper sleep than I have ever felt. I want to keep my eyes open, to see if the light returns, if objects re-materialize. It's useless. As soon as it occurs to me that perhaps I am dead, I am.

I feel the air passing over me when they cover me with a sheet. I don't listen to what they say. It holds no interest for me.

They left me then, alone with the dead man that I was. My ears, however, pick up the slightest sounds. One drop of blood remains in my rebellious heart, allowing me to direct my thoughts toward the one place I desire, but they return unaccompanied. The deepest thought of all carried with it the word "Loki," and the name came back to guide me.

What a dark night!

Suddenly the unmistakable sound of battle. The whistle of projectiles spraying dirt when they explode. A man's scream as he advances with blind courage to defy the bullets, drawing others with him. The trenches are hollows created by the shells.

Machine guns devour the lines. Rifles wear out from overuse. For each soldier that falls, twice as many emerge.

Everything grows silent.

Softly comes the murmur of water flowing downstream. The river is beside me, carrying away all that is useless. It streams into my eyes. Trees float past, the leaves on their branches swaying in the wind. A coolness penetrates my chest as the water rushes over me.

# NIGHT
# AND FOG

**If all of us here could return to the womb, half would be trampled** to death by those who fight to get in first. A womb is warm, dark, enclosed.

I used to tell myself to play dead. That was before I realized I was a shadow. Now I keep quiet. There is no possible justification for them to have turned me into a shadow. In other countries, the wind still blows, there are still trees, still people. I was filled with a hunger for those people, more than a hunger for food. When that mania came over me, I was ready to smash my head against a wall. The more deaths that occur here, the better I feel. It fills me with such a deep sense of joy, so complex it can't be described. Meier died some time ago. He stank. All of them do. That's why I used to have this hunger for people. People sleep, get up, wash their hands, know that roads are for walking, chairs for sitting. People are neat. They do their business in a corner, closing the door so no one will see them. They use a handkerchief, turn off the light to make love. Meier used to piss all the time. *"C'est pas de ma faute,"* he would say at first with that grotesque accent of his, as a way of excusing himself. Then he stopped talking. He slept in my bed. The first time I felt my thigh damp and warm; a wave of wild anger rose to my head. With all my might I thrust my spoon into his neck. I heard the rattle coming from his throat, right by my ear. Suddenly he kneed me in the stomach. My arms went slack, and I let him go.

They caught me in Bordeaux on 14 March 1943. Six days in a French prison, seven beatings till I bled.

At home, when I was little, we had a fishbowl with three red fish. I would spend hours watching them. They never bumped into the side of the glass. I used to think, "If they don't see it, how do they manage to sense it and turn at just the right moment?" One afternoon I was alone. Father was working and mother had gone to the hospital to visit a friend who had a tumor on her back. I went over to the fishbowl and grabbed a fish. It struggled frantically in my hand, then opened its mouth, eyes bulging, all shiny and round. (It had a white spot on one side. The other two fish were completely red.) I returned it to the water. When I thought it had recovered, I took it out again. I put it back in the water, then grabbed it again. I continued the experiment until it died. I was playing a game: I wanted to see what the fish would do. I didn't want it to die.

They dragged me out of my cell, then returned me. They took me out to beat me and sent me back to recover, so they could beat me again.

That's why here in the camp I was so glad I didn't have a white spot. Sometimes I was afraid I'd develop one. I would've been calmer if I had a mirror. I'd look at myself every morning and wouldn't have to bother a bunkmate.

"*Tu connais?*" The guards showed me a picture. It was a young girl with a strand of hair that practically covered one of her eyes. "*Connais pas? Connais pas? Salaud!*" One of them grabbed my nose and was twisting it like he had some pliers. "*Fais pas l'imbécile, voyons . . . avoue.*" He got all worked up. When I couldn't stand it any longer, I seized his hand. I felt a terrible wallop to my stomach, followed by many more. "*Connais pas la poule? Avoue!*"

If everyone would just stay still, fewer would die. I should have warned them. "Reserve your strength." But if I had told them, fewer would have died. When I think of the walks I made Meier take! "Go get some sun, go on: walking in all that air will dry out your trousers." He believed me. The idiot didn't realize that the more he ran through the camp, the more he pissed. If I could send them all out to walk, the ordeal would end sooner. This mass of men, these dregs, would slowly vanish, but then I'd be left alone. And the guards would spot me. I'd be visible. It might be better if they hung *me* out to dry.

One day a truckload of sick men arrived. No one mistreated them; they were just put out to dry. They were taken off the truck and seated on a bench outside. You couldn't even hear them walking; the soft snow muffled the sound of their footsteps. You could almost touch the sky with your hands. It was overcast, gray, heavy. Once all the sick men were seated, they were never given another thought. The following morning seven were still alive. A frozen corpse is quite pretty. Clean. One had his shrunken legs spread apart, his hands over his eyes. The Belgian slipped his arm under the right knee and called to me, "Grab him by the other handle." We carried him like that to the pile. When we went back, I noticed his head had made a groove in the snow. Some of them still weighed a good bit.

They haven't come. Maybe they won't. They should've come the same day, in the afternoon.

When I arrived, the camp seemed like paradise. The tall, wide door and the watch towers made it look like a fortress, but inside . . . By the entrance, around a little square, stood some wooden huts, a fresh green color, with flower boxes. They weren't for us, of course. A gentle slope. The first thing they did was take everything we had. Everything. They led us naked to the shower. The skin on my back was still raw. Freezing shower, boiling shower. We queued for an hour to get our clothes: striped trousers and jacket. And get on with life. And shouts of *"Schwein! Scheisse!"* Get on with life.

If you want to see some black satin pajamas, you can find them in the prostitutes' hut. When I was still working in the tunnel, I used to imagine that one night we stormed it and made flags from the black satin, traveling around the world, like a parade of shadows. Literary reminiscences. That's when I started thinking about the girl in the photo. I remembered her in great detail, almost as if I had known her. Even more than if I'd known her. A narrow forehead, a long nose with wide nostrils, one bright eye open, thin lips. Very dark. That strand of hair falling over her left eye. Sometimes, when I was in the tunnel, I would feel a sudden anguish. Like the day I left my wallet on the table at the Préfecture, the section for *Service étrangers*—foreigners. As I was walking down the stairs, a dark uneasiness made me realize I forgot the wallet. I felt it all of a sudden when I was pushing a wagon or digging. I spent a long time—couldn't tell you just how long—without knowing where that anguish came from. Sometimes it almost kept me from breathing. One night I discovered where it came from. It was that wisp of hair over the girl's eye in the picture. That was what troubled me. I had this intense desire to push it back, leave her face free and naked. That face was the last human thing I saw. I had no wish to stroke her forehead, just the irrational desire to move that strand, place it behind her ear.

My only longing was to breathe the wind that came off the hill. It was pure air that seemed to carry the scent of flowers, making me think of a Sunday afternoon I had spent by the river, in the reeds. That was then, but now . . . I still used to wash and undress at night, despite the cold. I still noticed the lice. Whenever I could I would lie facedown and spend long moments with my head between my hands, contemplating the blades of grass, the ants, the only living things in that world of wood, rails, and cement. Now, when I think about the tender leaves on trees that seemed transparent against the light, the sun on the water, the flowers, the little blue and gold insects that climb up stems, the spongy, damp moss, it all seems excessive, useless, greasy, too oily, the world's tropical disease, the disease of gray and snow. I think about it and nausea fills my mouth with spit.

When Meir died, I kept him in the bed for two days. I made it seem like he was still sick, so I could eat his soup. Dead, he wasn't so disagreeable at night, because he didn't piss. And dead men . . . Night after night I'd sleep with my head against the thin wooden walls of the hut. Mountains of dead bodies, a hundred, two hundred were piled on the other side. On the second day the Belgian realized. He didn't say a word until they distributed the soup, and then he took Meier's ration from me and stared. "Thief," I yelled at him, my whole body shaking with rage. He raised the bowl to his mouth as he looked at me. I jumped on him. They had to separate us. His mouth was covered in blood; my face was swollen for three days. When I lay down on the bed, I saw they'd taken him away. I was filled with a profound sadness and almost wept. That was the last echo of the shining world from which I was removed the day they applied the pliers to my nose. The last palpitation of the complicated, marvelous feelings of this world. I still used to think occasionally, "If I get out of here alive, what will I be like? I'll always feel like I'm transporting a stream of corpses. I'll only beget children with the huge eyes of the starving, their monstrous sex hanging within the thin arch of their thighs."

*L'amor che move il sole e l'altre stelle.* "Come to dinner son, hurry before your soup gets cold." "Change your wet shoes, son; the damp is bad for you. You'll be full of aches and pains when you're old." "Brush your teeth."

"Look at me," Staub cried the day they gave him a beating. They had just finished purging him because he swallowed the diamond. "Look at me!" He howled, naked and raging, apocalyptic. They had knocked out some of his teeth; those that were left fell out like rotten pears. He wandered around, scratching his chest. From their bunks three or four men raised their heads to look at him, their faces moonlike, like a beheaded Pierrot, the look men have here when they can't endure the hunger. Maybe Staub thought the sky would open and his Yahweh would give a sign. He fell to the floor on his knees: "I can't stand." The day they hanged him in the tunnel, he was the second corpse in the row. When we filed past, I saw that the right leg of his trousers was ripped to the knee. His head was bent, like he didn't understand.

"Comb your hair, son, comb your hair." I don't have any.

Sometimes I think: "How have you survived till now?" Some want to be saved and that saves them. Some think that one day they'll get out, and that saves them. Get out: why? Some want out so they can continue. If I were part of the resistance or a communist . . . But I'm not a communist; I've never done anything. I haven't helped blow up a train or delivered any secret password. Maybe I don't even hate them. That's why the first days were hard. I was more distressed by the terrible misunderstanding than by the blows I was dealt. This unsettling feeling seemed to be coming from my stomach. It was like I was the only one who recognized an obvious error in a problem, and I couldn't make others see it. Get out to take revenge? For what? On whom? One day they called me to help unload the soup thermoses from the truck. It was freezing cold, and while I waited I put my hands in my pockets. The guy raised his fist to hit me in the face. He must have been twenty years old. I thought, "He could be my son," and I looked at him, waiting for the blow. I don't know what he said, but slowly he put his arm down and started shouting to the others. I felt a shudder of shame. First for him, then for me. What could he have seen in my eyes? If he could have pulled them out! I don't know what the last person I hated looked like. I never hated Meier. It was the day they showed me the photograph. He must have been in the office next door. He opened the door and without looking at me told the guard who was beating me: "*Écoute, toi: fais pas tant de bruit, quand même.*" It's hard to hate a man if you've never seen his face.

The first two blows are the ones that hurt. If they hit you on the head, sometimes only the first hurts. Hide your face. The canons yesterday evening excited a few of the men. *"Partir, partir,"* the Polish guy said feverishly, *"Fini, fini."* His teeth started chattering: *"Par . . . tir, part . . . tir."* They must be nearby. Yesterday they made us line up five times. Took away a lot of men. To start over in this world of oily things, honey-sweetened and peremptory? Start what? No. During the first months here, I kept thinking about the day I'd leave, the day the misunderstanding would end. Not because I wanted to leave, I later realized. It was instinctive for me to have something to anticipate. I had always lived with something on the horizon: exams, the end of my military service, the competition for a job, the end of the war. It was a way of escaping the vertigo of the future, of death. In this camp I have gradually sunk into an infinite, serene marsh. Perhaps death installs itself in people long before it finishes them. As if it wounded them. Be invisible. Invisible like an object. Eyes only slide over you, a brief outline. Be almost an object, like I was the day of the beating when they showed me the photo. I was just an object to that faceless man I hated so deeply.

To return to the womb, doubled up, drowsy, enveloped in warmth. In this corner, the sun is warm. A few days ago two guards found a man hiding here and beat him to death with a shovel. They made me collect him with a cart. It was distressing. He was so heavy I felt like my arms would drop. I didn't even recognize him. His face was covered with clots of blood. Black blood. Hide your face. Now they come two or three times a day to see if they find anyone there. But what are they waiting for today? What are they waiting for? This breeze that makes the grass sway must still be cold. The wind must blow that wisp of hair. From time to time she must push the strand of hair back. What are they waiting for? Maybe I've taken too long to come, to make up my mind. Maybe I should have come the same day, that afternoon, or the following. I didn't know they were so close by. The first two blows are the most painful. Lower your head, hide your face. After that, it doesn't matter.

# ORLÉANS, THREE KILOMETERS

**Whenever she asked, "Is Orléans very far?" he was filled with** a dull rage that surged upward till it reached his throat and choked him, causing him to cough. At least he spared himself from responding. They were entering a town. A group of people were gathered in front of a house, and they crossed the street to speak to them.

"What town is this?"

No one paid any attention to the couple. Everyone was anxiously standing around two men in shirtsleeves who were distributing wine. Like the rest of the town, the tiny tavern was abandoned. Smoke billowed from a window, and the air carried the smell of gunpowder.

"Bring bottle, give you wine. Give wine from cellar. Everything abandoned, wine go bad, better to drink it." The person had no more than imperfect French. He was a tall, thin black man, middle-aged, dressed presentably. A poppy was stuck in the lapel of his jacket; only one petal remained, the others had been winnowed out by the wind.

"Hey, take a look at that suitcase," the woman exclaimed as she elbowed her husband. The black man was carrying a small pigskin suitcase. It was new, its locks gleaming in the sun.

"Quiet, woman. If he hears us—"

"If you're afraid he'll understand us—"

Addressing the Negro, the husband asked, "Would you know the name of this town?" The man raised his hand (dry with long fingers, the color faded from his palm) pointing it upward. A sign was perched on the top of a pole with the name of the town marked in shiny, black letters. Artenay.

"There's some wine left. Who wants more?" offered one of the two men who were moving back and forth between the cellar and the doorway. Their trousers and shoes were drenched in wine. A woman approached them with a ladle.

"Look what I found. In the house on the corner. The door was blown away and the kitchen's full of all kinds of utensils. They must have just abandoned it, because the milk on the alcohol burner was boiling over."

"You got nothing to put wine?" the Negro asked the couple who had arrived last. "No? I look for vase or bottle." With a smile, wishing to be helpful, he had moved over to the couple. He held out his arm as if he were going to ask them to keep the suitcase for him, but changed his mind. His body stiffened as he tightened his grasp, and the suitcase was fixed to his body, like a continuation of his arm. Calmly he left the group and sauntered along as if he were made of cloth or his arms and legs were broken. One of the men distributing wine came up from the cellar, filled one more bottle and the woman's ladle, then announced that the wine was all gone.

"Planes, planes!" Everyone looked up. The sky was limpid with the sweet color of blue that the sky takes on in France. Not a cloud. Suddenly there was absolute silence, as if the dozens of people in the street had magically vanished. You could hear the airplanes but couldn't yet see them.

"Look! There they are, behind the chimney on the white house, directly above." An old man with a white mustache and eyebrows pointed to the house opposite. Suddenly five gleaming specks of silver flashed across the sky, growing larger and larger.

"Down to the cellar. Everybody down the stairs!"

"I can't move."

"Don't be afraid. They aren't coming for us. They've been bombing Orléans since last night. They'll pass right over us."

The drone of the engines drew nearer, and the planes took on the appearance of swallows. The men and women started down into the cellar, serious and silent. Their eyes were steady, as if they already held death. The cellar gave off an unbearable stench of wine, and the floor was muddy. Someone had drawn wine from a full cask and left the valve open. The men who were distributing wine had gone into the cellar and found the cask half empty, the floor flooded. After the brightness of the street, the cellar seemed like a skyless night. The last night of all. A child began to cry. A ray of light filtered down the stairs. Once their eyes became accustomed to the dark, they could make out rows of barrels lined up across the room. All of a sudden the ceiling shook as if it were going to collapse, and a furious clamor resounded through the cellar as it filled with dust. The child abruptly stopped crying, as if he were holding his breath. The women screamed. A man's trembling voice kept saying, "Keep calm, calm, calm." Silence returned. Then two or three distant, less violent explosions could be heard.

One of the men risked going outside, then leaned back down the stairs, calling, "It fell in the middle of the street; there's a crater large enough to hold us all."

Everyone hurried up to the street. The light blinded them. Everything was brighter than before: the day, the sun. The woman who was carrying her baby was weeping.

"Come on, let's get going."

"I'm dying of thirst. I feel like my mouth is full of gunpowder."

"The problems will be over when we reach Orléans."

"Is it very far?"

They followed along the streets, first to the right, then to the left, until they reached the village square. In the center stood a fountain. It was dry. The bombings must have cut off the main water line. A few tall, leafy plane trees, very green, cast bluish shadows on the sun-drenched ground and the church façade. A tavern, larger than the one they had just left, stood in front of the church. *Au bon coup de rouge.* Its wrought iron door, with the sinuous design, was broken off the hinges. They entered. At one end of the counter was a vase with fresh daisies and cornflowers. They stepped over the broken glass. Not a single bottle remained on the shelves. Most of the chairs and tables were broken, their legs pointing upward. Not a glass or mirror was intact. Through the open door at the back you could see a vegetable garden in the bright sunlight, to the right of which lay a lettuce patch and a fat, round daisy surrounded by a swarm of bees. They returned to the room. On a shelf beneath the counter they discovered a half-empty bottle of anise. They downed it as if it were water.

"Are you sure this won't hurt us? We haven't eaten anything since yesterday morning."

"Don't worry about such a small thing."

Wheat fields fanned out on both sides of the road. The stalks were full and ripe, bent to the point of bursting. A breeze sent golden waves rippling through the land. The evening was misty as the crimson sun began to set, throwing mauvish tones across the countryside. An occasional poppy raised its head among the wheat stalks, tired of being still for so long. The road was flooded with people who didn't know where they were going. Wagons passed, piled high with furniture, cages filled with thirsty, famished poultry, mattresses, kitchen utensils, tools.

"Will you give us a lift?"

Invariably, the owner would be walking alongside the wagon, striking the animals' haunches from time to time, encouraging them to continue. He would always respond:

"The horses are exhausted. They're already carrying too much weight and haven't stopped moving day or night for a week.

"We haven't eaten in two days."

"This is the war."

The stern man knit his brow and continued on his way, his entire fortune piled onto the wagon.

A military truck had broken down and pulled off to the side of the road.

"Can I help out?"

A barefoot soldier in shirtsleeves glanced at the couple.

"Hey, you, pass me the wrench," came a voice from beneath the truck as a hand stretched out.

"The wrench?"

"It's behind the seat, wrapped in a bag."

"Where?"

"Wrapped up, behind the seat."

"Ah, I thought you said . . . Come here and take a look at the motor."

The soldier came out from under the truck. First his head, his torso, his legs, then he jumped to his feet. He was blonde with steely blue eyes and enormous hands and feet.

"If I give you a hand, will you take us to Orléans?"

The man who had been under the truck glanced at them. His companion replied:

"I wouldn't mind. But we don't know if we will make it. Right now, this hippo has broken down on us. We only have gas for about two kilometers, and the Germans have probably reached Artenay by now. You'd better keep moving. Don't hang around here."

People began to shout. The horses pulling the wagon stopped, their ears straight up. A dull sound traveled along the road, a mixture of voices and shouts of fear.

"What is it?"

"Nothing. A bunch of silly people must have seen a plane. It never fails. They scream; the plane appears. There it is, I can see it now, but it's a reconnaissance flight. They've been pestering us all morning. Watch out: they use those machine guns."

As they approached Orléans, the road grew more and more crowded as people streamed into it from the neighboring towns. Every road, every path was overflowing with people who were fleeing. The road dipped gently, and in the distance you could see houses on both sides.

"You can't get through, you can't," shouted a boy on a bicycle headed in the direction of Artenay.

"Why not?"

"The bridges've been bombed. All Orléans is on fire."

"Don't pay any attention to him. He's a spy. A spy."

"Everything's burning."

"It's true, everything's ablaze. They kept bombing, all through the night."

But people and wagons continued toward the city. The houses on either side of the road were empty, their doors and windows open. Some roofs had been ripped apart by the bombs, displaying the inner beams and canes. An old woman dressed in black, a scarf around her head, was seated on a low chair in the doorway of a house.

"We have to help her."

"She's enjoying the fresh air, like in the old days."

"She's dead. Shut up, she's dead."

As they passed, everyone stared at her, leaning down to see her face. They kept repeating, "She's dead."

Orléans appeared on the horizon. Tiny and gray, enveloped in smoke.

"If we don't sit down for a moment, I won't be able to walk any more."

They sat on the ground, in the ditch alongside the road, watching the mass of people streaming past. Tied to the top of a wagon were a sewing machine and four sad children with plump cheeks sitting on a mattress. The muzzles of the horses pulling this tiny world were covered with a thick, greenish foam.

"It's going to be night soon, and we won't know where to go."

A quiet, sickly light began to fall across the scene. The asphalt was still warm from the sun. They stood up and began walking. Some soldiers were standing in the middle of the road, their bayonets pointed downward. They were directing the avalanche of wagons and people toward a path to the right.

"At the end of the path you'll find the road to Tours. This morning they bombed the bridges of Orléans. It's impossible to get through. To the right, all of you, to the right. The bridges are down."

The path winded past well-tended gardens filled with vegetables; the earth was rich and dark. Everybody walked slowly, mechanically. Everyone walked without knowing why. Suddenly the crowd flattened against one side of the path, and a group from a colonial cavalry unit rode by. A horse reared up with a desperate neigh.

"Stand right up against the fence and hang on tight. You don't want to fall under the horses' hoofs."

From the gardens came the scent of green, of fruit. Some wilted sunflowers gave the appearance of being asleep. A man was stretched out on the ground, his hands swollen, his face covered with a blue and white checkered handkerchief. His chest and the handkerchief were stained with blood.

"Close your eyes. Don't look."

"I'm going to fall. I can't go any farther."

"We'll enter the first house we come across and spend the night."

"The Germans have been in Paris for days now. I saw the flag with the cross at the Arc de Triomphe."

"The Germans in Paris?"

"Yes, yes, Paris."

"You must mean Artenay."

"Those are just tall tales from people who aren't getting any sleep. The Germans will never get to Paris."

"Watch out they don't catch up with you in Tours."

"Our army would never allow it."

"Take a look at our army," a man said, pointing at three soldiers who stumbled along, holding each other up. They were barefoot, weaponless, their epaulets ripped off.

A house appeared between the dense foliage of the trees. It lay isolated, outside the town, surrounded by a large tract of land, flat as the palm of your hand. In front of it stood some linden trees and a garden full of tulips and rosebushes, the last roses of June. At the gate by the road was a wall of oleander with pink and red flowers. As if trapped by the enclosed garden, a thick scent of honeysuckle and privet reached them. To the right of the house stretched a huge field, so large you couldn't see the end of it. Long rows of very short pear trees had been planted, trees no taller than a man's arm, cultivated like a vineyard, their branches tied to a wire espalier. It was a two-story house, the front facing Orléans. Behind it stood a garage, a shed for washing clothes, tools, wood already cut and stacked. Beneath the roof was a sundial. The windows on the second floor were beginning to turn pink with the burning of Orléans.

It was dark when they reached the house. They pushed the

gate; it creaked as it swung open. They crossed the garden slowly so as not to run into the trees. A cat slipped between their legs, frightening the woman, making her heart pound. A wave of heat rose from her throat to her forehead.

"Let's go," she said, tugging at her husband's jacket.

"Leave me alone."

They reached the massive wooden door with two lion heads for knockers. They pushed. The door didn't give. Again, using their shoulders, they pushed as hard as they could. The door shook but didn't open.

"The wood's swollen, but we'll get in. You'll see."

"I help."

They gave a start. Behind them a shadow was leaning over, wanting to be helpful. The man commenced shoving the door with his shoulder. Hard. All at once the door opened, and they almost fell inside.

"Me too enter. Legs no good. Tired, tired."

Roca lit a match and the man's teeth and black eyes shone in the flame.

"Look for the switch."

"There's no electricity."

A dank sickening odor of garbage, smoke, humidity, and putrid food hit them. The match went out and Roca lit another. On the table stood a plate of rotten meat and a few empty bottles of what had been good wine. The large room must have been the dining room. On the ledge above the fireplace a row of copper pots cast a dark gleam. Beside a glass tube with a pansy was a photograph of a young couple. He was wearing the uniform of a French officer, she a white dress. She was holding a bouquet of little flowers.

"Hungry, go look for something good."

When they were alone, the woman grabbed her husband's arm anxiously.

"It's the Negro from Artenay."

"I'm scared."

"He looks like a good man. Want to go upstairs and see what we find?"

"And if we run into him on the stairs?"

"Stop worrying. Come on."

They went upstairs. You could see all of Orléans ablaze, as if the furious fire had waited for night before igniting. The light from the flames flooded the room. They could move from one room to another without needing matches. In a small room, beside a bed covered with a crocheted spread, was a shiny, sticky area.

"Someone spent the night here and vomited."

There were two more very large rooms, connected to the smaller one through a barely visible door that had been wallpapered over to look the same as the wall.

"Can you hear that? It's a duel: artillery. They'll never stop. It's getting louder and louder."

"And the Negro?"

"He probably got lost."

"I hope so."

"Wonder what he's carrying in that suitcase. When he went to get us a bottle of wine in Artenay, did you notice he didn't want to leave it?"

"He was right. What if he had to hide during the bombing?"

Neither the main door nor the bedroom doors had locks. They stretched out on the bed. The legs of the bed were broken and the mattress dipped.

"Do you really think we'll get some rest here?"

"I'd be able to sleep on a bed of brambles. You'll see."

"Did you hear that?"

"What?"

"Planes. Listen. They're really close. If they weren't, they wouldn't sound like canons."

The red glow enveloped Orléans like a throbbing halo licking the sky. At short intervals a tongue of fire circled into the air, straightened up like a sword above the roofs, then disappeared mysteriously into the heart of the immense forge. Soon after, another appeared, higher and brighter.

"The planes are dropping bombs."

The house shook and the open window banged shut. You could hear the sound of breaking glass.

"Cover your face, cover it!"

He stretched his hand out, feeling for the floor. Bits of glass lay all around the bed. The artillery battle continued, without stop.

"I'm dying of hunger. Not found anything."

They hadn't heard him enter. The Negro was standing at the foot of the bed, looking like an abandoned ghost. The metal locks on his suitcase gleamed in the bright flames, casting fleeting green and red reflections.

"Don't think any more about food. Just go to sleep."

"I don't want to think, but—" he dropped the suitcase on the ground with a loud metallic sound and leaned down to pick it up. "But hand scraped, not let me sleep." He sat down at the foot of the bed, causing the wood to creak. "My name is Wilson. When little, picked cotton in America, poor parents, servant rich folks. Was alone in Paris when war lost, bosses on summer holiday."

"You'll find a bed in the next room."

"Feel lonely, very scared. Can I sleep near you, on the floor near you?"

The night seemed drunk with stars, sound, and fire. A never-ending stream of people and wagons passed the house.

"I drag cabinet from dining room, place behind front door. Nobody comes in to bother."

It was hot, not a leaf moved in the garden. The Negro stood before them, between the bed and the window. They looked at him, and the Negro returned their look. Suddenly a breath of air made a branch from a linden tree dance across the wall.

"You might die there, if you keep standing."

"Wilson want to sleep near you."

"Do whatever you please, but shut up."

He lay down on the floor, right by the bed, hugging his suitcase. Roca ran his hand through the space between the mattress and the bedpost and discovered a bottle. He smelled it: wine that was slightly off. He waited a long while, until the Negro was asleep. When he thought the man was no longer in this world, he drank slowly and silently, then handed the bottle to his wife. The blasts sounded as if they had calmed somewhat. He was falling asleep when his wife leaned over and whispered in his ear:

"See if he has the suitcase."

"Yes."

"Maybe he's carrying jewels."

"Go to sleep."

"I'm wide awake. I can't stop thinking about this man. We don't know who he is or where he's from. Do you hear me?"

"If you were as tired as me, you wouldn't be talking nonsense. Go to sleep."

He suddenly jumped straight up, screaming and running from one side of the room to the other.

"What is it, what's the matter?"

"Maybe we should have just thrown him out the window."

"Shut up. What's the matter?"

"Oh, oh, there's rats. House full of rats, bring bad luck. Run over face, slowly, over face, like Wilson was dead and worms begin to eat. Eat cheek, eat nose, eat strength, rats." He was standing in the center of the room, moaning, his body swaying from side to side as he made a low squeal, like the lament of a night animal. "I like quiet, very quiet. Noise terrible. Want to return to America."

# THE THOUSAND FRANC BILL

**"I'm fed up with being poor."**

She put on her old, worn-out coat and opened the door with a jerk. At the other end of the landing her neighbor was in the midst of waxing the parquet floor at the entrance to her apartment. It was too late when she realized: the woman had already seen her.

"You look really lovely. You're even wearing eye makeup." Still on her knees, the woman straightened up and looked at her in amazement, "And you've curled your hair. If I had your hair . . . Will you be long?"

"I don't know. I'm going to see my friend, Isabel, she's very sick," she said as she double-locked the door. On the street, the bright light surprised her—the afternoon was winding to an end. All of a sudden she felt weak in the knees, as if her will were about to abandon her, but her mind was made up. Nothing was going to stop her.

The first man to pass her whistled and came to an abrupt halt as he looked at her. "I've put on too much eye makeup. I must look like . . . exactly what I want to look like!"

At that time of day only a few people were walking along Boulevard Rochechouart. As always, Zuzanne was at the corner of rue Dunkerque with the flower cart, wrapping carnations in transparent paper. "Don't let her see me with so much makeup on." Just as that thought came to mind, Zuzanne raised her head.

"Good afternoon. Any flowers today?"

She would have taken the whole cartful. The carnations must have just been picked, and the round bouquets of Parma violets seemed to be waiting for ladies dressed in gray with veils on their hats, who would take them away to die in crystal vases inside polished rooms with soft lights and velvet armchairs.

"Later, when I come back.

She held the empty wallet against her chest. Someone was following her. In a shop window she saw the man who had whistled and turned to look at her. She waited in front of another window to get a better view of him. She stopped, her heart pounding. How could she manage to look at him? Her eyes were bothering her. She had put on too much makeup.

"Can I offer you a drink?"

Despite the anguish, she noticed he was young and slender. He was wearing a trench coat and a bottle-green felt hat. Without replying she began walking again. When she reached Place Pigalle, she crossed to the center, glanced at the magazines at a kiosk, then headed toward the entrance to the métro. She stopped and leaned against the rail. Suddenly, when she thought she had lost the man who had whistled, she saw him cross the street. All the men were looking at her. She shook her hair energetically and heard a warm voice by her ear.

"You want to come with me?"

She looked at him steadily, calculated, and said in a low, determined voice: "Five hundred."

A cold shiver ran up and down her body. She couldn't see anything. A muscle in her leg was throbbing and her head hurt. He took her by the arm and murmured in a dark voice:

"You're worth twice that. A thousand!"

She held the wallet against her chest. Her lips were pale, unpainted. With a sharp gesture she brushed the hair away from her forehead and said, looking at the violets, "One bunch. The one at the very back. It's the prettiest." Zuzanne smiled, "Take whichever one you want."

Timidly she stretched out her hand and took it. It was beside two bunches of carnations. Zuzanne wrapped it in the transparent paper, making the flowers seem even more mysterious. She took the thousand franc bill out of her wallet. Zuzanne looked at it. "I don't know if I have enough change." The woman gave her the violets, took the bill, and left it lying on top of the flowers. She began to fumble through her wallet.

"No, I don't have enough. I'll go to the bakery, I'll be right back."

While she was waiting, a lady stopped at the flower cart.

"How much are the carnations?"

"I don't know. If you'll wait a moment, the florist went to look for change. She'll be right back."

She was middle-aged. Her cheeks were round, her makeup a tender, rose color.

"The flowers are fresh today. If the Parma violets had a nice smell, maybe I'd buy some, but you see my daughter is wild about carnations. Your bouquet is beautiful . . . Was it very expensive?"

She was about to answer when Zuzanne arrived. Scratching her cheek with one finger while looking at the bill, she said, "Your bill is fake. Look at this. You can tell by the lines: they should be purple but they're bluish. If you know who gave it to you, you can still give it back."

She left the violets in the same place where she had picked them up, beside the large bunch of white carnations. "Don't worry; you can pay me another day, take them," Zuzanne told her.

"No, no. Thank you."

She walked along quickly, the bill folded in her hand. A surge of liquid rose from her stomach to her throat, so sour it made her close her eyes. She breathed deeply, her mouth closed. She entered the apartment. There was a smell of tomatoes and onions frying: it was from the air shaft, no doubt. She put the bill inside an envelope, and with four thumbtacks nailed it underneath the last drawer of the wardrobe with the mirror. She raised her hand and touched her cheek: it was burning. She looked steadily at the wall: she had never realized that the branches on the wallpaper looked like a swan. The muscle in her leg began to throb again. "Now what?" Suddenly she leaned over, jerked out the thumbtacks and removed the envelope. When she had lit the gas, she moved an edge of the bill toward the flame and waited for it to burn. Her fingers hurt from grasping it so tightly. Then she went to the foyer, took off her coat, hung it up, and began preparing supper. Her husband would be home soon.

# PARALYSIS

*Il faut savoir mourir, Faustine, et puis se taire,*
*mourir comme Gilbert en avalant sa clé.*
—P.J. Toulet, Les contrerimes*

**I looked up the word "foxglove" in the dictionary. "I always asso-**
ciate you with flowers." Such an ugly word, "associate." A plant
with purple flowers shaped like a thimble. Digitalis. No. Not just
purple, lots of colors. Sky blue as well. I've taken all the clothes
off the shelf and started throwing them on the floor. I have just
enough time to arrive a few minutes early and relax in the waiting room, sit in the armchair next to the sofa looking at the painting of the tree, rock, sheep. I mean with enough time so I won't
be nervous or my heart . . . Sky blue. If I wear the red, it'll seem
like . . . The black would be more appropriate, but it's too tight. A
doctor in Barcelona examined me once without even asking me
to take my dress off. It was hot like today. I was stretched out, and
he was feeling my stomach, asking me if it hurt. It was a blue and
white silk dress, from *The One Thousand and One Nights,* several
shades of blue. Long sleeves, but with two openings at the top
that left my shoulders bare. Where the devil is that blue slip? I'll
have a real problem on my hands if I can't find it. I still have to
wash. Maybe the bottom shelf. My foot hurts when I walk and
when I move it from side to side in bed. But it's fine if I'm sitting
up nice and still. I have to tell him the tendons in my leg are sore.
If foxglove came in just one color, like garnet red . . . Geneva.
Foxglove. Leaves erect. Are you Genevese? The grass in the parks
is starting to look parched, and the trees are turning golden even
though it's still summer. A city of leaves, green paths, gardens
filled with flowers that seem to have sprung up on their own.

212

Like the difficult path toward naturalness. Or spontaneity. Am I
not Catalan? Mediterranean. Sirens and dolphins, lots of Ulysses.
Thyme, rosemary, broom. Land of gorse and furze, lavender and
fennel. I haven't worn the blue slip for a long time. If I can't find
it and have to wear the red, what kind of impression will that
make? I'll tell him he's nice, because it's true, it'll make him happy.
It takes so little to make a person happy. What if suddenly I ask
him if he likes foxglove? I'm sure nobody's ever asked him that. A
drop of blood. Seated on the examining bed, legs dangling, he'll
have me place my hand on his knee as he sits beside me. He'll
soak some cotton in alcohol and rub my fingertip, then, quick,
he'll prick my finger with the needle, all the while keeping his eye
on me. I'll bear the pain and try to keep the muscles in my face
from flinching. I'll breathe lightly so it won't be noticeable. He'll
attach a suction tube and draw blood, fill it half way, then stand
up, add a liquid to the tube, go back to his office as he tells me I
can get dressed. Shoes, slip, dress. I'll reappear, sit in the chair in
front of his desk, and trams and autos go past, I mean cars and
more cars, and the afternoon will wind to an end as he holds the
tube with my blood up to the light and adds a few more drops of
liquid. Seventy percent. I lower myself into the bathtub, quickly
soap myself, and shower away the suds as the mirror fogs up and
smells permeate. I brush my teeth, comb my hair quickly. The
slip. I phone for a taxi. Cornavin. It's coming from the Cornavin
taxi stand. I go down to wait for it. The driver closes the door; I
glance at my address book for the house number, I can never remember it. The dizziness begins. Just a bit, very slight. The same
reaction I used to get when I was little, when I would smell the
varnish on the trams. Ring-ring. The plane trees along Passeig de
Gràcia. Starlings soaring above Plaça de Catalunya, tracing tri-
angles and circles in the evening sky, a fury of wings and shrieks.
The peacock tower near Plaça de la Bonanova. Under the bridge,
near the church. Buy a votive candle and place it on the right side,
straight up so the flame won't gutter. Pull the wick up before you

light it. Let's walk the tram smells bad. Ring-ring and the tram passes us along República Argentina, heading down the hill. Be sure to buy the newspaper for the obituaries. Pont du Mont-Blanc. The Salève is unattractive, barren in places, but higher up the snowy summit is lunar. Majestic peaks the solitude of the snow-drifts sky crossed by eagles black wings snow storms hurricanes. The mountain that metamorphoses: distant, near, invisible in the fog. The fog off the Arve, down by the river, close to the ground. The bridge of the desperate, where the waters mix, the clear with the turbid, the Arve and the Rhône. Those who jump from the bridge are dead when they hit the water. The idea of suicide makes me feel important, and I sit up straight in my seat and watch Geneva drifting past: "Je pisse vers les cieux bruns, très haut et très loin, avec l'assentiment des grans heliotropes." Going around a curve the taxi throws me against the door. How can I explain the anguish? The desire to scream. It's wrong for him to do what he's doing to me. Boulevard des Philosophes. I have to put one foot in front of the other to go down the stairs, and if I need to get up at night for a glass of water, I have to hold on to the wall as I walk because my foot . . . Ghastly. Nerves are a bad thing. All those days of sitting down did me no good at all. Nor did the scalding foot baths with salts. Just the opposite. Will it ever get well? Life is such a fragile thing, so difficult to keep it balanced till the end. I asked for little and gave a lot. What if I'm wrong, and I'm exaggerating what I did? I don't think I'm deceiving myself, playing tricks on myself; I wasn't brought into this world to play tricks. I get out of the taxi, pay, and go inside. The stairs are sad, the elevator ancient. The nurse is just a girl, young, short, her flaxen hair poking out from beneath her cap. She looks at me carefully, speaks very slowly, as if weighing each word, spelling it letter by letter. The correct words emerge, sure of themselves. I'm in the waiting room with the painting, rock tree sheep. I pull back the sheer curtain and gaze at the street. Fox-glove. The elastic waistband has stretched and my panties are sliding down. I pull them up. I glance at myself in the mirror in front of the sofa, pick up a magazine, and sit down. According to the statistics, Geneva is the city that has the most cars in Europe and rains the least. I hear a door shutting at the other end of the apartment. I stretch out my leg and slowly move my foot from side to side. It hurts. I'm drowsy. I put down the magazine but don't feel like looking at another. When I realize that I am filled with this terrible despair, I think about what he's doing to me, though he denies it, says I'm just obsessed, the anguish settles under my heart like a huge beast and won't let me breathe. There's nothing to know I don't want to know. Break this silence! Watching cars isn't enough, I need something stronger to drive away the anguish that's devouring me. All the pain I've caused him . . . just something he invented. It's all fairy tales, fiction, tall tales. I shouldn't complicate things. Nothing matters. What's important today won't be important two or three years from now. Not at all. Not to middle-aged me. Me, right in the middle of my life. The odor from the tram always used to upset me, and when I got home I needed to smell cologne and sometimes even lie down. How much is the foxglove compared to the Royal jasmine, the starry flower clambering up the wall along the ivy path? Above the white stars in the heart of Sant Gervasi de Cassoles, all the way up to the rooftop. Doing the shopping in the cool early hours. Every morning in front of the grocer's lies a sad, shaggy dog whose owner pretends to tie him up with an invisible rope to an invisible pole, and he lies there calmly, convinced he's tied up. In the early morning the gardens are still withdrawn; they must think night perseveres. If plants had eyes, they'd realize it's never clear when night will end and the sun will begin to gild them and finally annoy them. They've closed the door, and I assume a reasonable face. Now he and the nurse must by tidying up, throwing away cotton, changing the linen sheet, disinfecting scissors and tweezers. He'll wash his hands and come to get me: tall, wearing his impeccable white coat, calm, a smile on his face. So, tell me how you are. My foot aches, and nothing eases the pain. He was recommended by one of Rafael's coworkers, and while taking his pulse at the house the doctor raised his eyes and saw the woman I'd painted on Canson paper, madly, with a damp cloth, soaking the paper. What is it? A fish? No, it's a woman. And, still taking Rafael's pulse, he doubled over with laughter. I showed him more of my paintings. I think I broke the elastic waistband when I sat down. It would be . . . Halfway along the corridor I'd be paralyzed, not a true paralysis but because my panties would fall to the floor and shackle my feet. I have a strong urge to laugh and mask it with a tiny cry and cover my mouth with my hand. What is it? Is it a woman? No. It's a fish. No. It's a woman. Blue, purple, pink. A triangle for a head, half of her face streaked with fine lines, broken here and there by a wipe of a damp cloth. I showed him to the bathroom to wash his hands, and while he was sudsing them he whispered, "I don't believe he's ill; he's pretending so he can be with you." I was silent, but when he left I studied myself in the mirror in the foyer. A friend of mine once told me, there's something inexplicable about your manner, something about you that I can't put my finger on. I'm uncertain about what's changed, but I've seen it coming on slowly, day by day. Stained teeth? Face full of pores? The whites of the eyes? The whites of her eyes are a bit blue, my grandfather used to say, have you ever noticed? Now it isn't white or blue, but tending toward ivory, streaked with the odd blood vessel. What does a burst blood vessel mean? Just a little vein that comes and goes. I mean it appears then suddenly dissolves. If my red corpuscles were what they should be . . . They're always low, and I have to take iron. My neck muscles have twitched. Tired of being in place since that first cry. Rebellious, these neck muscles. What's the matter? Me and my neck against the light. When I laugh I raise my face, but when I'm worried like now because of the pain in my foot . . . What's the matter? The look he gave me made me cover my neck with my hands. As he was washing I heard him say something about a disinfectant and

I went over to him. What did you say? And he turned and whispered, his hands under the faucet, "There's nothing the matter with him. He just wants to be with you." When he left I went out on the terrace; he placed his satchel in the back seat and, standing by the car, looked up at me and waved good-bye. I closed the door to the balcony and gazed through the glass at the bruise-covered Salève. Nice man, the doctor. You should give him a watercolor. The one with the nest full of birds, their beaks stretched wide-open, spilling out, heads raised, more like seals than birds. Earlier, he'd said nothing was the matter with Rafael, he was only pretending so he could be with me, and I mentioned that my foot hurt. Told him I'd ask for an appointment so he could examine it, been troubling me for a couple of months. But I didn't say we'd sent for him because Rafael and I had a fight, all through the night, no sleep, and he hadn't gone to work and needed a a note from a doctor for an excuse.

"Do you like foxglove?" I like you just the way you are now, so attached to flowers. *God first planted a garden.* I can get by without flowers, get by perfectly well. Vases filled with flowers are scattered around the terraces of the buildings in front; they bring them out at night so the flowers won't wither. There are boxes with white petunias and red geraniums. Whiter than white when the sky is low and gray and threatening to rain. The gardeners in the park below bend over the plants, caring for them. The most profound thing about it . . . I mean I believe it is profound. More profound than simply falling in love. I get a lump in my throat when I think about the garden at home, wretched but full of flowers. The flowers at home . . . the ordinary rosebush that I grafted to the finest rosebush of all, and the graft killed them, took all the sap for itself. Deep inside that impalpable, pulsing thing is what we call a soul. Man is the wisest of all. All of him primed so that his brain lives. King man, tiger man, lion man. Man man. If the world is man then I too am man. But man is more because all of his ribs are his, while woman is made from a man's. Woman bound to man associated with man rib wrenched from his ribs bones of man she is all man fading disappearing. The tragedy of living that man must endure from the moment he is born. War, revolution, incomprehension, stupidity, love. And death that laughs as it strips the flesh from bones, aided by white, eyeless worms, moving and moving, piled on top of each other, slithering through the windows of eyes between the teeth when no tongue is left no uvula or palate no pink gums embellishing the teeth. Like a man, and as such, my pleasure in flowers is the greatest expression of the will of God. One part feminine one part masculine. The artist. Half of an apple embedded in the other half I don't know what I'm up to. In this weather the vases are filled with gladiolas proud flowering swords. Maybe there are people who love them, I'm referring to flowers, but there are probably few like me who want to weep because suddenly the sky is gray threatening rain and words spring to my mouth: lilac camellia love-lies-bleeding Joseph's coat . . . King Jaume Royal jasmine, starry jasmine that climbs as it arbors up the marquee, sunroot chrysanthemums dahlias flower of bergamot mad flower of the coral pomegranate and first of all to bloom the almond tree blossom. The white rose delicate flower flower of the Japanese almond tree pregnant with hard almonds placenta of roasted almonds. Angelica. Behind the flesh within the flesh I am the flowers. You, whom I have loved so deeply, what do you think? That if I weep . . . many people rejoice when they make others weep. The pleasure derived from domination, victory! It has taken me a long time to realize. At this moment the pure truth my truth is that the worn-out elastic waistband will trip me half way along the corridor. I am the flowers and this allows me to vanish, do without them. I have just put on the Kreutzer sonata. I am no longer at the doctor's office, I do not think about anything that I am saying, I am not excited. I am writing. I am writing but I can't communicate the tremendous jumble of impressions I want to communicate. In real life no one can. Attempts, trials, experiments. Indian skirmishes with the Sioux who are the cleverest. Doesn't make sense. The sonata on the turntable as I fill pages. I talk about myself. But I don't. Then someone intelligent will come and say: There she is with all the cleverness of a writer who wants to deliver but can't and when she confesses to the Lord, she'll find herself empty-handed. I'll say nothing. I'll talk without talking about myself, offering nothing. I'm paralysis itself. But I'll be empty-handed because truth is spoken by no one and besides it's slippery. Water that slips away. And the Kreutzer sonata reminds me of my first reading of Tolstoy, when I was transported. I stop writing and listen. It is true that it is hot, I am listening to a sonata, the flower boxes on the terraces have petunias and red geraniums. Here in Geneva. And it is true that I am myself if I'm not someone else. The knob turns, the door opens, and the doctor greets me. With a gesture he has me walk before him down the corridor and nothing happens to the worn-out elastic. I enter his office. The lamp has a green shade. A porcelain hand, palm upward, sits on the table, a sign of friendship. In a corner stands a vase with red roses. Seven. I have only a moment to glance at them. The doctor sits behind his table reads my medical history raises his head and I explain the story of my foot. I have an unorganized foot, been like that for a couple of months. I explain to him all the home remedies I've applied. He doesn't laugh sits seriously. He's Swiss. As I speak I unfold myself and look at the light on the balcony, the sliver of sky, tiny piece of sky, color of Lac Leman, just a speck of sky behind the glass door to the balcony. The doctor's hands on his desk and my file, my name, my age. I tell him my right arm was once half-paralyzed for four years and I couldn't even write my name because I couldn't hold a pen and didn't have a typewriter never had a serious illness except a serious operation in Limoges after the French withdrew an old doctor performed it, had a little white beard, his blue eyes examining me. So far away. Everything disappears. I don't know what I tell the doctor who looks at me and I ask him if he wants to know anything else. He doesn't reply. I could initiate a corny little scene, talk about the scent of the roses in the vase, the quality of the petals, *une rose d'automne est plus qu'une autre exquise,* but a few steps away the melodic contour of the violin takes flight, all because a man had madly scribbled notes across five lines—I could have said a staff but that wouldn't be me, I would have said five lines. It is true that the roses in the vase are highly perfumed they were christened nocturne it is true that the doctor is silent and a curious complicity is established. A man and a woman. A chastity belt used to serve as an innocent defense because of this mysterious thing that is suddenly created between a man and a woman, imperceptible, but present. As slight as the dust of butterfly wings. I feel the need to explain many things and quickly. Liking Geneva didn't come easily. I was bored to death without the Louvre, the museums, the old streets, the wide avenues. Rue de Prony. I was settled in Paris for God knows how many years. The Jardin du Luxembourg with all the saintly queens of France Saint Clotilde was missing a finger can't remember if it was the right hand or left. When I say that the Salève is unattractive the national pride is offended and a voice reaches me from the mouth above the white coat framed by the light from the balcony. From above, seen from below. The magic fades. The sonata that inspired me I now find irritating. It's much too good, too, too much. Stop that blasted violin, stop it. No, it wasn't on the day of the red roses that I told the doctor that the Salève was the most hideous mountain in the world. The sonata made me write it. I grind my teeth the typewriter ribbon is stuck I fix it. I. We all stop living at the age of twelve. That's why I continue to have this passion for flowers. It can't be explained, nothing can. Men are asses. Sheltered by the mother hen from infant to school to university the first girl we don't know what to do with life. Swirling skirts, an embrace and let's get married. My wife's pregnant and then the cliché children are the greatest thing of all for his children a father must be willing to die mother too they are all dead because of a germ that will slowly devour you forever. Very careful pregnant again maybe this time it'll be a boy since we already have a girl and everyone thinks how nice to have the pair and then it's another girl. The skin on my chin is rough and my hair is falling out. A lotion? Is there a remedy for baldness? The stomach swells and the tailor has to alter the clothes, stomach spilling over trousers. The children grow up all of them are away for the summer now I can enjoy myself a bit. The children laugh at their father and the father grows old. A man can go blind lose the use of his voice be ravaged by rheumatism but they say his desire never ceases. A woman passes by and he's consumed by . . . Yes, there are excellent husbands and loving children. I like flowers what a bore stop talking stop saying that your life came to a halt at the age of twelve as if you had died with soft skin and teeth of pearls and clear eyes like water sparking green beneath leafy trees. *I honour you, Eliza, for keeping secret some things.* Why did Sterne sneak in here like that? To establish in an unsubtle way that I'm a cultured person who reads Sterne. I've never finished a book of his. Not *Letters from Yorick to Eliza* or *Tristram Shandy* or *The Sentimental Journey.* But then maybe I enjoy tricking people and I actually do like Sterne. No way of knowing. Other emotions other manifestations of tenderness.

As it happens I now like Geneva and the barren Salève. After years of feeling suffocated in Geneva I've finally discovered it. Let's agree that I have just now told the doctor Mount Salève is hideous. We move into the examining room, the glass cupboard filled with surgical instruments and cotton balls in a glass jar, scales, a bed. I undress. I'm wearing the black slip! I can hear my voice explaining how the problem with my foot began. Walking up the Parc des Cropettes. A sting on my ankle as if a glass had broken inside it and tiny pieces had pierced the cartilage. Impossible. It must be rheumatism and I'm just a bundle of nerves. I didn't tell him that as I was walking up the park, all of me—all my skin, the part that can and cannot be seen—began to tremble, and the nerves settled in my left foot. I was limping by the time I got home. What's the matter? I don't know, must have twisted my foot. It hurts, but without noticing the hurt, like when I get a bruise sometimes and realize I've hit myself because I see the bruise. This was some time ago. I thought it'd go away but it hurts more and more. The address of an orthopedic doctor. My foot has a fallen arch, massages, foul-smelling white ointment and my friend had told me that the ointment had to be black, made from iodine. Makes me start thinking. I've gained five kilos. I want to lose them. Recently, with the bit about the foot, I haven't taken care of myself, eaten a lot of sweets. You can't imagine how much I enjoy a cup of tea in the afternoon, scones. He looks at me without opening his mouth. No, no. I suppose I can get rid of the extra weight in a month. I don't know, no will power. Lie down. Close your eyes. He rubs the nail of his index finger against the sole of my sick foot. No reaction. He hammers my knee, the leg doesn't budge. The other does, jerks right away. He makes me walk up and down, up and down. The too-tight slip gives me a complex, I feel even fatter. He has me squat down with my hands extended in front of me, heels off the floor, tells me to stand up. I can't. A drop of blood. He pricks my finger with the needle. It's the first time I lose control: I grimaced, a slight contraction around my mouth. He examines my eyes, feels the glands in my neck, takes my blood pressure. I don't ask, don't want to know. He goes into his office while I dress and I hear him say: only fifty-five. That's the percentage of red corpuscles. I enter his office, still zipping up my dress. He adds more liquid to the tube. Playing with my blood. Tells me my blood pressure isn't good either. Writes a prescription. Then he suddenly looks up. We'll start you on a rigorous treatment, clear this up quickly. A tranquilizer, lots of vitamins, infrared sessions, plenty of vitamin B. He gives me the address of an orthopedic doctor. I don't want to wear braces inside my shoes. He arches his eyebrows, looking at me in surprise, an intense look. We stand up. He puts his arm on my shoulder. Suddenly he stops and makes me stop. I'd like to see your husband. We shake hands. On the wall at the end of the corridor hangs a map of Geneva. But the view, high up there . . . The nurse opens the door for me and I'm on the street again. The light is strong, the sun high, the afternoon hot. I have to return in three weeks. I'm afraid to cross the street because the cars in this country all charge about as if everyone were late. If my foot didn't hurt so much I'd walk home. You won't do anything crazy now, will you? He said just that, anything crazy. None of the other nervous manifestations had caused me any pain. I'll cross the Bastions, see the ivy-covered wall that serves as the backdrop for the leaders of the Reformation. Geneva: the eagle, the key. I catch a taxi. I'd like to scream. I breathe deeply when I enter the apartment. I lie down on the bed and think how bright it was outside. My spine hurts. The light in the study is different because it faces the east. I smoke a cigarette. I'll have to go to the pharmacy to buy the whole arsenal. What did the doctor say? Nothing. What's the matter with you? I don't know. Rheumatism. I'll fix supper. We eat on the terrace. The air is heavy and the Salève shrouded in fog. Do you know what foxgloves are? No. See those smudges of colors beyond the boxwood shrubs? That's foxglove. How do you know? Because they're shaped like a thimble. When he doesn't look at me I look at him. It's risky because the person who is observed without observing always realizes he's being observed. Then my eyes move to the lake where a white sailboat is passing. Did you put on a record? The Kreutzer sonata while I was writing. I don't feel like listening to music. I don't feel like little round dots on five lines. The light fades to gray and the streetlights come on, all at the same time. I pick up a book, Plutarch's demonology, and lie on the bed again. I'll wash the dishes tomorrow. I get up to go look for . . . I lie down again. When I came back from the doctor the first thing I saw as I entered the bathroom was the blue slip on top of the ironing. I read:

A chattering crow lives out nine generations of aged men, but a stag's life is four times a crow's, and a raven's life makes three stags old, while the phoenix outlives nine ravens, but we, the rich-haired Nymphs, daughters of Zeus the aegis-holder, outlive ten phoenixes.

I slept badly. I woke up filled with anguish and this tells me what I should do. Leave. I'll die if I don't. My heart . . . Alone in the morning, I pack two suitcases with clothes from the wardrobe. I take only half of them. I have to go to the pharmacy. The first thing I need to do is cure this sick foot, I couldn't even board the train, not unless there's a porter. I read the prescription calmly. I'll go to the pharmacy after I wash my face. The pharmacy is just around the corner.

# IT SEEMED LIKE SILK

**One windy day toward the end of September (I can't recall the** year), I entered the grassy cemetery for the first time, not because I knew anyone buried there, but to enjoy the sense of peace that cemeteries radiate and, more especially, to escape the wind whose wings swirled my skirts, filling my eyes with dust. The man I loved had died. I can't keep him company, but every day I saw his face on the wall. His brothers and sisters wanted to have him buried in the village because they had a niche there. It was far away. You had to take the train to reach it, and I couldn't afford the ticket. I knew I would have less and less money because my eyesight was getting worse. As things stood, I could only work in the afternoons, and soon I wouldn't be able to go to people's houses and sew.

There was less dust in the cemetery than on the street, but the wind's wings shook everything. A wreath, its flowers still fresh, was blown off a niche—I couldn't tell you which one—and a small bouquet rolled till it came to a stop at my feet. I strolled among tombs with statues on top. One looked like a little house, round with a roof over it, covered in ivy and surrounded by agaves so old they scared me. I walked further, pausing in the center of a more sheltered path so I could think about something. I didn't hear it coming, but suddenly a powerful gust of wind, like a tremendous flapping of wings, would have knocked me to the ground had I not grabbed hold of a tree trunk. The wind seemed to laugh as it blew through the cemetery, whistling and raising leaves. I stood in the middle of the path, thinking that earth is earth, no matter what color it is, no matter where it is, and that meant the earth in the cemetery I had just entered was the same as in the cemetery where my poor dead man slept. The realization consoled me. I moved away from the tree—a twisted olive tree, canted to one side, tortured by the wings of every wind—and right beside it I noticed a very simple tomb, which I immediately liked because the sun and the night chill had gnawed at the stone, giving the impression that it was abandoned. To make it mine, I stroked it. A cluster of weeds, with yellow flowers so shiny they looked like porcelain, had sprouted in the crack between the horizontal slab and the headstone that bore the name of the person who had died. My poor dead man would have liked those flowers. After that I couldn't get them out of my mind. I saw them in every patch of sun, on a girl's yellow scarf, on yellow-striped flags. I explained all this to the face on the wall, which appeared as soon as the light was switched off, emerging from a smudge the color of bile. First the eyes and mouth. The forehead and cheeks—the flesh—took longer. The face was partially rubbed out; it didn't disturb anyone, didn't make me want to run away or scream. Sometimes it wept. The entire face would grimace, and a glistening tear would spring from the right eye; the tear would tremble a moment, till it detached itself and rolled down the cheek. Nothing, however, remained on the wall the following day during the sunlit hours.

"We don't like visitors using this holy place to eat lunch. This is the last time!" I had never laid eyes on the gravedigger before. I'd gotten in the habit of going to the cemetery daily, for more than a week, ever since that windy day. He must have noticed me right away, because twice I had eaten only a tiny piece of bread with chocolate, seated by the tomb, so I wouldn't waste time going home for lunch. I stared at him as if I hadn't heard a word he said; he grumbled as he walked away, a small wrinkled man pushing a cart filled with leaves. I wasn't at all happy about it.

I arranged the little yellow flowers so they would drape across the letters on the headstone, concealing them. I would have erased them had I been able, because they kept me from believing what I wanted to believe: that the dead man I loved, mine, was buried there. From time to time, I brought him a flower, sometimes large, sometimes tiny. The gardener around the corner knew me by now, and without my ever asking him, he would wrap it in silver paper to make it pretty. I would lean down, positioning the flower just right; then I would gaze at it from the olive tree, my arm around the trunk. I prayed. You can't exactly say I prayed, because I've never been able to say an entire prayer. A buzzing fly distracts me. Anything does, even if it *isn't* moving. Sometimes I would think of the dead person I didn't know inside that tomb and try to imagine what he looked like, walking along the street, dressed up and breathing. Or I would talk to Jesus, whom I loved the moment I saw him on those cards at church. But thinking about the Holy Ghost had always made me laugh; what can you expect of a dove? "Dear Jesus, help me to be able to afford the flower, and keep the gravedigger from scolding me." Sometimes, instead of talking to the sweet, blonde boy who walked the world barefoot while his father made little wardrobes and cupboards, I would long to know what kind of blue the distant sky was. Or at night, as I gazed at the face on the wall gazing at me, I would take a piece of sky and spread it over me.

All Souls' Day was approaching. I stopped going to the cemetery the week before. It was like a circus, filled with families cleaning tombs and niches, taking bouquets of chrysanthemums and lilies to their poor little loved ones. I missed my visits so much that I was almost ill. It was as if I'd been thrown down a well and the light had been extinguished. I dreamed about the yellow flowers, the iron-colored agaves with their bayonet-pointed leaves, the avenue with its rows of cypress trees on either side. By the time I decided to return, I had wings on my feet. When I reached the beginning of the path, I stopped short, dropping the flower I was carrying. I didn't recognize my tomb. Someone had painted the letters, just a splash of gold, not black or gray, and the flowers in the crack were gone. A few yellow petals lay drying on top of the tombstone. I picked up three. I didn't know what to do with them, but instinctively I hurried over to the olive tree, the petals in my hand. I wept and wept until nightfall. The thought of quitting the cemetery upset me. I felt as if something terrible would happen the moment I left, but I was cold and my eyes stung. Before starting off, I glanced around me. Everything seemed sweet and light, but my legs felt heavy as lead, and I was afraid that the gravedigger might have already shut the gate. Suddenly I heard the sound of wings above the cypress trees, as if a huge bird had caught its feet in a tangle of branches and wanted to escape but couldn't. Then the wind started blowing.

I slept terribly. The sheets, my arms, the face on the wall— everything harried me. When I got up, I was more tired than when I'd gone to bed, but I was determined not to be frightened. I would find another clump with the little yellow flowers and plant it in the crack between the stones; there had to be plenty of them in the cemetery on the paths I'd never taken. When the plant grew tall, I would train it to cover the letters. The rain would remove the paint. A surprise awaited me: on the tomb lay a bouquet of flowers, pink and young as morning. I hugged the olive tree, breathing fast, my lungs demanding air. The sky that had been serene began calmly to fill with clouds. When the rain started, careful that the gravedigger didn't see me, I grabbed the bouquet as if it were a nest of vipers and hid it in some shrubs.

Nothing could reassure me. I visited the cemetery at every hour of the day, trying to determine who had brought the flowers and pulled up the plant. Just when I was about to believe that the person never existed, that it was all the gravedigger's fault, I discovered a dozen white chrysanthemums, tied together with a shiny ribbon, on the tomb. I felt ill. I knelt down on the ground and leaned against the olive tree, sobbing and drinking in my tears. I could afford only *one* flower. I have no idea how many hours passed, but I realized it was late because the sky had turned pitch dark. Something fluttered in the darkness: was it a shadow, a huge, extended wing? The thing blended with the black night so much that I told myself my senses were playing tricks on me, that what I saw wasn't true. When the tomb was taken from me, I could think of nothing else, I was so desperate, and from then on I never again saw the face on the wall. It had probably never existed. The face wasn't on the wall but in my thoughts. My poor dead man didn't remember me, he couldn't. It was I who remembered him. To reassure myself, I exclaimed out loud, "It's a dream." So is the wing, and I too am inside the dream. It was all false. But directly above my head some real wings fluttered, making me duck, and the wind tousled my hair. "I'm locked in the cemetery." I raced down the barely visible paths, not knowing where I was placing my feet, thinking constantly that I was going to fall and chip a tooth. The gate was shut. I was terrified at the thought of spending the night among the dead, with the sound of wings and shadows, gusts of wind springing up out of nowhere, soughing in the branches. I raised my eyes to the sky, pleading for mercy, and as I was looking, the hinges began to creak. Someone I couldn't see had opened the gate. "Thank you, dear Jesus."

All night I tortured myself, wondering whether I should return to the cemetery or not. Then, in the early hours of morning, the cart of souls appeared. It was flying up to the moon, but the bad souls fell to the ground just as they were about to climb aboard. The good souls, however, immediately began grazing in the fields of the sky, eating the grass of the blessed, a wing over their foreheads.

I was ill in the morning, wandering mechanically about the house, not knowing what to do, not sure what I was searching for, what I wanted, the thread of memory enshrouded, lost. I went without lunch; I had burned it. I could no longer tolerate the battle with life, and when the hour of terror arrived, I left the house. Everything within me led me where I didn't want to go. I walked quickly up the streets. Once, when I breathed in, the stink of tar filled my nasal cavities. Everything was so still I should have realized I was being followed. I didn't hear the footsteps, but, oh yes, someone was following me. There were seven of them, all more or less the same size, with waxen faces and closed eyes. If I had stretched out my hand behind me I could have touched the one who was closest. It was me when I was seven years old, wearing an apron with pockets and black woolen stockings. Enveloped by silence, I stood in front of the cemetery and again breathed in, then out, my spirit and heart calmed.

You could see a light in the gravedigger's house. The gate was half shut. Twisting my body to become as thin as possible, as if I were passing through a mangle, I slipped past and entered the cemetery. Instead of heading to the right, I went to the left. I would have to go the long way round, walking through the area where the rotting wreaths were piled, but I would avoid the avenue of cypress trees where the gravedigger could see me. There's no telling what he might have said. I stopped beside the tomb. The creatures that had been following me had vanished. For a moment the terrible solitude was disturbing. Not a blade of grass moved, not one sad leaf. Everything seemed so tender my eyes couldn't get enough of it. Finally, with my arms extended, I whispered—not addressing anyone—that it was all mine. The garden of the dead, from wall to wall, and far within, down to the deepest roots, the sky toppled so you never know where it begins or ends, with a sliver of moon dappling it with yellow near the sea. There was no trace of the chrysanthemums, but on the ground, embedded in a stone, something black gleamed, long and narrow as my arm. A feather. I was dying to touch it—it seemed so strange—but I didn't dare, and it was so large that it frightened me. What wing, what tail could possibly have borne a feather like that? I leaned over breathlessly and stared till I couldn't stop myself any longer. Then I ran my finger over it. It seemed like silk. "How beautiful you'll look in a vase," I said. When I was on the point of picking up the feather to take it home, a flapping of wings and a strong gust of wind thrust me against the olive tree. Everything had changed. The angel was there, tall and black, above the tomb. The branches, the leaves, the three-star sky were all from another world. The angel was so still that it didn't seem real, till finally it leaned to the side, almost falling over, and very gently—was it to calm me?—it began to sway from side to side, side to side. Just when I thought it would never stop, suddenly, it fled upwards like a moan, slicing the air, then dropped to the ground, diaphanous. Right beside me. Help me, legs! I ran like mad, dodging tombs, stumbling into shrubs, doing my best not to scream. Once I was convinced that the angel had lost me, I stopped, my hands on my heart so it wouldn't escape, but dear Jesus, there it was, standing before me, taller than night, made of cloud, its trembling wings the size of sails. I looked at it for the longest time and it at me, as if we were both under a spell. With my eyes trained on it, I stretched out an arm, but a flap of its wing made me draw back."Go away!" cried a furious voice that I wasn't sure was mine. Again I stretched out an arm, again the wing flapped furiously. I began to scream, as if I'd gone mad, "Go away, go away, go away!" The third time that I stretched out my arm, I bumped into some agaves. I don't know how I managed, but I curled up behind them as fast as I could, certain that the angel hadn't spotted me. The wedge of moon that was now in the center of the sky spat fire from the edges.

Lying on my stomach, using my elbows, I crawled along the ground like a worm; I got caught on everything, ripped my clothes on some kind of thorn. I wished I could just go to sleep forever on the bed of rustling leaves, not knowing where I would end up or if I would be able to leave the cemetery. With tremendous effort I finally reached the cypress trees. The bitter scent of sun-warmed mandarin flowers reached me. Where could it be coming from? It was making me dizzy. Keeping my eyes shut in order to kill the angel, I pushed aside the branches that kept scratching my arm and came to a halt by the nearest cypress. My arm hurt, and blood was oozing from my cheek where an agave spike had cut me. On the other side of the path, still as death and suffused with starlight, the angel was watching me. I didn't move again. The exhaustion was more powerful than fear.

Was it midnight or was I dreaming that it was midnight? My poor dead man was weeping far away because I had forgotten him, but then a voice from behind a chalky, moon-like sun told me the angel was my dead man and nothing lay inside the tomb. No bones, no memory of the person at rest. There was no need for me to buy another flower, neither large nor small. Nor should I shed any more tears. I should only laugh till that hour when I too would be an angel. I wanted to shout loudly—so that my hidden voice could be heard—that I didn't like wings or feathers and didn't want to be an angel. But I couldn't. My voice ordered me to look. A low-lying fog was spreading over the cemetery, like a sheet made of all the dead who lay there, and I was filled with a sense of well-being. Many scents reached me: honey, grass that grows only in starlight. I was no longer by the cypress tree but in a little square surrounded by tombs. The angel was sitting on a wooden bench, his wings stretched out on the ground, as if he had been waiting for me since the day I was born. I remember thinking, "If he drags his wings around like that, some of the feathers will come off, and they'll get lost in the cemetery." The fog grew whiter and thicker, causing my legs to freeze, moving forward. Not the fog, me. I was slipping down an incline of frost. Against my will, I drew nearer the angel, who never took his eyes off me. When I stood beside him, he rose suddenly into the air till his head touched the moon, and the scent of grass turned into the scent of good, black earth—the kind in which anything can grow—and the scent began to envelope me. You could hear the sound of water and see a gleaming thread of something coming from the tombs and the dead leaves, and the angel spread his wings wide, when he had me right beside him, when I could feel his sweetness blending with mine . . . I'll never understand why I needed to feel so protected, but the angel must have understood, for he wrapped me in his wings, but without squeezing me, and I, more dead than alive, stroked them, searching for the silk. I remained wrapped inside forever, as if I were nowhere. Imprisoned.

# THE
# SALAMANDER

**I strolled down to the water, beneath the willow tree and through**
the watercress bed. When I reached the pond, I knelt down. As
always, the frogs gathered around me. Whenever I arrived, they
would appear and come jumping toward me. As soon as I started
to comb my hair, the mischievous ones would stroke my red skirt,
with the five little braids, or pull at the festoon on my petticoat
full of ruffles and tucks. The water would grow sad and the trees
that climbed the hill would gradually blacken. But that day the
frogs jumped into the water, shattering the mirror in the pond,
and when the water grew still again, his face appeared beside
mine, as if two shadows were observing me from the other side.
So as not to give the appearance of being frightened, I stood up
and, without saying a word, began walking calmly through the
grass. But the moment I heard him following me, I looked back
and stopped. A hush fell over everything, and one end of the sky
was already sprayed with stars. He stopped a short distance away
and I didn't know what to do. I was suddenly filled with fear
and began to run, but when I realized he would overtake me, I
stopped under the willow tree, my back to the trunk. He came
to me and stood there, both arms spread wide so I could not run
away. Then, gazing into my eyes, he began to press me against
the willow, my hair disheveled, between the willow and him. I
bit my lips to keep from screaming; the pain in my chest was
so great I thought my bones were on the point of breaking. He

placed his mouth on my neck, and where he had laid his mouth I felt a burning.

The trees on the hill were already black when he came the following day, but the grass was still warm from the sun. Again, he embraced me against the willow trunk and placed his open hand over my eyes. All of a sudden I seemed to be falling asleep, and the leaves were telling me things that made sense but I did not understand, things spoken more and more slowly, more and more softly. When I no longer heard them, I asked him, my tongue half-frozen in anguish: What about your wife? He responded: You are my wife, you alone. With my back I crushed the same grass that I hardly dared to step on when I combed my hair; I used to tread lightly, just enough to capture the wounded smell. You alone. Later, when I opened my eyes I saw the blonde braid hanging; she was leaning over looking at us with empty eyes. When she realized I had seen her, she grabbed me by the hair, whispering "witch." Softly. She promptly released me and seized him by his shirt collar. "Ah, ah, ah," she kept saying. She began pushing him and dragged him away.

We never returned to the pond. We met in stables, haylofts, the root forest. But ever since the day his wife took him away, people in the village have looked at me as if they weren't looking at me, some furtively making the sign of the cross when I walked by. After a while, they would rush inside their houses and lock the doors when they saw me coming. Everywhere I heard a word that began to haunt me, as if it were born from light and darkness or the wind were whistling it. Witch, witch, witch. The doors would close and I walked through the streets of a dead village. When I glimpsed eyes through parted curtains, they were always icy. One morning I found it difficult to open the front door, a door of old wood split by the sun. In the center of it, they had hung an ox head with two tender branches wedged in the eyes. I took it down—it was heavy—and, not knowing what to do with it, left it on the ground. The twigs began to dry, and as they dried, the head rotted; and where the neck had been severed, it swarmed with milk-colored maggots.

Another day I discovered a headless pigeon, its breast red with blood. On another, a premature, stillborn sheep and two rat ears. When they ceased hanging dead animals on the door, they began to throw rocks. They were the size of a fist, and at night they banged against the windows and roof tiles. Then they had the procession. It was toward the beginning of winter, a windy day with fast-moving clouds. The procession, all purple and white from the paper flowers, advanced slowly. I lay on the floor viewing it through the cat hole. It had almost reached the house. I was watching the wind, the statue of the Saint, and the banners when the cat wanted inside, frightened by the chanting and large candles. But when he saw me, he screeched and humped his back like the arch in the bridge. The procession stopped. Again and again the priest gave his blessing, the altar boys sang, the wind twisted the candle flames, and the sexton marched up and down as the purple and white paper flowers swirled madly about. At last the procession left, and before the holy water had dried on my wall, I went in search of him. I couldn't find him anywhere. I looked in the stables, the haylofts, the root forest. I knew every inch of the forest; I always sat on the white, bone-smooth root, the oldest root.

That night, when I sat down, I suddenly realized I had nothing left to hope for: my life faced the past, with him inside me like a root inside the earth. The following day, they scribbled the word "witch" on my door with a piece of coal; and that night, outside my window, in a loud voice so I would hear, two men said that I should have been burned at the stake when I was little, together with my mother, who used to escape into the sky with vulture wings while everyone was asleep. I should have been burned before they needed me to dig up garlic, bind the wheat and alfalfa, and pick grapes from wretched vineyards.

I thought I saw him one evening at the entrance to the root forest, but he ran away when I approached; I couldn't be sure whether it was him or my desire for him or his shadow searching for me in the trees, lost like me, moving back and forth. "Witch" they cried and left me with my misfortune, which was not the one they would have wished for me. I thought about the pond, the watercress, the thin branches of the willow tree. Winter was dark and flat, leafless: there was only ice, frost, and the gelid moon. I couldn't leave the house, because to walk in winter was to walk in sight of everyone, and I didn't want to be seen. When spring arrived, its leaves tiny and joyful, they built the fire in the center of the square and gathered dry, well-cut wood.

Four of the oldest men in the village came for me. I called to them from inside, saying I wouldn't accompany them, but then some young men with large, red hands appeared and smashed the door with an axe. I screamed because they were taking me from my house, and when I bit one of them, he struck me on the crown of my head. They picked me up by the arms and legs and threw me on top of the pile of wood, as if I were just another branch; they tied my hands and feet and left me there, my skirt up. I turned my head. The square was crowded: the young people were standing in front of the elderly, the children in their new Sunday smocks in a corner, holding olive branches in their hands. As I gazed at the children, I noticed him: he was standing beside his wife with the blonde braid. She was dressed in black, and he had his arm around her shoulder. I turned back and closed my eyes. When I opened them again, two old men were approaching with bright torches, and the children began to sing the song about the witch who was burned at the stake. It was a very long song, and when they finished, the old men announced that they couldn't light the fire, I wouldn't let them. Then the priest walked over to the children with a basin filled with holy water and had them moisten the olive branches and throw them over me. Soon

I was covered with olive branches, all with tender leaves. An old, hunchbacked woman, small and toothless, started laughing and left. A moment later, she returned with two baskets full of dry heather and told the old men to scatter them on four sides of the bonfire. She helped, and after that the fire took. Four columns of smoke rose, and as the flames began to climb, it seemed to me that everyone heaved a sigh of relief and peace, a sigh that came from deep down in their chests. As the flames mounted, following the smoke, I watched from behind a torrent of red water; and behind the water, every man, every woman, every child was like a shadow, happy because I was burning.

The bottom of my skirt turned black, and I could feel the fire on the small of my back. Every now and then, a flame bit me on the knee. It seemed to me that the ropes that bound me had burnt away. Then something happened that made me clench my teeth: my arms and legs started to become shorter, like the tentacles on the snail I once nudged with my finger; and below my head, where the neck joined the shoulders, I felt something stretching and poking me. The fire screeched and the resin boiled. I saw some of the people who were observing me raise their hands; others were running and stumbling into those that hadn't budged. One side of the bonfire collapsed, sending embers flying. When the logs caught fire again, I thought I heard someone say: She's a salamander. And I began to move across the coals, very slowly, because my tail was heavy.

My face was level with the ground as I scurried on my hands and feet. I headed toward the willow tree, following along the wall; but when I reached the end of it, I turned and from a distance I could see my house burning like a torch. No one was on the street. I made my way to the stone bench, then to the house and through the flames and embers, hurrying toward the willow and watercress. When I was outside again, I turned back because I wanted to see the roof burning. While I was watching, the first drop fell, one of those large, warm drops from which toads are born. Instantly more drops fell, slowly at first, then fast, and soon all the water from above fell, and the fire was gradually doused, spouting huge columns of smoke. I stood still, and when I could no longer see anything, because thick, black night had fallen, I started crossing puddles and mud. My hands enjoyed plunging into the spongy sludge, but my back feet kept getting stuck in the mud and were tired. I would have liked to run, but I couldn't. A thunderclap stopped me short in the middle of the path; then came a bolt of lightning, and between the stones I spotted the willow tree. I was panting as I approached the pond. Once I was beyond the mud, which is formed by dirt on land, I found the marsh, which is dirt deposited in water. I moved into a corner of it and stayed there, half suspended between two roots. Then the three little eels appeared.

In the morning—I'm not sure if it was the following day or another—I slowly emerged and glimpsed the high mountains beneath a cloud-dappled sky. I scurried through the watercress and stopped at the willow trunk. The first leaves were still inside the sprouts, but the sprouts were beginning to turn green. I didn't know which direction to take; if I wasn't paying attention, the blades of grass poked me in the eyes. I slept among the blades of grass until the sun was high. When I woke up, I caught a little mosquito, then hunted for worms in the grass. After a while I returned to the marsh; I pretended I was sleeping, because the three playful eels promptly reappeared.

There was a big moon the night I decided to return to the village. The air was filled with scent, and the leaves on all the branches trembled. I took the stone path, being very careful because even the smallest thing frightened me. I rested when I reached the front of the house: I found nothing but rubble, stinging nettles, and spiders spinning and spinning webs. I crawled around to the back and stopped in front of his garden. The sunflowers were growing beside the rose-scented geraniums, their round flowers on the verge of bending. I proceeded along the blackberry hedge, never questioning why I was doing it. It was as if someone were telling me: Do this, do that. I squeezed under the door and entered. The ashes in the fireplace were still warm. I stretched out there for a while, then scampered around a bit before crawling under the bed. Dead tired, I fell asleep and didn't realize when day dawned.

When I awoke, it was night again and I glimpsed shadows on the floor; his wife was moving back and forth with a lit candle. I could see her feet and part of her legs in white stockings, slender at the bottom, swollen toward the top. Then I saw his big feet, the blue socks falling over his ankles. I saw both of their clothes fall to the floor, and I heard them sit on the bed, their feet dangling, his beside hers. One of his feet moved up and a sock dropped, and she pulled off her stockings with both hands. Then I heard the sound of sheets being pulled over them, and they spoke in low voices. Much later, when I was accustomed to the dark, the moon entered through the window, a window with four panes separated by two crossed laths. I crawled over to the light, directly beneath the cross. I began to pray for myself, because inside me, even though I wasn't dead, no part of me was wholly alive. I prayed frantically because I didn't know if I was still a person or only an animal or half-person, half-animal. I also prayed to know where I was, because there were moments when I seemed to be under water, and when I was underwater I seemed to be above, on land, and I could never know where I really was. When the moon disappeared, they woke up, and I went back to my hiding place under the bed, and with tiny bits of fluff I began to make myself a little nest. I spent many nights between the fluff and the cross. Sometimes I would leave and go down to the willow tree. When I was under the bed, I listened. It was all the same. You alone, he would say. One night when the sheet touched the floor, I climbed up the sheet, hanging on to the folds, and slid into the bed, near one of his legs. I lay as still as a corpse. He turned over, and his leg weighed me down. I couldn't move. I had trouble breathing because he was smothering me. I rubbed my cheek against his leg, being very careful not to wake him.

One day she cleaned the place. I caught a glimpse of the white stockings and the crumpled broom, and when I was least expecting it, part of a blonde braid hung down to the floor and the broom swept under the bed. I had to escape because the broom seemed to be looking for me. Suddenly I heard a yell and saw her feet running toward the door, but she returned with a lighted torch and hid half her body under the bed. She wanted to burn my eyes out. I was slow and ungainly and didn't know which way to go. Blinded, I bumped into everything: bed legs, chair legs, walls. I don't know how, but finally I found myself outdoors. I headed to the puddle beneath the horses' trough and the water covered me. Two boys saw me and went to look for canes and started poking me. I turned my face toward them, my entire head out of the water, and looked them up and down. They flung the canes down and ran away, but they came right back with six or seven older boys who threw rocks and handfuls of dirt at me. A rock hit my tiny hand and broke it. Terror-stricken, I dodged the poorly aimed ones and managed to escape into the stable. She came after me with the broom, the screaming children waiting by the door. She poked me and tried to drive me out of my corner in the straw. Blinded again, I bumped into buckets, baskets, sacks of carob beans, horse legs. A horse reared because I bumped into one of his legs, and I grabbed hold of it. A thrust of the broom hit my broken hand and almost tore it off, and a black thread of drool rolled out of the corner of my mouth. I was able to escape through a crack, and as I was escaping I heard the broom prodding and poking.

In the dark of night I headed to the root forest. I crawled out from beneath some shrubs that shone in the moonlight. I wandered around, lost. My broken hand didn't hurt, but it was hanging from a tendon, and I had to raise my arm so it wouldn't drag too much. I stumbled along, first over roots, then stones, until finally I reached the root where I used to sit before they took me away to the fire in the square. I couldn't get to the other side, because I kept slipping. On, on, on, toward the willow tree, toward the watercress and my home in the marsh, in the water. The wind blew the grass and sent pieces of dry leaves wafting through the air and carried away short, shiny filaments from the flowers by the path. I brushed one side of my head against the trunk and slowly made my way to the pond and entered, holding my arm up, so tired, with my little broken hand.

Through the moon-streaked water, I could see the three eels coming. They blurred together: linking with each other, then separating, twisting together and tying knots that unraveled. Eventually, the smallest one came up to me and bit my broken hand. Some juice spurted from my wrist; in the water it looked a little like smoke. The eel was obstinate and kept pulling my hand slowly, never letting go of it, and while he pulled, he kept looking at me. When the eel thought I was distracted, he gave me one or two jerks. While the others played at twisting together like a rope, the one who was biting my hand suddenly gave a furious yank. The tendon must have been severed, because the eel swam away with my hand. Once he had it, he looked back at me as if to say: Now I have it! I closed my eyes for a while, and when I reopened them, the eel was still there, among the shadows and splashes of trembling light, my little hand in his mouth. A tiny bundle of bones fitted together, covered with a bit of black skin. I don't know why, but all of a sudden I could see the stone path, the spiders in my house, their legs hanging from the side of the bed: white and blue, as if the two of them were sitting above the water, but were empty, like laundry hanging on the line, rocked by the lapping water. I saw myself beneath the cross formed by the shadows, on the color-charged fire that screeched as it rose and didn't burn . . . While I saw all of these things, the eels played with that piece of me, let go of it, snatched it again, and the little hand passed from eel to eel, swirling like a tiny leaf, all the fingers spread apart. I was on both sides: in the marsh with the eels and partially in that other world, without knowing where it was. Until the eels tired and the shadow sucked up the hand, a dead shadow that little by little scattered the dirt in the water, for days and days and days, in that corner of the marsh, among grass and willow roots that were thirsty and had always drunk there.

# LOVE

**I'm so sorry to make you open the door, just as you were closing,**
but I was needing a notions store, and yours is the only one I
pass when I leave work. I've been looking in your window for
several days. I guess it must seem amusing for a man my age,
covered in cement and exhausted from working on the scaffold
. . . Let me just wipe the sweat from my neck. The dust from the
cement gets into the cracks of my skin and the sweat irritates it.
I'd like . . . Your window has everything except what I want. But
then maybe that's because it's not a good idea to display it. You
have necklaces, needles, all kinds of thread. From what I can tell
women go crazy over thread. When I was little I would rummage
in my mother's sewing basket, and I would string the spools onto
a knitting needle and play at spinning them around. I was a real
devil of a boy when I was little, so it's curious I'd amuse myself
like that. These things happen. Today's my wife's Saint's Day and
I'm sure she thinks I'm not going to give her anything, won't
remember. Shops like this sometimes keep what I want in big
cardboard boxes. What do I think about giving her a necklace?
She doesn't like them. When we got married I bought her a glass
necklace, beads the color of dessert wine. I asked her if she liked
it and she said: Yes, very much. But she never wore it, not once.
When I asked her—just occasionally so as not to bother her—why
she didn't wear the necklace, she would say it was too dressy. Said
she'd look like a showcase if she wore it. I could never convince
her otherwise. Rafelet, our first grandson (he was born with a

full head of hair and six toes on each foot), used the glass beads of the necklace to play marbles. I can see I'm delaying you, but some things are difficult for a man. I have no trouble shopping for food, any kind, and I'm not embarrassed to be seen carrying a shopping bag. Quite the contrary, I like to choose the meat. We've been friends of the butcher's since he was born. Or pick out the fish. The fishmonger—I mean her parents—used to sell fish to my parents. But to buy things other than food, that's a different story. I'm like an owl in broad daylight. What would you advise? What do you think I should give her? A few dozen spools of thread? All different colors, but mostly white and black, colors you always need the most. Maybe that would be to her taste? Who knows? She might just throw them at me. Sometimes, when she's in a bad mood, she treats me like a child. After thirty years of marriage, a man and a woman . . . It's from over familiarity. That's what I always say. Too much of the same thing, always sleeping together, too many deaths, births, too much of this our daily bread. Maybe some sewing tape? No, of course not. A nice lace collar? Now we're getting somewhere. She had one with roses—buds and leaves. The only thing you're missing are the thorns, I used to say every time she'd sew it on a dress, to make her laugh. But she doesn't fix herself up any more. Her life's all wrapped up in the house, a woman who lives only for her home. You should see how she makes everything shine. The glasses in the sideboard: gracious, she must wipe them three times a day with a linen cloth. She picks them up so gently she hardly touches them, places them on the table, and on and on she goes, swirling the cloth around inside them. Then she puts them back, lines them up one beside the other, like soldiers with wide caps. And you should see the bottoms of the pans! It's like she cooks the food somewhere else, not at home. The whole house smells clean. You think when I get home I stick my head in the newspaper or listen to the news? No, I find a washtub of warm water out on the gallery. She makes me soap down, then rinses me off with the watering can. We have a thick curtain, green-and-white striped, just for this. So the neighbors won't see me. In winter I wash in the kitchen, and all that water on the floor that she has to clean up. She scolds me if I wear my hair too long. Cuts my fingernails every week. Well, what we said about the collar, I'm not so sure. Some skeins of wool to make a sweater? But I don't know how many she'd need. And to buy her wool now when it's so hot, and to give her something that would mean work for her . . . Let me read the labels so I'll know what's inside the boxes. Buttons: Gold, silver, bone, buttons that don't shine. Bobbin lace. Children's T-shirts. Fancy socks. Patterns. Combs. Mantillas. I can tell I need to make up my mind or you're going to push me out of the shop. Now that we've gotten to know each other a bit, I can tell you what I'd really like. Some ladies' underpants. Long, with crimped lace that forms a ruffle on the bottom and a ribbon strung through the holes of the lace (before the ruffle's made), with the two ends tied together in one of those bows that looks like an artichoke. Would you have that? Here it's been so hard for me to say it. She'd be just wild with joy. I'll lay them out on the bed without her seeing me, and she'll have a wonderful surprise. I'll say, Go change the sheets. She'll be taken aback, but she'll go to the bedroom and find the underpants. Careful, the top of the box isn't quite on. These big boxes aren't easy to open or close. There we go. Here I was so worried about nothing. I like the ones with the wavy kind of lace, like foam. Blue ribbon? No. The pink's more cheerful. They don't tear easily, do they? It's because she works so hard, she's never still. At least they should be reinforced. They look strong enough, and if you say so. It's cotton, no? Nicely sewn. You can believe she'll notice, and she'll tell me so. I like them, she'll say. Nothing else. She's a woman of few words, but she says what she needs to. What size? Now I'm really lost. Let's see, hold them up. She's, well, round, like a pumpkin. The leg openings need to be as wide as the waist. You say this is the largest size you have? They look like they're for a doll. They would have fit her perfectly when she was twenty, but we're old now. Nothing you can do about that. Or me. The problem is I don't see anything else she might like. She always wants something useful. Now what am I going to do? I can't show up empty-handed. Unless I buy something from the bakery on the corner. But that's not the thing to do. A man who works all day has so little time to do things to please, show him in a good light . . .

# WHITE GERANIUM

**Balbina died on a warm night, amidst the last stars, the fog ris-**
ing from the sea. I was forced to open the door from the dining
room onto the balcony to create a draft from the street window, because as soon as death took Balbina from me, the whole
house filled with her smell—the smell of decaying flowers. I sat
in a low chair by the glow of a candle while Balbina was dying,
never taking my eyes off her. From the time she had fallen ill, I
watched her like that every day and every night till I reached the
brink of sleep. I would lie beside her feverish body and gaze at
her almond-shaped eyes: they looked at me unseeing, shining in
the dark like a cat's. The warmth of her protracted illness had
kept me company, forcing me to close off the house for so long
that it had grown damp and the wallpaper had started to peel.
When Balbina died, she had no cheeks, nor flesh on the back of
her hands, and the dimples in her knees—I adored them so—had
vanished. She was fading, her eyes already protruding, when I
lay down on top of her, drinking in her final breath, wanting to
steal from her the last trace of life, wanting it for myself. As I was
about to open the door to the balcony, still holding the last bit
of life in my mouth, I realized that death would not leave. The
courtyard cast its spell of sun and mist, and a white geranium
petal fluttered into the room. On the railing over the street we
kept red geraniums. They were mine. On the railing over the
courtyard were the white geraniums, Balbina's. As I watched the
petal, I was reminded that I had waited months and months for

Balbina's death, always spying on her to see if her eyes closed with drowsiness, so I could wake her, keep her from sleeping, and be done with her sooner. The moment I heard her breathing calmly, I would slowly rise and cross the room to the wardrobe, climb onto the medium-sized chair, and take down the trumpet I had hidden at the very top.

One morning, some time ago, while I was at work chiseling marble curls for an angel, a tall, thin lady with a long nose and dry lips came in. She was holding a boy's hand and wearing an awkwardly tilted hat with a bird on it. The boy was dressed in a sailor suit, clutching a shiny, golden trumpet with tassels and red strings to his chest. The lady had come to commission a gray marble headstone for her husband's grave. Above the name and the words, she wanted three white marble chrysanthemums, standing upright, one beside the other, the first somewhat taller, the third shorter than the one in the middle. She wanted it made quickly. My employer told her that I would put aside the angel and make the headstone right away, but not with raised chrysanthemums, as if they had simply been placed on top of the marble, but engraved, gathered together to form a bouquet. But as soon as she had left, he told me the angel was urgent, the angel first, so I went back to pounding out the ringlets. Every evening when I reached home, I told Balbina that I was making an angel all by myself, because my employer had once told her that I wasn't good with marble and couldn't be trusted to make a complete figure. When I finished work on the day that the woman ordered the headstone, I noticed the boy had left his trumpet at the foot of a half-finished kneeling figure. The trumpet was so pretty, all gold and red, that I took it and hid it on top of the wardrobe, so Balbina wouldn't ask me where I'd gotten it. I didn't think about it again until one night, while Balbina was sleeping, I slid the chair over to the wardrobe, climbed up, grasped the instrument in the dark, and blew into it, just a little, softly, to punish her for her sins. Then I blew harder, and the sound it made was part

moan, part grieving wail, part music from another world. I heard
Balbina stirring. I replaced the trumpet above the wardrobe and
cautiously slipped back into bed. From that moment on, whenever
Balbina slept soundly, I would make the trumpet moan. After that
first time, I was on the verge of laughter as I waited for Balbina
to wake up, thinking she would talk to me in the morning about
the strange noise that had troubled her sleep. But she never mentioned that she had heard the trumpet. My eyes used to trail her,
fixed on her back as she moved between the dining room and
the kitchen. I was trying to see if my dagger-like glance, traveling
along her spine, could lead me to the thoughts she kept hidden in
her brain, in the corner that held another, smaller brain, which
gathers and stores all our secrets.

That was when her illness began. Always in bed, always lying
in bed, with her thread of a voice moaning, I'm tired, tired. While
I was watching her one night, I heard her breathing calmly, the
way trees must breathe, and all at once she opened her mouth
and stuck out the tip of her tongue, and with her tongue and
lips she made the sound of a trumpet. What I had been patiently
funneling into her ears now issued from her mouth.

When she had been dead for a while, her gaunt cheeks appeared to grow fuller, her lips taking on the shape of youth,
her body seemingly at rest. This miracle occurred before I had
crossed the room to open the balcony onto the courtyard. As this
change was taking place, I noticed the cat lying at the foot of
the bed. It had seen me drink in Balbina's last breath. I grasped
it by the scruff of the neck and flung it far away, but a moment
later it was again at the foot of the bed, as if it had never moved.
While Balbina was still warm, I dressed her, removing all her
clothes, particularly the dress she had worn since she first grew
ill. It made her look ugly, but I wouldn't let her change it, not
even to sleep. Suddenly I was charmed by the whiteness of her
lily legs. My hand circled her knee, round and round, grazing
the bone. The cat must have thought that I was playing, because

it stretched out one of its paws and touched my fingers. When I had dressed her and combed her hair, I shut her eyes and crossed her hands over her chest; one was so tightly clenched that I had to force it open. Finally, with much grief mixed inexplicably with wild joy, I slowly closed her mouth. I left her side, thinking the cat had stayed with her, but it must have followed me; while the geranium petal was floating in the air, the cat jumped up to catch it before it reached the floor. But I was taller and snatched it. The petal looked like a tooth, smelled like a milk tooth, the same smell as Balbina's mouth the first time we slept together. Before I realized what I was doing, I found myself standing beside her, a pair of pliers in my hand, wrenching out a front tooth, a tooth so firmly rooted and so hard that, when it yielded, I thought the whole jaw was slipping out. I held it up. It was clean, and I licked it to remove the red that stained the root, then stuck it in my pocket. The cat watched everything. From that day onward, I never again called him by his name—Mixu—I always called him Cosme, because Mixu was the name Balbina had given him when Cosme brought him as a gift. After I had decided I would call him Cosme, I lifted the dead Balbina's skirt—with respect, I did it very respectfully—and ran my finger repeatedly over her belly, as if I had nothing else to do, from her navel down to her pudendum. And when I calculated that Cosme had to leave home for work, I pulled Balbina's skirt down and left the house, the cat trailing me. I told Cosme that Balbina was dead. He couldn't have turned more pale because his blood had already lost its redness and grown watery from thinking so much about my Balbina, who would never be his, and had never been. Because in fact Cosme and Balbina were in love.

The gravediggers came and welded the lid of the coffin shut with a large flame, and I thought I must be in hell. Returning from the funeral I stopped at the tavern to drink a glass of red wine, one of those that help build up your blood, and when I left the tavern, wine-filled, Balbina's tooth in my pocket, the blue chimera began to materialize. It followed me as I entered the house. The cat brushed his belly up against my legs and made me stumble. I gave him a good kick. The moon, the stars, the water flowing from the faucet—everything was blue. Filled with the dream, I sat down at the table and talked to the cat, explaining to him that Balbina would soon be mere bones, and in less than a year her new pink dress, the one in which I had chosen to bury her, the one she had made so Cosme would fall in love with her— it would be covered with bones as white as the marble angel with extended wings and carefully combed ringlets. I showed him the tooth. He stared at it, closed his eyes, his honey-colored eyes, a black line dividing the honey in two, and his whiskers grew stiff. A moment later he glanced at the tooth again. I showed him the tooth every evening. One day, as I was leaning over to show it to him up close, he stretched out his paw, jerking it forward so fast that the tooth fell and rolled into a corner out of sight. I had quite a time finding it. I stuffed the cat in a pillowcase and beat him. Then I made a hole in the tooth and passed a thick thread through the hole. I would dangle it before the cat's eyes and pull it away when his paw tried to grasp it. We played and played until one day he opened his mouth and swallowed the tooth. A piece of thread was left hanging, however, and with sweet words I tried to calm him, and when I had him nice and calm, I pulled on the thread to bring up the tooth, but the thread, worn and wet with saliva, broke, and the tooth stayed inside him, the cat that Cosme had given Balbina soon after he was born and had always followed her around the house, the courtyard, the roof top.

I went out to look at the blue stars, frantic at having lost the tooth, the cat sitting beside me, looking up, just like me. I took him back inside, closed the door, and started pacing, and as I paced, I kept saying to myself, Cosme loved Balbina, Cosme loved Balbina, and now Balbina is dead and the fact that she *is* dead makes me very, very, very happy. They never had the opportunity to embrace because between them stood the marble worker who made angel curls. From his hiding place he used to play the trumpet to drive Balbina mad, killing her little by little so he could bury her, devoid of the tooth, in that pink dress she had made one spring because Cosme had placed a pink geranium in the window overlooking the street. In this way he could see her walking past on her way to mass on Sunday mornings, wearing the finest of veils dotted with black sequins.

I bought a fish covered with scales and ate it fried with tomato and parsley. I gave the head to the cat and forced him to swallow the thick hard spine that I turned the wrong way round so the bones would prick him if he tried to cough it up. Right away he began to heave and heave to disgorge the bone, and the more he heaved, the deeper the bone cut into the pink flesh of his throat. His stamina kept him from dying quickly. It took days of dry heaving and attempts to dislodge the bone before he finally offered up his soul, and while he was still warm, just as I did when I dressed Balbina, I slit him open, top to bottom, with a razor blade. I discovered the tooth in a corner of his swollen intestine, as white as ever. I washed it with soap and rubbed my fingers over it for a long time to make it shiny again.

That evening I buried the cat. I began to go out every night to determine when the stars would cease to be blue. I would stroll down the road until I reached the fields where the houses no longer obstructed the streetlight and the wretched vegetable gardens stood with worm-gorged cabbage leaves and insect-ravaged rue. Here too, with no houses to interfere, the glow from the streetlights was blue. I came to believe that everything was blue, not because I saw that it was blue, but because it had turned that color. I asked people, one after another, what color the stars were, what color the moon was when it had been stripped naked, what color when it wore a necklace. They would stare at me for a while, as if I had asked something outrageous, then reply that the stars were the color of a light bulb, the moon too. And the water flowing from the faucets was the color of water, nothing else. I continued to chisel the marble. My employer had finished the angel, and I the curls. The tombstone was ready, and I was working on the pleated skirt of the girl who had died and been laid out, but the first pleats came out uneven and my employer remarked, Your work has gotten worse since your wife died. That night I wandered further than before, beyond the vegetable gardens, beyond where I had buried the cat, beyond the cabbages and rue. The last streetlight was blue, and for a while I threw rocks at it, all of them aimed at the blue glow. The night was dark, and after hours of hurling rocks, I finally smashed the light bulb, causing it to shatter and fall to the ground. Then I sat with my back to the streetlight, alone, facing the dark night, and when the first star appeared and the windows in the distant houses had blackened, out of the blackness of night and the smell of untilled land came a meow, then another, another, always closer, and out of a clump of tall weeds emerged the noiseless shadow. The approaching shadow was a huge cat, as big as three cats together, and the pupils that I thought might be as blue as the stars were honey-colored, the color of old honey, and the honey was cleaved, top to bottom, by a black line. The cat brushed past me, rubbing his belly against my knees three or four times as he circled the streetlight. I stood up and took the road back; he followed me, but I turned around when I reached the first gardens and realized he had disappeared. The following day, as I was chiseling the pleats for the girl who was laid out, constantly coughing up marble dust, I pondered the blue glow, the bulbless streetlight, and the cat.

That night I returned to the farthest light. You could hear a multitude of frazzled, mad crickets singing. The huge cat showed himself again. He didn't appear out of the wasteland and tall weeds; I discovered him directly in front of me, his honey eyes staring at mine, blacker than the night of souls. He came every night. I would sit against the streetlight, waiting as the wind carried away the fallen leaves, and suddenly I would find him beside me, still as a corpse. I got in the habit of showing him Balbina's tooth, and when he saw it, his body would rub up against my legs and he would go *rrromm-rromm* over and over again, looking at the tooth with eyes like honey. On the last night I found him waiting for me. I pulled the tooth out of my pocket and began tossing it in the palm of my hand. Without even a glance, he began to circle the light as if he were a rope, and each time round he tied me to the streetlight, tying and tying me, tighter each time. I felt as if he were tying up my life forever. My thoughts floated beyond the gardens, toward the cemetery and back, but they never quite returned to the fields and the bulbless light, and as I gazed at the night before me to see if it had grown blue, blue from top to bottom, back to front, with the knot at my throat, my tongue protruding, the night turned blue and tender, like the stars Balbina had embroidered on a tablecloth, because Balbina did needlework, and in addition to embroidering blue stars, she embroidered pillowcases and sheets with letters that looked like flowers and branches, and the blue of the night was blue like the stars made of thread, blue like Balbina's blue eyes. When I first met her, I called her the girl with the blue eyes. But then I forgot she had them.